And All the
Phases of
the Moon

Also by Judy Reene Singer

In the Shadow of Alabama

Published by Kensington Publishing Corporation

And All the Phases of the Moon

JUDY REENE SINGER

KENSINGTON BOOKS
www.kensingtonbooks.com

KENSINGTON BOOKS are published by

Kensington Publishing Corp.
119 West 40th Street
New York, NY 10018

All Kensington titles, imprints, and distributed lines are available at special quantity discounts for bulk purchases for sales promotion, premiums, fund-raising, educational, or institutional use.

Special book excerpts or customized printings can also be created to fit specific needs. For details, write or phone the office of the Kensington Sales Manager: Kensington Publishing Corp., 119 West 40th Street, New York, NY 10018. Attn. Sales Department. Phone: 1-800-221-2647.

Kensington and the K logo Reg. U.S. Pat. & TM Off.

eISBN-13: 978-1-4967-0948-6
eISBN-10: 1-4967-0948-9
First Kensington Electronic Edition: June 2018

ISBN-13: 978-1-4967-0947-9
ISBN-10: 1-4967-0947-0
First Kensington Trade Paperback Printing: June 2018

10 9 8 7 6 5 4 3 2 1

Printed in the United States of America

To all those creatures that inhabit the seas. May you forever be protected from harm, from nets, and boat propellers and sonic testing and poisonous waste and blocked migratory routes and all the other evils perpetuated by my ignorant species. May the more enlightened among us grant you safety and aid.

ACKNOWLEDGMENTS

Many heartfelt thanks to the folks at the Center for Coastal Studies in Provincetown, Massachusetts, for the heroic work they do in rescuing the many whales, seals, and other marine life that are caught up in nets and the many discarded items that litter our waterways. They have a dangerous job and have saved numerous marine animals as well as have provided crucial educational programs. I urge everyone to support their important and necessary work.

Thank you to my favorite attorney, Steve Gottlieb, for his advice on the court stuff. I hope I got it right.

Thank you to the Dolphin Fleet of Provincetown for the many, many, many hours I have spent in the Atlantic Ocean with them, observing the marvelous humpbacks and other marine life at close range. I also appreciated the Dramamine and oyster crackers.

Thank you to my dear friends Richie and Jackie Chiger, devout animal rights people who brought me on my first whale watch so many years ago.

Chapter 1

I have walked this beach a million times.

It's just a long, thin spit of land that nestles inside the curl of Provincetown and points off into Cape Cod Bay like a finger, as though warning the bay not to forget us. And not to forget the ones it took.

I grew up here, in this quiet village called Fleetbourne, which neighbors the beach. I know everyone here. They are all like family to me, every one.

I feel the same about the water.

Felt the same.

I spent my life on the bay; it has been part of my family since the beginning of time. We took our sustenance from it. My grandfather fished here; my crazy grandmother danced in its waters long before I was born. My father always swore that our brains were wrapped in seaweed. When I left for college, he made me promise not to forget where I came from. Small towns are easily forgotten.

* * *

I come here every night when I am finished with work and stand on the old wooden pier to stare across the bay. I used to come here every night when I was a child, too. I stood right here, on these same old boards, and watched over the bay. I knew the water so well. Even when it changed—one minute dark silver, mirroring the looming clouds, the next a thoughtful blue that pulled the sky down into its depths. I carried its every iteration in my heart: the white foam that lightly rides the swelling surf onto the pale gold sand, the waves thrashing under a driving rain, the bay sitting serenely under a full moon when the tide is high and so proud that it swallowed the beach in one gulp. I knew all of it. Still do.

Every night I pick my way over the broken shells to get to the pier. They are everywhere. Once they held tiny creatures that gathered together in life and ate and drowsed peacefully in the ocean beds. Now only their shells remain. This is a beach of broken shells.

I used to walk alone. I am especially suited for walking alone. I was very shy when I was a child, and awkward, and was happiest when I was left to myself, to comb the beach for shells and sea glass and the skeletons of sea horses and star fish and try to imagine where they came from. There is as much life below the sea as above and I wanted to know about it all. It was a great and solitary preoccupation. But now, every evening, no matter the weather, I am accompanied by a pit bull. He has made a career of following me.

My name is Aila Cordeiro and I own and run the Galley. It's a little general store that I inherited from my father two years ago, and it sits right in the middle of town, just off the main street. We handle the mail and sell a little bit of everything, including the traditional sweet golden Portuguese muffins, which were brought to Cape Cod by the original Portuguese settlers and are very popular. Everybody eats them. In the morning, I serve almost the whole town as they come, sometimes one by one, sometimes in a group, following one another like lemmings, into the store for milk and fresh muffins, eggs, and, for those who keep a post office box here, their mail. The first breakfast I ever remember my grandmother feeding me was a toasted Portuguese muffin dripping with butter and beach-plum jam, accompanied by coffee served in my favorite blue enamel mug and so diluted by milk, it was the palest beige. My breakfast is still a toasted muffin and the lightest coffee that can still be called coffee, out of the very same mug.

I work every day. I haven't missed a day since my father died. Not even Christmas. I keep the Galley open for Christmas.

Here's how I got a pit bull. One morning, about a month ago, I arrived to open the store and found him sitting in front of the door. He had practically no fur; his skin was covered with lesions. And his broad chest, thick neck and legs, and square chiseled head reminded me of a wrestler, except he was skeletal thin. His eyes had intelligence but spoke of pain and he scooted away if you came too close.

"Who is this?" Shay had asked. Shay Williams is my dearest friend and very beautiful. Growing up, we used to pretend we were twin sisters, even though I am as pale as an oyster shell, with red hair and gray eyes, and she had glowing mocha skin and thick black curls loose as a garden of wildflowers. She cared about everyone, was the first to offer help. I always thought she had the perfect heart. Growing up, I was prone to bouts of shyness; she always had a wide, friendly grin that drew people to her as though she were magnetized and guaranteed her a parade of never-ending dates during our teen years. I counseled her through a variety of broken hearts, and she always answered my panic calls in the middle of the night when my mother grew very ill. I can never repay her for that. We split up for college but promised that we would always be part of each other's lives, returning to Cape Cod to spend every summer together.

She even introduced me to Dan, my husband.

Excuse me.

Late husband.

Dan and Shay and Terrell—Shay's boyfriend, now husband—

played music together in a little group they called the Baytonics. Corny. Dan played the guitar; Shay, the piano; and Terrell, the fiddle. They all sang. Folk tunes, spirituals, easy pop. Sometimes, at Shay's insistence, I sang with them, holding harmonies against her sweet, clear voice.

"Whose dog is that?" Shay asked when she saw the pit bull. She was wearing cutoffs and a tee, practically the village uniform, and was carrying her usual bouquet of cut flowers from her garden. She had squatted down to pet the dog, but he quickly dodged away, only to sit again, out of reach. "Where did he come from?"

"I don't know," I answered, pulling the store keys from my pocket and opening the door, quickly shutting it behind us after Shay and I ducked inside. My habit is to feed anyone or anything that needs a meal and I immediately grabbed a bag of dog food from one of the shelves. The dog crept up to the front door and watched through the glass as I cut the bag open and poured some food into a mixing bowl. I couldn't take the chance of letting him in. When you own a store, you can't take chances on stray dogs. Especially his breed.

Shay laughed. "You just made the biggest mistake of your life," she said, watching me fill the bowl to the top. "But a good mistake!"

"He's so thin," I explained, bringing food and water outside. He darted backward and sat down, looking at the food and then at me, but not quite meeting my eyes, as though it embarrassed him to be caught begging.

"Go get it," I said, then returned into the store. He walked to the food, his nose extended, sniffed, then gulped it all down, drank some water, and sat by the door, staring in at us. I was struck by his dignity. "I hope somebody is looking for him," I murmured more to myself than Shay.

There were things to be done. Shay and Terrell are music teachers and come back to the Cape every summer from New Jersey. Her mother is a dentist and her dad a math professor, which meant neither had a summer job opportunity for Shay, so she and I helped my father by working together at the Galley through the busy tourist season. Even after we both got married and had started good careers, we would return every summer. Shay and Terrell, me and Dan. It was a reunion in the best way, reliving old times and laughing through new ones, all summer, every summer, until she returned to what she called her winter life. I had a winter life once, too, returning to Boston with Dan at the end of the season. I was head of the science department in a private school.

Summer life, winter life. That's all changed.

After my father died, I inherited the store and soon made Shay my "summer partner," splitting the profits with her from June until the end of August because she worked so hard, side by side, with me. I work here every day now. I think, once in a while, about how Dan and I used to live in Boston and how I used to love the change of seasons and our location.

Now my life is the same, summer, winter, summer again; it never changes.

I stared out at the dog for a few minutes, then started mine and Shay's daily choreography. We both know exactly what we had to do while staying out of each other's way, working as smoothly as dance partners in an old routine. First thing, we put on our aprons, snow-white, with *The Galley* embroidered over the left side in little blue letters. Then she filled a big mayonnaise jar with water for her flowers, placing it on the counter next to the register. Daffodils, pink and yellow, and tiny purple grape hyacinth, quiet flowers, almost no scent, but they were rich in color.

Next, I turned on the big flattop behind the front counter, to heat it up for breakfast orders. Shay opened the side door and brought in the day's delivery of Portuguese muffins and fresh doughnuts and crumb cakes on huge foil-wrapped trays. I took the bowl of eggs from the cooler and set them by the flattop, then piled the par-cooked bacon on a platter next to them. The bacon would be "finished"—fried as needed—for orders. I filled the coffee grind, set it to "fine," filled the pot with water, stacked cups and napkins, my hands and body performing it all automatically. The last thing I do is write the Marine Conditions, which I get from NOAH, with a felt-tip marker on a whiteboard up front. My great-grandfather always did it, then my grandfather, then my father, and I still do, and even though I know it's an anachronism, it comforts me.

I find great consolation in my work. It promises me that though I have suffered my loss, had my life ripped apart when I lost Dan, I still have a place to be, an anchor, working as I have always worked. The sun rises, the sun sets, month after month the moon returns full and round and glowing, and I can ignore it, until its life passes and it shrinks down to nothing and disappears and can do no more harm. And still I work here. I survive. I will come back tomorrow and open the Galley, and the next day and the next. There will be no more changes for me.

It's all okay. I like the work and the rhythm of the work, the repetition, the comforting, blessed, deadening sameness.

Chapter 2

The rich smell of fresh-ground coffee fills the air. I have coffee every day. Almost exactly at the same time every day. I need it to wake me up. I don't sleep well and my mornings start off a bit fuddled.

I grab one white porcelain cup for Shay and the old blue enamel mug for me. I pour a hefty dollop of light cream in mine. "Shay?" I called out. "You want coffee?"

"Just have to get the newspapers!" she called back from behind the rows of shelves. Like the breads, the papers, too, had been delivered to the side door to be sold throughout the day. She carried them to the front and stacked them on a low shelf by the register. I sorted the morning mail, which had been left in a locked pouch clipped to the front door, quickly sliding envelopes and magazines into the mailboxes that lined the back wall. We finally finished.

"You need me to do anything else?" Shay asked.

"Everything's done," I replied. "Help yourself to breakfast."

She scrambled some eggs for herself; I toasted two muffins,

poured coffee, and sat down on the stool next to hers to eat. We always have our breakfast together.

"I swear, you are drinking a cup of cream," she said, laughing.

I looked into my cup. "I love it this way." It felt like my grandmother was still taking care of me, which she did, more or less, in her own idiosyncratic way.

"So, how are things going for you?" Shay asks me that every morning.

"Sailing against the wind." My usual response. "You?"

"Perfect." Her answer, as always, was accompanied by a contented grin.

"Have you given any more thought about adding a café onto the store?" It's the first time she has asked me that in a long time and it hurt. Dan was an architect and was going to design a little café for my father, since there was really no place in town to sit down with a cup of coffee and a snack and read a newspaper. I admired my father, but he didn't do everything that I approved of. For instance, he was thrifty, which is a polite way of saying cheap. I still have a ton of white tees, all of them misshapen because my father got a discount on them—he thought that as long as they had a neckhole and two armholes somewhere on them, they were good enough to wear. Even when they have *Fleetboom* written across the front.

"Even if I built a café, who would help me run it?" I returned her question with another. "You're gone in the winter and help is hard to find around here."

"There's plenty of people—okay, kids—that you can hire," she said. "You do the cooking and they can run the deli and wait tables. You're a great cook."

"I'm not ready," I murmured. "And kids aren't the most reliable."

She started to offer her usual rebuttal, but the bell hanging by the front door tinkled, signaling that our day had officially begun. Our first customer was always Mrs. Skipper. She was the mayor's wife, and since it was town custom to address him as The Skipper, it seemed logical to call his wife Mrs. Skipper. Actually, I don't even remember if The Skipper was actually an elected official; he had always been in charge, since I was a child. He and Mrs. Skipper were quite elderly now, maybe in their nineties, but he always carried himself erect and with a certain authority. Mrs. Skipper was tiny and thin, with wispy silver hair in a librarian bun, while her customary dark blue wool sweater covered her bony shoulders, no matter the temperature. She had always been brusque with me, and I had always chalked it up to some personality glitch. She gave Shay her daily order—two cherry Danishes, one for herself and one for The Skipper. "Make sure they're fresh," she always warned, as though the soft, glistening crust and moist cherries swirled with streusel crumbs weren't proof enough. Mrs. Skipper watched intently as Shay grabbed a small square of wax paper, picked out two Danishes, and put them in a bag.

"Thank you," Mrs. Skipper said, taking out her tiny gold beaded change purse and paying. She left, clutching the bag and her purse tightly to her chest in her two thin blue-veined hands.

Most of the population of Fleetbourne, like groupies, followed her, one after another, exchanging greetings and gossip and corny jokes. They mixed with the tourists, who spend their summers in the little rental cottages that line the main road and are within walking distance.

As usual, tourists and "Fleeties" alike emptied us of bread and milk, jars of the Cape's famous homemade beach-plum jam, plus enough bacon and egg sandwiches to feed breakfast to Disney World.

The tourists are really no problem. They shop quickly and leave, sometimes checking the whiteboard where I post the Marine Conditions or repeatedly asking for directions to the many local tourist spots; but the good people of Fleetbourne linger. They seem to share a relentless need to delve into one another's lives, blithely poking around personal business like beachcombers looking for lost engagement rings. I had already endured ten "Are you dating yet, honey?," six "You must be lonely rattling around that big old house all by yourself," and four promises to introduce me to perfectly lovely men who'd just been divorced, released from jail, or finally having great success with their new meds. I generally shrug them off.

But the last question left me rattled.

Martha Winston, who owns the florist shop, leaned across the counter, clutching her coffee and a half-pound plastic container of fruit salad, and asked me in a confidential tone, "I often wondered, honey, did they ever find the boat?"

"Shay!" I called out.

"Coming."

Dear Shay. She immediately took my place at the counter while I sneaked off into the little kitchen in the back of the store to regain my composure. The boat. I had almost stopped thinking about the boat. Almost stopped looking for it. Waiting for it. Listening for its soft growling motor as it pulled up to the dock.

No, they never found the boat.

Baking calms me down and whipping up a few cranberry-pecan loaves was what I suddenly needed to be doing right now. After I mixed the dough, I sat on a stool and watched them bake through the glass oven door as their moist paleness slowly gave way to a rich brown. It's called the Maillard reaction, this process that caramelizes their crusts and transforms them into proper breads. I was so proud of them.

The little kitchen felt comforting and protective. The ceiling fan creaked overhead, driving the scent of fresh loaves throughout the store. The shelves surrounding me were laden with glass canisters, neatly labeled, holding a variety of flours, brown sugar and white, almonds and pecans and walnuts, chocolate chips, bottles of boiled cider, molasses, and honey, all kinds of flavorings. There were shining copper-bottomed pots and pans hanging from the wrought-iron ceiling rack and cookie sheets and rolls of parchment paper and aluminum foil stored in a corner. My father had collected ingredients and kitchen tools. If I had nothing else, I had the neatly labeled canisters and glass jars that he kept in stock, the big silver mixer, the measuring cups and scoops and dented tins, every one of them a piece of my heritage, and every one of them reminding me of him.

When the loaves cooled, I wrapped them in aluminum foil ready to be sold.

Usually my cakes and cookies and pies became spontaneous gifts to friends and good customers, but these loaves will all be sold, because my heart has frozen over. I bake now only to make extra money for the store.

I peeked outside to see if the pit bull was still there. To his credit, he was staying out of the way, tucked under a nearby tree and curled into a ball, his eyes tightly shut. His stomach was full, he had found a place to sleep, and, too much like me, he was content with that, as little as it was.

Chapter 3

The dog was waiting for me again the next morning, sitting by the front door of the Galley, his square lug-nut head tilted; he was watching me intently as I approached. He looked hopeful when I greeted him, his stumpy tail wagging very hesitantly, before he turned his face away as though he didn't want to intrude. One eye was swollen shut and crusted over, and he had only one ear, the right, which had been cut down into a small triangle, the way they do with pit bulls that are used for fighting. It looked like the missing left ear had been ripped off; the edges had healed close to his skull in a lumpy line. There was a map of white lines tracing across his muzzle and right shoulder and down his front legs. His skin looked raw; thistles of reddish fur poked through crusty scabs that covered him like a threadbare blanket. He backed up a short distance and whined softly, then looked away again.

"I know," I said to him. "I'll feed you."

Mine was a simple reaction. He needed to eat and I wanted to feed him. I let myself into the Galley, grabbed the dog food, took two clean bowls from the dishwasher and filled them, food and water, and left them several feet away from the door. He waited until I went back inside before he started eating.

Turning on the flattop was next. It was exactly six a.m. I had been up since five. I had showered and dressed, jeans and a tee, then walked the five blocks from my home to the Galley. I try to walk to work every day, straight down Mainsail Road, which cuts the town in half, five blocks, a right onto Beach Six. The Galley is on the right side.

Alone. I always walk alone.

Our village is safe and quiet, twenty-two blocks long and ten blocks wide. My house is on Beach One Street, sitting right on the sand. The village ends at Beach Twenty-two. I like walking past the small Cape Cods painted in pale Easter colors, blue or green or pink or yellow, all with white shutters and doors. I know whose children are getting up for school, who has left for work, who likes Danish with their morning coffee, who likes buttered rolls. I like that the cross streets are named for sea things, Neptune Road, Anchor Road, Mooring Way, all of it fenced in by low white wooden posts and rails and looping white-painted anchor chains and white buoys hanging here and there. It's the perfect seafaring landscape come to life. You would think the Little Mermaid lived here. The Galley is seven hundred steps from the corner and is painted a soft gray with marine blue trim. Everyone knows the Galley.

I arrive the same time every morning. Five forty-five. I live by routine; its rigidity and repetition keep me together.

"I knew he'd be back," Shay announced from the front door at six a.m. She had more yellow daffodils. Her hair was wrapped in a yellow scarf; she was wearing long, yellow bead earrings and looked like a flower herself. I had to admire her style. She always looked so pulled together.

I shrugged. "I don't think it's personal," I said. "He came for the food."

"Probably." She nodded in agreement. "But you should adopt him. It looks like he could use a friend and you need something in your life again."

I had to turn away, so powerful was my reaction. My stomach cramped, sending a wave of nausea through me. I had a sudden vision of Dan, in our living room. It was a winter evening and we were lying together on the rug in front of the fireplace. His face was glowing from the fire he had just built in the hearth. Life was wonderful. I was chairing the science department in a private school that I loved. And we were both euphoric because Dan had just made partner in the small architect firm in Boston where he had worked since graduating from college. He was going to design us a totally green house, he said with a wide grin, with four bedrooms, because we were going to need the extra space. We had just agreed to try for a baby.

Shay put her hand on my arm. "You don't want to live alone forever, Aila."

I held up my hand to silence her. "It was never my intention to live alone."

"I know." The conversation was finished. She left for the side door to bring in the bakery items. I took out the eggs and the bacon and ground the coffee and put fresh water into the pot. I saw with satisfaction that three of my six loaves had been sold the day before. When they were all gone, I would make more. Mix the dough, watch it brown, sell the loaves, make more.

Routine.

Routine is my savior.

The rest of the morning passed quietly. I usually close the Galley at four, but Shay came over to me much earlier. "When is the last time you took a break?" she asked.

"Never," I said, laughing, then stopped abruptly, realizing I didn't want a break.

"There's hardly anyone coming in," she said. "Why don't you knock off early? Do something else."

"What would I do?" I was genuinely puzzled. I hadn't taken a day off in two years. Not one day. I even opened the Galley on Christmas in case anyone needed something. My mother was in a nursing home; I visit her every Saturday after work and this was only Thursday. What else was there to do?

"Get a haircut," said Shay, tugging gently at a strand of my hair. "Your hair could use an update."

"Miss Phyllis says the David Cassidy look is coming back," I protested. Miss Phyllis owns Phyllis's Follicles, the local hair salon. It featured an ugly name, two chairs, and hairstyles from the seventies.

"Then buy shoes," Shay continued "Or take yourself out for an early dinner at the Lobster Pot. I can close up and drop your keys off later." She handed me my striped canvas purse and pushed me out the door with a firm good-bye. I walked home. The dog started to follow me.

I turned around to face him. "Go home," I commanded.

He blinked at me and looked away; his stump tail drooped.

"I'm not kidding," I said firmly. "Go away. I can't take care of you. Go find your owner."

I continued walking—I admired the sight of one pastel house after another, almost all of them flanked with magenta and cerise beach roses in full bloom—ending at my house, and yet fully aware that he was following me anyway.

Late June is the best time of the year. The weather runs from mellow warm to meltingly hot, the breezes blow fair, as my father used to say, the tourists are plentiful, and the public beaches are dotted with colorful umbrellas and laughing children. Our village beach is private, dotted mostly with shells and pebbles and an occasional human, and we like it that way. That day it was empty.

I stood on my deck and stared out over the bay. But this time, the dog was also standing on the deck, across from me. He had followed me up, one hesitant step at a time.

I sat down on the top step. He sat down where he had been standing. I considered having dinner at the Lobster Pot. It had been a longtime family favorite and they knew me there, but I pictured myself as they would, the pathetic young widow, sitting alone at a small table with her outdated haircut, staring through the big glass windows that overlooked the bay, watching the water and sipping white wine. *Thinking about* him, they would say, and they would be right. I hate clichés.

I cleared my throat and the dog stood up as though we were going to have a formal discussion. "You can't stay here," I told him. "I have to work every day and I don't think it's a good idea to have a pit bull at the store. Also, I don't want to get involved with a dog. You need somebody better than me to take care of you." He tilted his head and sighed, like he had heard it all before. I got up and went through the back door that led into the kitchen. He crept up to the storm door and peeked in through the glass. We stared at each other, him using his good eye. He licked his lips. I took a Portuguese muffin from a plastic bag, buttered it, and opened the door to toss it at him, but the muffin fell to the deck outside while the dog bolted in. It wasn't what I intended. He immediately sat in one corner of the kitchen and trembled, as though realizing his lapse in manners. His eye certainly looked infected and needed to be cleaned off. I took a paper towel, wet it with warm water, and slowly approached him. Holding my breath, I extended my hand toward him. He held his neck rigid and trembled even more. I spoke softly and finally touched his face, wondering which finger I could live without. But he squeezed his eyes shut, and after a minute or so I was able to turn his muzzle to me and gently wipe his eye.

It's not like I don't care about animals. When I was a child, I tried to save every living thing that crossed my path. Nestlings that fell out of trees, abandoned kittens, baby mice after their mothers were killed in traps behind the store, broken butterflies, even worms that had been dug up by the local fishermen and discarded on the beach at the end of the day. I would bring them to the Galley and set up a nursing unit in the back. Everything has a right to live. I do have a heart, but it's been gated, much like the front door of the Galley when I leave at night. I lost too much when Dan died and a gated heart is necessary because it locks out pain and protects everything left inside.

"I'm not looking for a dog," I said softly while washing away the accumulations that had gathered around his eyes. "And even if I wanted a dog, I kind of like poodles." He looked up at me, his chunk of a head resting ever so lightly in my hand. "I don't know where you came from," I said, "and maybe someone is searching for you right now." He sniffed the air as if to double-check my statement. Then he sniffed my hand.

Dogs have 140 million scent receptors, more or less, and he was evaluating me. I noted his tattered ear, then the snipped ear, his prominent ribs, the scars, the wretched skin draped like tattered crepe around his bones. No, it wouldn't be such a good thing if he was found by the person who had allowed him to get like this.

I buttered him another muffin and left it on the floor as a goodwill gesture. He crouched toward it, ate it slowly, then licked all the crumbs from the floor, leaving it polished clean, also a goodwill gesture. We were one for one. We sat there for a while, both of us thinking.

"Well, you're not a poodle," I pointed out. He crawled a few inches on his belly, toward me, apologizing for not being the right kind of dog. I stared at him. I knew this much: that if I opened my heart it would crack apart from pain. I couldn't have that.

He was shivering. I knew it wasn't from being cold. How could I not respond?

"I'm cranky most of the time," I warned. "And I can't allow myself to love you."

He knew. It was okay with him; he had nothing else. Our eyes met; then he looked away in deference. There was such misery in his face. "Oh, okay," I heard myself saying. "Listen, you can stay on. Trial basis and all that. Don't expect me to love you, but I will care for you. You have to eat, and you need medical care, which means the first thing I have to do is take you to the vet. You look like shit."

He wagged his tail very slowly, his eyes still averted. Oh, he knew.

"And when I find you a good home, you will be leaving," I said. "It would really be better for you."

Yes, he agreed, it would be better.

It seemed I now had a houseguest, more or less. I didn't want one, but I don't think that was important to him. I sighed; he sighed back. We needed a walk on the beach to seal the deal.

Chapter 4

I cannot forgive the bay for taking Dan and my father, but I still need to see it every day. I need to stand watch on the old pier and supervise the movement and cadence of the water, to make sure that it is behaving, though I know it flows without a conscience. I rail at it sometimes, for being so selfish.

The beach was quiet, waiting for early evening to start. The water was flowing shoreward, ebbing and returning, giving and taking, trading old shells for new, old pebbles for new glistening ones, adding fresh seaweed to the clog already on the shore, as though all that swapping should appease me, but it is never a fair trade. It takes lives and never returns them.

The gulls, unfazed by the dog following me, walked behind us in a straight line, waiting for their bread. I always throw them stale bread, but I had nothing today. "Tomorrow," I promised them aloud. "I'll bring you food tomorrow." They cried at me in disappointment before flying off, dipping and hovering over the water, looking for something else to eat. Ahead of me was the town dock, really a collection of old wooden boards fastened to weather-beaten pilings and fenced in by a wobbly rail.

There is a staircase on one side that goes down to a lower pier, where the boats are nestled in their slips. I have a need to stand there every evening and stare across the water, listening to the wood creak from the undulating waves, and feel the boards sway under my feet. I always hope, without any reason to, that I will see a certain boat.

Everyone here owns a boat, and like their owners, they are practical and unpretentious. They were just ahead of me, boats of all sizes and colors moored in their slips like captured horses in their stalls, bobbing and tugging at their chains, impatiently waiting for their masters. I start thinking maybe I should have packed a few sandwiches from the store, for the two of us, dog and me, to spend the evening sitting on the dock. I would bet a dollar that the dog knew all about boating. He was behind me every step, keeping his distance, but there was longing in his eyes to come to me, though he couldn't allow himself to do it. I understood that.

I had picked up a slow jog when my foot caught a coil of thick pink Asian seaweed. It twisted my ankle out from under me and landed me flat on my back, flailing like a fish fighting for its breath on the sand. I was wrapped in putrid seaweed and furious at myself. I know better than to run in flip-flops. I pulled myself to my feet and stood for a moment, testing my ankle, not sure what to do next. I felt a stabbing twinge, but it seemed tolerable, certainly not a reason to give up what little was left of the afternoon. I could make it to the dock if I walked carefully, but by the time I got there my ankle was swollen like a melon, and throbbing bitterly.

There was a pile of old blankets lying against one of the wooden benches along the pier. Sometimes people leave things to pick up later, especially if they are carrying a lot of fish home. Blankets, food chests, gear, all of it stays safe until they return. We are an honest town.

The dog sniffed at the blankets and started barking loudly. The blankets moved and I jumped.

"Miss, please," a deep voice rang out, "call off your dog." The blankets rolled and sat up and I quickly realized there was a person wrapped inside. One of the blankets fell away, revealing a man—jeans, plaid shirt, thick beard and mustache, his head covered in an unkempt pile of dark brown curls. It took me another minute to realize that the dock was isolated and I was disadvantaged by my ankle.

I backed away and started to call the dog. After all, what is a pit bull for, if not a deterrent? The first problem was that the dog didn't have a name, at least not one mutually agreed upon yet, and the second problem was that he wasn't particularly inclined to run to my side.

I mustered some authority and gave the dog a stern look. "You! Come!" I ordered. "*You!* Come here!" I pointed to my feet. He barked at them.

I was on my own. I lurched away, my ankle sending up waves of pain. The man unrolled a silver cane from the blankets and hoisted himself up in a most unusual manner, one leg stretched out, before staggering to his feet and steadying himself with the cane. The dog trotted over to sniff him.

"Please, ma'am," the man called to me, "I don't want him to bite me!"

Not being able to vouch for the dog's spirit of hospitality, I called him for the second time. "Dog!" He still ignored me. "Come on!" I started hopping away, hoping the dog would follow.

"You don't have to leave, ma'am." The man's face fell into disappointment. "I'm sorry. I didn't mean to complain about your dog. I like dogs. Please stay."

Right.

I didn't answer, just hopped off on my good foot, trying to spare my useless ankle. The dog could stay and make a new best friend and follow him to the moon, as far as I was concerned. Pit bull or not, he was doing me no good. The man rolled the blankets into a soft bundle and tucked them under his arm, then started after me, leaning on his cane in a slow, careful, side-to-side swinging walk. "Don't go, ma'am. You don't have to go!" he called after me. "I live around here."

Ma'am? Ha! He couldn't possibly be local. No one around here was that polite.

"I'm a good guy."

That would be for me to decide, I thought. But the dog apparently believed him and was now trailing him closely.

It looked like a turtle race. A woman, slowly limping away from a man who was slowly lurching after her, the metallic click of his cane against the wooden pier coming closer, and a pit bull bringing up the rear in a leisurely stroll.

But where to go? It struck me that I was only leading the man back to my empty house on an empty beach with an empty street on the other side.

"I live on Beach Six Street and Neptune!" the man called after me, as though to reassure me. "Honestly. I just come here to nap. I bet you even know my aunt."

I kept hopping but mentally rummaged through all the people I knew on Neptune Road. One. I knew one.

"I'm Phyllis Reyes's nephew. My mother is her sister!" he called out again.

Bingo.

"I just moved in with her this week," he added. "Me and my mother."

Miss Phyllis. Well, his hair could have used her help.

He stopped. "Please?" he said softly.

Against my better judgment, I stopped, too.

We were facing each other now. He was taller than me, maybe six three or something, an oak tree kind of guy, large and solid. His face—what wasn't obscured by the thick beard—and his neck, though he had an olive complexion, were burned red from the sun and he had dark brown eyes. His plaid shirt and rumpled jeans looked clean; I was the one who looked like she spent the morning rolling in seagull droppings. My tee was covered in wet sand and gull poop. I had seaweed dangling down from one shoulder like an epaulet, shells and barnacles still tangled in my hair. And I was moving like I had a wooden wheel.

"I'm Sam Ahmadi." He gave me a rueful smile and ran his hand through his hair as if to tame it. "I'm really not what I look like." He offered his hand and we shook.

"Aila." He didn't need to know my last name.

"What's wrong with your foot?" he asked, peering down at it. "Let me see it." He leaned awkwardly on his cane and bent over to inspect it closely. "I don't think it's fractured but maybe a bad sprain. What happened?"

"I tripped," I said. "On seaweed."

He straightened up. "Need help getting somewhere?"

"You're limping yourself," I pointed out.

"I'm used to limping," he said, and pulled up his pants leg. Instead of a left leg, there was a silver and blue prosthesis, a space age replacement that started from inside his sneaker. I gasped even before I realized it. "How did that happen?"

"IED," he said softly. "Afghanistan. I was a Navy SEAL."

I dimly recalled almost two years back when I received, simultaneously, my usual bad haircut and a long family history from his aunt. Nephew blown up serving in Afghanistan. This man had obviously been the subject of her story.

"So, am I okay?" he said. There was a teasing note in his voice. "Enough to help you home?"

Well, yes.

He dropped his blankets. "I'll get these later," he mumbled, and moved next to me, holding his arm for me to lean on. "May I help you?"

"Thank you."

We lurched a few steps together—I was the destabilizing force—then paused for a moment before taking a few steps more. We were in sight of the small parking lot just off the beach and I could see that it contained a single car. I recognized it. It was his aunt's car, a 1970 iridescent pink Cadillac Eldorado, with *Follicles* written in gold script on the doors. He gave the parking lot a quick glance. "Well, that's my aunt's car, but I don't see yours."

"I don't need a car to get home; I live right there." I pointed to my house ahead, standing on its stilty legs, like a flamingo. His face launched into a goofy smile. I've always loved that reaction when people find out where I live.

"Whoa!" he exclaimed. "That's a great house. The water's practically in your back door."

"Yeah." I gave an ironic chuckle. "And sometimes that is exactly the problem." He held me close, allowing me to lean a bit. It felt awkward, but his arm was strong around my waist and supported me easily. The dog followed us, politely staying back a few feet.

"I can get up from here," I told Sam at the bottom of the steps, hoping to make it less complicated for him. "Thank you for your help."

"I didn't mind at all." He stepped onto his good right leg, then swung his left leg out to the side and set it down carefully on the step before putting his weight on it. "See? I can do steps," he said as he slowly climbed to the deck. The way he said it, the wonder and triumph and pride in his voice, caught me. He sounded like a child tying their shoes for the first time all by himself. "But I can't help you, sorry. Just hop up on your good foot and hold the railings."

I followed him up.

When we finished, he looked around, carefully studying the landscape before pulling the rocking chair against the house and plunking himself down. Now I would have to make polite conversation, I thought with some regret. I hate small talk.

A breeze blew in from the bay, twisting his curls into strands that stood up from his head like he was being electrocuted. I smiled at the sight. He patted them down, but the wind blew them right back up.

"Can't tame the wind," he said apologetically, "or my hair. Both very independent." The dog climbed the steps and sat himself in a corner. Sam put his hand down to summon the dog, who gave him the squint-eye and remained where he was.

"He's not very friendly," Sam commented.

"He does what he needs to do," I said, hoping I made the dog sound vaguely protective, just in case.

Sam leaned back in the chair. "Aila," he said, then repeated it. "Well, Miss Aila. This is a great location."

"Belonged to my folks," I said, then regretted saying even that. It would only lead to more conversation.

"So, you grew up around here."

I nodded. "What about you?" He didn't look like a local—the ones who grew up here tend to look alike, with crooked teeth, sandy hair, and a hooty-snarky laugh. Shay says it's because the whole town is inbred and that's why we had to find husbands in out-of-state colleges.

"I was born here, but we moved to Jordan when I was six. I came back to the States for my last year of high school. Lived with my aunt on the east end of Long Island," he explained. "Wading River. I never could stay away from the water."

"Is that why you were sleeping on the pier?"

He pointed to his leg, or rather where his leg should have been. "Can't get sand between my stump and the leg, and it's not good to get the leg wet with seawater, it gets corroded, so I nap on the pier, except the wood is full of splinters, so I roll up in blankets. Besides, I have lung problems and the air is good here."

It made sense.

"You need a lift to the doctor or something?" He nodded toward my foot. "I can drive you."

"Thanks, I can take myself."

"Maybe you should call someone—your husband?" he said, glancing at the wedding band I still wore.

"He's dead," I said. The pain returned. Boats and search-lights and bad news under a full moon. Suddenly I couldn't, didn't want to talk to him, or anyone, anymore. "I have to go," I said, and hopped to the back door. I rattled the doorknob, hoping he would think I was fiddling with a key, though, in truth, the door had been unlocked the whole time.

He stood up, too. "Listen, put some ice on that," he said firmly. "I'm pretty sure it's a bad sprain, but you never know." He reached into his pants pocket and fished around, pulling out a Swiss Army knife, then a gold Cross pen and a few scraps of paper. He scribbled on the paper and handed it to me. "Here's my cell. Call me if you need a ride to the hospital or whatever. I don't mind." He took a breath. "I mean if you want to. I don't want to push myself on you." He sounded apologetic.

"Hey, thank you. It's very kind of you." I didn't want him to think I was ungrateful, but I felt a wave of relief when he finally lowered himself down each step to the beach. He quickly scanned the shoreline, then looked up at me.

"I'll check in with you tomorrow to see how you are." Our eyes met only for a moment; he looked away immediately. "If that's okay," he added softly. "I tend to take over."

"I'll be fine," I said.

"It's no problem," he said. "Honestly."

"No, really," I said.

"No, really," he said, walking away. "I'll check in on you tomorrow. You need to get that looked at."

He stopped and pointed to the dog. "That's not your dog, is it? You don't look like the type of person that would have a dog in that condition."

"No," I admitted. "I just found him."

"I figured," he replied. "He needs a vet—he looks like shit. Medically speaking." He gave me a quick wave and in his slightly stiff gait walked across the beach, back to the pier, to pick up his blankets, then made his way, slowly and carefully, across the sand and the broken shells, to the parking lot.

I watched him for a moment. I didn't want to make new friends. I didn't want to talk to anyone; I didn't want to start anything. I opened my door, then ducked inside to the kitchen and shut it behind me, turning both locks, leaving him and the dog outside.

Chapter 5

I don't sleep well anymore. I see ghosts along the wall that are made of moonlight. Sometimes the bay calls me through my bedroom window to come outside. When the moon is shining, my bedroom lights up silver; the little statues from my childhood glow on the bookshelf as though they are coming to life. There is a picture hanging over my old bureau, of Dan and me on our wedding day, and the lace on my dress shimmers. I am wearing a tiny, delicate necklace that Dan had given me when we were dating. It's a shell, a wentletrap, with a fine silver chain threaded through. The shell is unique, a porcelain spiral of tan and cream swirling upward, like a tiny staircase. Even in the picture, the delicate ribbing caught the tiny shred of moonlight. "A staircase to the stars," Dan had told me as he put it around my neck. "And I'll always be waiting for you at the top." If I stare at the two of us long enough, I can hear wedding music and Dan whispering into my ear, telling me he loves me. I fight sleep. It can be my friend or my enemy and I never know which one the night will bring.

* * *

Sometimes I wake up in the middle of the night still stuck in a dream: I am talking to Dan while we are eating dinner and he reaches across the table to take my hand. I feel his fingers close around mine; their warmth and strength, the texture of his skin, make my heart beat so fast it could lift me off my chair. And then I awake to nothing. Sometimes Dan and my father are getting into the boat, the wind is up, and the clouds on the horizon are just starting to look moody. I yell at Dan, *Stop, don't go out, stop!* And he listens! He and my father get out of the boat and we all go home and everything is back to normal and I wake up pulling long, noisy breaths of relief thinking that I *did* it, I saved them! For a moment, the dream hangs there, like a cloud draped on the air before dissipating, and then I sit up and realize, again, I am left with nothing.

That night there was a new moon, a sliver of itself, selfishly hoarding its light, letting dark shadows devour the bedroom.

Wanting the day to be done with, I had eaten a bowl of left-over chicken stew, showered, and limped off to bed. Maybe it was the way I had been bracing against the pain in my foot, but I fell asleep almost at once.

Something woke me.

It was very low, very soft, a cross between a moan and a whine, and I knew right away it was the sound of a lonely dog. I got out of bed and opened the door. He quickly ducked into the kitchen and disappeared. I started to go after him, but the bay called and I couldn't help but slip outside to stand on the deck.

The new moon was barely visible within the clouds. I used to think that new moons ushered new beginnings, the promise of another month, the promise of more time, of four more weeks for you to change things, find answers, make yourself better. Now I see that new moons assure nothing. They are too narrow, too stingy; they keep their light to themselves, leaving us in the shadows. I looked away.

The air was moist from a northern breeze, but even in the dark I could see thin white foam floating on black water. It was high tide; the waves rose up and fell like horses rearing, then dropping back into the water. The rocking chair sat immobile in a corner, waiting for me, but there would be no boats coming home tonight. No point in sitting there. "You took them!" I yelled across the sand, hoping my words would sink below the foam and penetrate the water. "How could you? How *could* you?"

I returned inside, locked the door, and looked around. The dog had seemingly vanished, but I knew right away where he had gone.

He was stretched across my bed, his eyes closed tight, his breath deep and relaxed, like he had been waiting for this forever. I stared at him for a minute.

"Hey," I said. "You can't sleep there."

He squeezed his eyes tighter, as if that would lock out my voice.

"You're dirty and it's my bed, and I don't want a dog," I said. There wasn't even a break in the rhythm of his breathing. "I would like to go to sleep now, in my bed. Alone, if you don't mind."

He didn't move. If a dog could have a look of imperturbability—and ownership of his surroundings—this one did. How could I wake him? How could I take this away from him? He had nothing. I decided to let him sleep there, just for the night, because how do you get a strange pit bull out of your bed? I would launder my sheets and blankets in the morning.

And find him a home.

I sat down on the bed. *My* bed. His body looked like the plastic dog skeleton I used for the comparative anatomy classes I taught. His prominent ribs rhythmically rose and fell under his scruffy skin, but his face looked peaceful. Okay, he seemed to be a gentle dog. A good and gentle dog who had come to terrible harm. He deserved one night of total rest; I could give him that. Careful not to disturb him, I grabbed my pillow and my robe and curled up on the floor, next to my bed, staying there for the night, immobile, staring up at the ceiling.

"Good night," I murmured, wrapped in my robe. I left him

alone. The night passed; I listened to his breaths and let the darkness escort me into sleep.

Five o'clock the next morning we both awoke. I let out a yelp when my foot hit the floor. The ankle was nearly unbearable. I opened the back door to let the dog out, since walking him was out of the question. I have a small fenced yard on the side of my house and I keep the gate open, but I knew I wouldn't be able to get to it. I was hoping he would use it and certain he would return, since I didn't think dogs ran away before eating breakfast.

I had to see the doctor. And I knew the dog needed a vet. I also knew that the vet would ask his name and I was not going to name him because naming implied I had an emotional investment in him and I couldn't give him that. Well, the vet could just call him John Doe Dog.

It was getting late. My first priority was the Galley. I called Shay. Dear Shay. She answered sleepily and promised to open the store and get things going. What would I do without her?

Not having the foresight to bring dog food home, I made the dog a bowl of oatmeal. And a bowl for myself, with the addition of my usual big cup of light cream—coffee for me. I dressed quickly as I waited for the dog to return from his morning business. After a few minutes, he scratched at the back door to come in. I turned around to find the shadow of a man across the glass.

There was a polite knock, and the voice from yesterday. "Miss Aila?"

I hobbled to the door and cracked it open to a new and improved Sam. He'd apparently had an intervention by Miss Phyllis. His hair had a fresh buzz cut; the beard was gone, the mustache tamed, revealing a handsome, strong-featured face with high cheekbones and a commanding nose. Gone, too, were the rumpled jeans and plaid shirt, replaced by fresh khakis and a new, clean tee with *Fleetbourne* across the front—damn those shirts, they were everywhere and I was mostly responsible.

The dog bolted in and ran straight for the oatmeal, then, when he was finished, hid in a corner under the kitchen table.

"I took the liberty of coming here," Sam started. "To see how you were getting by. How's your ankle?" He waited politely at the door, his shoulders at an angle, his eyes darting out to survey the beach every few minutes. "I am offering to drive you to the doctor."

I was taken aback for a moment. I remembered he had offered the day before, but I hadn't taken him seriously. I was planning to call the one cab that served our village, though the driver didn't start until ten a.m., usually stopped for a snack at eleven, lunched from two to three, and ended the day around five.

"That is very kind," I started, "but—" But what? I could barely move my leg without a wave of pain now traveling up to my hip. I made a quick decision to invite him in. The dog was giving me courage. What is a pit bull for, if not for courage? Even if said pit bull was lacking his own and, at the moment, quivering under my table.

"Would you like some coffee?" I asked, opening the door wider.

He stepped into the room, his wide shoulders filling it, looked around quickly, took a chair, and placed it against the wall before lowering himself into it. "Yes, ma'am," he said. "I would love some."

Military training. He was charmingly respectful and I girded myself against him. I was not going to be taken in by good manners and kindness. I walk alone. Okay, limp. Another shot of pain as I pivoted to get the coffeepot from the stove reminded me that I might want to scale back my independence. I poured him coffee. "Would you like a bowl of oatmeal?"

"Thank you, ma'am, but I already had my breakfast."

"I'm not old enough to be ma'amed," I joked. "Please call me Aila."

"Yes, ma'am. You know, before I knocked on your door, I took the liberty of checking out your car," he said. "The red one on the side of the house? I see it's a manual. You won't be able to drive it with that foot."

I looked down at my foot. It was now about the size of a cranberry-pecan loaf.

"There's nothing wrong in letting someone help you," he said gently.

"You're right."

"And," he ended, "it would be my pleasure."

"Thank you," I said. "I do appreciate it." I did. He didn't know me and yet he was giving up his morning to help me. He was a good person.

I was very grateful.

And—yes, despite myself—charmed.

Chapter 6

Getting a reluctant pit bull from under a table and into the backseat of a car is not an easy undertaking. He was obviously afraid of men, and one just doesn't whisk a dog like that out of hiding and carry him like a sack of turnips through the back door. Nor does one push him, pull him, roll him, or in any way cause undue agitation. I eventually lured him out of the house with a Portuguese muffin, after which I quickly slipped an old clothesline from the back deck around his neck. He'd apparently had some training and walked next to me as though we hadn't just had a major tussle lasting fifteen minutes. But when he saw the car door open, he planted himself like an anchor before jerking backward in terror.

"I bet he was thrown out of a car," Sam said. "He thinks it's going to happen again."

Hoping that the dog might still be motivated by food, I put a fluffy green beach towel on the backseat and covered it in day-old muffins from the store. He took the bait, hopped in, and ate them at the rate of a mile a muffin while Sam drove slowly and carefully, using his normal leg to capably work the gas and brake pedals. He didn't seem the least bit embarrassed to be driving us to Urgent Care in a bright pink Eldorado touting hair follicles on each door.

"So, how do you like Fleetbourne?" I asked as he navigated us through town.

"I haven't seen all that much of it, ma'am," he said. "Just the beach."

"You don't have to ma'am me," I corrected him. "Do you get to the beach much?"

"Yes, ma'am." He nodded. "Every day. Usually early in the morning. I don't want to bother anybody with the way my leg looks. You know, sometimes I take it off."

"I don't think anyone would be bothered," I murmured. "It's very stylish."

He chuckled, then asked, "When do *you* go? The beach, I mean."

"I prefer to go at night," I answered. "I like to look at the moon. It's a personal thing we have, me and the moon."

"The moon is very nice, ma'am."

"Don't ma'am me."

"No, ma'am."

"Severe sprain," diagnosed the doctor at Urgent Care after my foot was X-rayed, rotated, and squeezed like a loaf of day-old bread before it was wrapped. "Stay off it for a while." I was given a soft cast, an extra ACE bandage, a prescription for crutches, and a starter bottle of painkillers.

"Demodectic mange," said Dr. Susan, the vet at the animal hospital, after examining the dog. "And a deep scratch across his eye." The dog was about eighteen months old, she said, and a red-nosed pit bull, which made him sound festive, like a reindeer at Christmas. I was given a paper bag filled with medicated shampoo, ear mite drops, eyedrops, heartwormer, an appointment to remove his doghood when he was stronger, and a bill for $312. The dog got a warm, sudsy bath from the vet's groomer, three shots, a new bright green leash, a leather collar, and, even though he shook violently and held his head and tail fearfully between his legs the whole time, a bag of cookies for being brave.

"What are all these weird marks?" I asked the vet, pointing to the white lines that covered the dog's chest and muzzle.

She peered at them. "Scars," she said. "It looks like he was used as a bait dog. They always get torn up pretty bad around the front part of their body."

I touched his head gently and let my hand linger.

Oh, he *had* been brave. He had been so very brave.

"You want to go back home or to the Galley?" Sam asked me as we rounded Beach Fourteen.

"How did you know about the Galley?"

"When I mentioned your name to my aunt, she told me all about you," he said. "She said you were a lovely person and a loyal client."

Yep, her salon was so conveniently close I had reluctantly joined the ranks of loyal clients with bad haircuts.

"She told me what happened," he said. "I'm sorry for your losses."

"Thank you."

"If you ever want to talk to someone," he added softly, "I'm a good listener."

"I'm not a good talker," I replied.

Shay was tidying behind the counter when Sam opened the door, her face registering surprise as I hobbled through, Sam and the dog following, but not before Sam gave the interior a quick glance over and placed his back against an aisle of cereal.

"It's demodectic mange," I announced.

"On your ankle?" she asked, surprised.

"On the dog." I pointed to him. "I have a bad sprain."

"Oh! I was so worried." She gave me a hug. "I was afraid you had broken it. Why don't you go home, so you can stay off your foot? I can handle things."

I laughed. "When is the last time I took a day off?"

"Never," she said, making a face. "Does it hurt a lot?"

The painkillers had kicked in by now "No," I replied. "It's quite *excellent*. I'm actually enjoying it."

"And it looks like you made a friend," she added. "I knew you two needed each other."

Sam flushed and looked at his shoes.

"He spent the night with me," I said. "Crawled into my bed without my permission." Sam turned even redder. Then I realized what he was thinking. "The dog," I quickly added. We all nodded at one another in relief.

Shay was on top of things. "And you are?" She held her hand out to Sam.

"Sam," I introduced him. "We met on the pier after I sprained my ankle. He was kind enough to drive me to the doctor this morning." Sam shuffled in embarrassment.

"Shay is my best friend," I said to him.

They shook hands solemnly. "Well, thank you for taking care of her," Shay said. "Aila is too independent sometimes. I worry about her."

"It was my pleasure," he replied, and gave her a shy grin.

Shay surveyed him. I just knew she and I were going to have a meaningful conversation after he left. Something along the lines of how happy she was that I was finally reaching out and letting my guard down and that he seemed like a very nice man.

She invited him to join us for lunch. "We usually make something special for ourselves that we call the Sandwich," she explained. "It has to be spoken with a capital *S*."

"Liverwurst with Swiss cheese, tomato, anchovies, pickles, potato chips, and extra mustard and mayo," I added. It was listed on the Galley chalkboard as the S&A Sandwich Special although there was very little call for it. The ingredients in the sandwich had evolved over several years, growing more populous with passing time. The chips were fairly recent.

"On rye," Shay said. "The rye is crucial."

He didn't flinch. "Thank you," he said, "but I'd better be going. I can see you're going to have a busy day and I promised my aunt I'd do a few repairs around the house for her."

"Then you have to let me give you my homemade bread," I

said, hopping behind the counter to retrieve a loaf of pecan-cranberry bread. "I really appreciate your kindness today."

He took the bread and thanked me. I thanked him for driving me. He thanked me for offering him lunch, ma'amed me half a dozen times while I thanked him for being so polite. After finally running out of pleasantries, we both took a deep breath. He smiled at me and left.

"So," started Shay, pouring us coffee while I made two Sandwiches. "I'm happy that you're finally letting your guard down. He seems like a really nice guy and it's about time you allowed yourself to reach out."

"I knew you were going to say that," I said, throwing the dog a thick slice of liverwurst so he would stop salivating on my soft cast.

"I knew that you knew," Shay said, taking a bite of her sandwich, then holding it away from her mouth, as though she was reluctant to chew it.

"What?" I asked. "Not enough chips?"

She shook her head, started to take a second bite, and stopped, finally putting the sandwich back on her plate. "I don't think I'm very hungry."

Something was up. How anyone could turn down the Galley Special was beyond me. "Toothache?" I asked. "Headache?"

"It's nothing." She got up and wiped off the counter, then restacked the newspapers, then took the liverwurst from the cold cut case and rewrapped it, then wiped off the counter, then started a fresh pot of coffee, then wiped off the counter—

"Okay, what's going on?" I asked.

"Just want to get—you know—stuff done so, you know, you don't have to hop all over the place on your foot."

"Liar."

She paused for a long moment before taking a quivery breath. "Okay. There is something I need to talk to you about."

"Okay," I said. "I hope it isn't that you are happy that I'm finally letting my guard down and reaching out—"

"No," she said, interrupting me. "We covered that already." She stood facing me, her expression serious. I looked up into her eyes, dark and kind and full of affection. "I can't eat the Sandwich because it's making me sick."

"What? How is that possible? It's our favorite! We always—"

She put her hand on my arm and interrupted me. "Aila, I'm pregnant."

"Shay!" I exclaimed, jumping to my feet. Actually, foot. "I am so happy for you!"

I *was* happy for her and stricken at the same time. We had always promised we would try to get pregnant together so that our children would grow up and become sisters. And now it had just become impossible. Forever impossible. She looked uncertain. I threw my arms around her and hugged her. "I *am* happy for you," I said truthfully, lavishing kisses all over her face. "Thrilled and filled with joy."

"Really?"

"Oh yes!" We hugged again. "It's the best news! You're going to have a beautiful baby! And I am going to be the crazy aunt, and feed it ground-up liverwurst and pickles in its morning bottle."

She gave me a glorious smile.

We worked together for the rest of the day, trying to come up with names for the baby, although she had no idea yet what it was.

"Oceana, if it's a girl!" I called out.

"Tug for a boy!" she called back, giggling.

"Anemone!"

"SurfDude!" We were practically rolling on the floor by now.

That was our last name; we were stumped after that. And after preparing forty-five sandwiches, selling twenty *Fleetbourne* T-shirts—extra large—plus all the rest of the pecan-cranberry loaves, we were ready to close. It was four o'clock. Shay gave me and the dog a lift home. I kissed her on the cheek and watched her bright yellow Fiat whiz down Beach One until it was out of sight.

And then I burst into tears.

Chapter 7

The fading sun spread soft peach light across a pale gray sky, drizzling it through the clouds and over the beach, like warm jam. The breeze toyed with my hair but didn't intrude as I sat in the rocking chair on the deck, my leg propped up. The dog seemed to understand that my foot hurt and was sitting a safe distance from me with a concerned expression. The seagulls weren't so forgiving; they dove at the deck, squealing angrily at me for having forgotten their bread again.

"It's not like it would have definitely worked out anyway," I told the dog. "There's no guarantee that I would have gotten pregnant. And our kids might have even hated each other."

He looked up at me solemnly.

"I want the best for Shay," I added. "She deserves it." He sniffed toward the water. The beach was empty. Small power-boats zipped across the bay; a guy was water-skiing behind one of them and waved to me. I waved back, though I was certain we didn't know each other.

"No beach today," I said. "It's just too hard to walk on the sand."

The dog stretched himself across the deck and stared up at me.

"We both wanted girls, you know," I continued. "Shay and me. I bet you it's going to be a girl." He crept a little closer, put his head down between his paws, his mangled half ear perking up, as though to say, *Go ahead; I'm still listening.*

"Maybe it's for the best. Maybe I should never have kids," I went on morosely. "My grandma was crazy, you know. I might have crazy genes." The boat turned hard; the skier slid sideways and wiped out. The boat powered a circle and someone leaned overboard to pull him back in. A member of his family? Other than my mother, I had no family. Maybe I would never have family. The dog was still listening.

"My grandma Ida was the town crazy," I began.

My grandmother Ida had long been known to the locals as Crazy Ida because she danced in the bay, fully clothed, no matter the weather, and sang, arms outstretched and her face turned full tilt to the sky. She was especially active when there was a full moon. I used to stand on the beach and watch her.

My sweetheart's the man in the moon. I'm going to marry him soon. . . .

Why she chose that song I'll never know. It dated back to the 1890s or so, but I thought everyone's grandma sang in public, with or without the water, until I hit third grade and realized she was the only one in Fleetbourne, in all of Cape Cod, possibly the entire world, or maybe the entire universe including the Milky Way and Andromeda, who did that.

During the day, my parents spent long hours running the Galley while my grandmother babysat me. Every morning she would wheel me in my stroller down to the water's edge, park me there, and then roll up her slacks and dance in the water as the tide lapped around her legs. On brisk days she layered herself in heavy clothing, swathed me in extra blankets, and parked me out of reach of the tide. Snow blended into her white hair and melted into the water, the wind turned her face scarlet and her hands nearly blue, but still she danced. Her voice carried far—it was said on windy days you could hear her across the bay and all the way into Provincetown proper.

Crazy Ida.

It was because she loved the ocean. Loved the way it smelled, the way it moved, the creatures it harbored, the stars it captured at night and reflected back. Her dance was a tribute to the sea, she once told me when I got old enough to understand. She would have been a sailor. She would have lived on the ocean, swum its entirety, traveled its lanes to every country in the world, sailed to the moon, if she could. But it was the wrong time. She could only dance in it, and let the water and her helplessness and her anger and her disappointment roll off her shoulders and fall back into the sea.

As I got older, I was teased. It wasn't easy being the granddaughter of Crazy Ida.

"Everyone has a little crazy in them, for all sorts of reasons," she told me once when she caught me crying bitterly after I had just gotten home from school after a particularly rough session from the class bully. "It's good to let it out."

"Everyone says you're crazy," I said through sobs. "And that maybe I am, too."

"And that's a good thing," she said, giving me a kiss on my head. "Because you can never be more free."

If I stared at the bay, I could almost see her figure in the water, her arms held aloft, her pants billowing around her legs.

My sweetheart's the man in the moon. I'm going to marry him soon. . . .

I needed her. I grabbed my crutches and hopped down the steps to the sand. The dog sighed and followed along.

The painkillers had worn off by now and my foot was throbbing meanly. It was exhausting to hop across the sand—the crutches dug deep holes each time I pressed on them, but I labored along.

As we drew closer to the pier, it struck me that I was showing an absolute lack of good judgment. It would have been a lot smarter to keep both my cast out of the sand and the sand out of my cast, but I was drawn to the pier. Standing there completed my day. It was the only way I could say good night to Dan.

Okay, maybe I was also a bit lonely and hoping to see someone.

My heart jumped when I saw Sam, sitting up, his blankets wrapped around his shoulders, his normal leg tucked underneath and his prosthetic leg stretched in front, shining silver, catching the declining rays of sun. His cane rested against the pier railing.

"Hey!" he called out, then coughed from the effort. "You're not supposed to be walking."

"I'm not exactly walking!" I called back, and he laughed.

He laboriously stood up and made his way down, swinging his prosthetic leg out over the step below, placing his cane carefully before transferring his weight onto both.

"Don't come down," I protested.

"I'm fine." When he got to the bottom, he shook out one of the blankets and laid it across a step. "You want to sit?"

I sat. The dog sat.

"He seems to be getting more relaxed around people," Sam remarked.

"I hope so."

We didn't speak. The water murmured against the pilings.

"I thought you came here in the morning," I finally said.

"I'm not comfortable doing it anymore," he said. "More people on the beach."

"Tourists," I agreed. "The summer crowd is starting. It's a private beach, but they wander across."

He looked at me and gave me a wry smile. "Is it okay if I come at night?"

"It's not mine personally; it belongs to the town," I said, then realized I sounded snotty. "I mean, everyone is welcome."

"We can share the moon," he said.

My stomach gave a lurch. "Don't trust the moon," I said. "Don't ever trust the moon."

* * *

We sat there in silence. The breeze became more insistent as the sun started its journey behind Provincetown. One by one, red, blue, green, and gold lights highlighted the restaurants, the little theater clubs, the boutiques. A long strip of gold lights illuminated MacMillan Wharf. Provincetown was waking up, ready to party.

"It will be dark soon," I said. The day was disappearing; it was getting harder to see his face.

"May I ask you something?"

"Of course."

"Would you like . . ." he started, then paused. "You are probably busy." He began again. "So . . . okay . . . yeah—so, what are you doing for dinner?"

I hadn't thought where things could lead. I wasn't looking for things to lead anywhere. I just wanted the next moment to be okay, and then the moment after that, to let me survive without pain. Still, I didn't want to hurt his feelings. "I was planning to open a can of soup and then go to bed."

"Oh. Okay," he said.

We left it at that, but I felt—what? Guilt? I should be sitting with Dan. Boston was over two hours away and Dan used to make the trip here every Friday and return to work on Monday. I should be sitting here with Dan. It was our ritual, summer nights on the pier. He would spend the day fishing while I spent the day helping my father in the store and then Dan and I would meet on the beach and swim in the twilight before we ate dinner. I should be sitting here with Dan.

Minutes passed. I could almost believe it was Dan breathing next to me, sharing the blanket. We were both too full of our own thoughts and the day finally tiptoed away without notice.

We left the pier, the three of us. Sam offered to walk me home.

"I'll be okay," I said, though I knew it wasn't the point.

Besides, I had the dog and what was the point of having a pit bull if I couldn't use him to escort me safely home? We all strolled to Sam's car and I thanked him again for driving me that morning.

I watched the Eldorado make its way down the road, a bright pink beacon shining into the dusk, and the old feelings came back. Dan and I walking home, hand in hand. Dan leaning over to give me a quick kiss on the neck. Dan and I killing off the last drop of wine, sitting on the deck, before we went to bed.

The loneliness suddenly stabbed me like a shard of glass. Why couldn't I finally let it go, give it all a kiss good-bye and reach out and take what was being offered me?

Was I going to spend my life in mourning, opening the Galley every day and baking bread and making sandwiches, and loving Shay's baby from June to the end of August, and closing the Galley every night and going home and standing on the pier to rail at the water and the moon until I was so empty of pain that I could allow myself to believe that perhaps *this* night, just this night, I would stop waiting for two dead men to return and I would be able to sleep? Did I want to spend my life waiting for two dead men?

Yes. I did.

Maybe you can't help it if your genes are crazy.

Chapter 8

The dog was not exactly a big hit at the Galley.

I insisted on going to work the next day; what else was there for me to do? The dog came with me. What else was there for him to do? Sam was kind enough to pick us up in the morning and take us home at night. I hadn't asked him to; he just appeared, the splendid pink Eldorado glinting outside my kitchen window just after sunrise in the morning, a flower just bloomed.

"I hope your aunt doesn't mind my dog in the car," I said to Sam as he drove us to the store.

"She doesn't know," he admitted. "I wipe everything down before I return the car, and then spray it with stuff to make it smell good. She thinks I have OCD." He chuckled softly.

"Well, I do appreciate it," I said. "You doing all that for me."

"Actually, I do have OCD," he added.

I took precautions with the dog in the store, of course. I couldn't leave him home alone—he needed medications throughout the day—and I couldn't leave him outside. He had been gentle, even timid so far, and I decided to keep him be-hind the counter with me. He had his new leather collar on, and a nice long leash that allowed him to luxuriate in his new red plaid bed and quietly observe the routine of the Galley.

Of course, Mrs. Skipper was the first customer of the day. Despite her age, she darted quickly through the aisles like a minnow, filling her basket, her long, thin fingers grabbing a box of detergent, a box of noodles, a bag of frozen vegetables from the freezer, two bananas, a dozen eggs, the mail from her box. She walked to the counter, bent from fighting the winds of aging, and ordered the usual cherry Danishes, one for herself and one for The Skipper, then stopped mid-sentence to stare at the dog. He was sleeping in his bed behind the counter.

"Where did you get that dog?" she demanded, pointing to him. "I don't remember a dog."

"Got him yesterday."

Shay stopped bagging Mrs. Skipper's groceries and turned around. "He's a lovely dog. Just needs some TLC," she said.

"You know what he is, don't you?" Mrs. Skipper was now stand-ing on tippy-toes in her little white orthopedic shoes, peering over the counter to get a better look.

"Yep," I replied. "He is a good dog."

"He's one of those killer dogs," she pronounced. "I think there's even a village ordinance against owning those things."

Shay picked up the groceries and carried them to the door. "I've lived here my whole life, Mrs. Skipper," she said gently, "and I've never heard of any ordinances about dogs." She held the door open and stood there, waiting.

Mrs. Skipper stood her ground. "This is a nice, quiet village," she said. "There has never been a dog in this store since your great-grandfather opened it and we don't need one now. Espe-cially that one. We don't want trouble."

I took umbrage. I do love the word "umbrage"; it sounds like an artist color—burnt umbrage. "He is staying right here, Mrs. Skipper," I said firmly. "I don't believe he's making any plans to storm the village, so he'll be fine." The dog was looking up at me, his ear stumps pulled back worriedly. He knew what we were talking about—pit bulls know. "He's my dog," I said. "I am taking care of him. Pete Vegara keeps his big shepherd with him at the hardware store and it's never been a problem."

"But this is a pit bull," she retorted. "We'll see if we're going to allow a killer dog in this village. In the general store, no less!"

"The dog stays," I said, trying not to let the tremble I felt in my knees show in my voice. "He's just a dog."

"A dangerous dog."

"He's done nothing," I countered firmly.

"Yet," she snapped. "He's doesn't belong in this town."

"You don't own it," I heard myself saying.

She looked me straight in the eye. "We run it, dear. And we're not going to let you drag in some mongrel to terrorize everyone."

"Do you want me to put your groceries in your car, Mrs. Skipper?" Shay called from the door.

Mrs. Skipper turned her attention to her. "Thank you," she said. "I better leave before I get ripped to shreds." She followed Shay out to her car, letting the door slam and the little bell tinkle behind her.

"People can be so funny," I said to Shay when she returned. "I mean, the dog is no threat. . . ."

"She's just an old crank," Shay reassured me. "She's never liked me. Don't let it bother you."

I looked down at the dog who hadn't broken his gaze from me during the whole conversation. It was the kind of stare that told me he was afraid of what my next words would be. The kind of stare that says, *I am throwing my heart out there for you to pick up, if you want to. Please don't ask me to leave.* I knelt down awkwardly on the floor next to him and reached out to touch his head. He flinched but let me touch him.

"I made you a promise that I would take care of you," I said fiercely, "and I don't break my promises. You're going to stay right here."

"Then you'd better get him a license right away," Shay interjected from behind me. "So he can stay right here legally."

* * *

The rest of the day went without anyone else commenting on him, except for an occasional murmur of surprise or an offer of a belly rub, which I knew he wasn't ready for and circumvented. He slept behind the counter, took his medicine wrapped in bologna slices, shared part of the Sandwich with me, and got up to yawn leisurely when Sam appeared to drive us home. He followed me into the pink Eldorado and while Sam drove, the dog smushed his nose, like he usually did, against the back window to watch the road, leaving huge nose prints all over the glass.

"My aunt needs her car back, so I'm planning to buy myself a car," Sam announced as he parked outside my front door. I eyed the back windows. His eyes followed my gaze.

"Artistic fellow, isn't he?" he remarked.

"Let me clean that before you leave," I said.

"Don't bother," he said, grinning. "I always clean the car before I return it to my aunt anyway. But I'm planning to get a car of my own, she needs this back."

"Good luck," I said. "They're pretty expensive."

"Well, I have some money saved up," he said. "I lived at home after I retired from the service." He paused. "I was hoping maybe you would go with me and help me find something nice. I don't know where anything is around here. Then your dog can mess up *my* windows." I liked his easy nature.

"I'll see how Shay is feeling. If she's okay, I can take the time off," I replied, and explained about the dog license. "Maybe we can get both things done in one day."

"It's a date then," he agreed, and then saw my face. "I mean, an adventure. Yes, ma'am, we'll have an adventure."

I thanked him for the ride and turned toward my house.

"You know," he called after me, "he needs a name if you're going to get him a license!"

I stopped in my tracks. "You're right," I said. "I can't just call him the dog."

"A proper name," Sam added. "It'll help him feel better about himself, too."

I looked at the dog, standing next to me, wearing his new green leash and leather collar, dressed for a new life. He was squinting up at me with his small almond-shaped pit-bull eyes, one swollen shut. He cocked his head, his broken ear pricked as high as it could go.

He did need a name.

But I couldn't allow myself to name him. It would have made him mine, it would have unsealed my heart, and I couldn't do it. A sealed heart seals out pain.

Dinner.

I poured the dog a bowl of crunchies and opened a can of soup for myself. We ate together on the back deck, the light glancing off the bay in the distance and fracturing into a jigsaw of pink and tangerine against the darkening blue sky. The water rolled across the beach like a cat, lithe waves purring softly. Someone walked by and waved; everyone knew me. I liked that everyone knew me. I liked that this was my place, sitting here on my deck and listening to the water hum its contentment along the shore.

The dog finished his food and came over to lie at my feet and watch with me. It was comforting, I realized, to eat with him. He was someone to talk to, someone to look at, someone to give a piece of chicken from my soup bowl and say, "Hey, try this, it's not bad for canned soup, right?" or just to call to him, "Hey, you're a good dog!" He seemed friendlier, more relaxed, the fear and sadness that had filled his eyes was slowly starting to dissipate.

I was not planning to walk the beach tonight. It was too much of a struggle through the sand, and my ankle was still aching from my earlier attempt. I knew Sam might be on the pier, rolled in his khaki wool blankets. He might even be waiting for me, but I didn't want to go. I didn't want things to evolve beyond where they were right now.

I was genuinely tired and went into the kitchen. The dog waited next to me as I washed our small collection of dishes, refilled his water, brewed myself tea. He whined by the door until I opened it and he vanished into the dusk for exactly ten minutes to do his business—in the yard, I hoped—before returning. He watched me as I locked the back door, locking the two of us safely inside, then sat by the tub as I showered, followed me into bed. He took over my pillow and quickly fell asleep. "Come here!" I called aloud to him. "Good boy. Did you know you were going to have a home?" I rephrased it: I didn't want to disappoint him. "A home with me, until I find you a forever home?" The stump tail wagged slowly, even though his eyes remained closed.

He knew.

I thought I would finally sleep. I was feeling the beginning of a sense of completion, a small oasis of peace opening within me, as I lay in bed listening to the dog breathe.

I thought about Shay being pregnant. She had a great family and I loved them. Her mother was affectionate and kind and funny; her father, strict and loving. They would honor this new life, surround it with goodness. Was I envious? Oh yes! *I* wanted that. But at least I would be part of it.

The dog whimpered in his sleep. I wondered if this dog had been sent to me. Why was I allowing him to pick at the corners of my heart, breaking its seal, allowing who knows what to creep under the layers? How could I not allow it? Tomorrow I would ask Sam to take us to Town Hall first thing. I needed to protect this dog, to make sure he could never be taken from me until I was ready to let him go. It was important for me to keep my promise to him.

A strangled cry, sent up from a bad dream, came deep from the dog's throat. I sat up to stroke his rough skin, rub a gentle circle around his broken ears, whisper soft words, my lips pressed against his heavy head.

The young moon, just a few days old now, tried to slip its meager light through the window, looking for attention. A waxing crescent, inexperienced, slight, too tender to press its arc fully against the night sky, supplicating, like a child, seeking my forgiveness for the full moon that had broken me.

I tucked the pillow around my head, rolled onto my side with my back to the window, and refused to look at it.

Chapter 9

The dog was sitting and facing the back door, whining softly, by the time I woke up. He knew Sam was coming and seemed impatient. I let him out to do his business, marveling at how fast animals pick up routines. Then I chided myself for also anticipating Sam's arrival so keenly. We were becoming friends. There was an easiness between us that I liked, a comfortable friendliness that seemed to work for both of us. I hadn't wanted anyone new in my life, but now there were two, a man and a dog, and it was okay. It was all temporary.

The dog was back in five minutes, to take up his station again at the door.

The pink Eldorado, glowing in the morning sun like a watermelon slice, rolled in front of the house right on time. I had already eaten my toasted muffin and had a pot of coffee on standby. The dog had a bowl of crunchies and a muffin. Sam would lean against a wall, have exactly one cup of coffee with one sugar, which he wouldn't finish, refuse a muffin because he had already eaten at his aunt's, and then stand politely, his back still straight against the wall, his hands clasped behind, while I washed the bowl and the cups and put them on the drainboard. Every day.

Routine was my savior.

Sam was dressed in a pair of navy slacks, a light blue shirt, and a charcoal sweater. The casual beach look was gone. The beard and mustache were shaved off, revealing a square chin and an open, strong face. His hair was combed neatly, and his dark eyes looked piercing under his thick brows. He was imposing, handsome even. I couldn't help but take a peek at his feet. He was wearing socks and shoes, looking as normal as anybody. I stepped back to admire him.

"Wow," I said. "You look really great."

He flushed and nodded his thanks.

I dressed the dog in his new collar and leash and we left the house.

"I don't have a checking account," Sam informed me as we walked to his car. "So I brought all my money with me. In my pocket."

Shocked, I stopped in my tracks. "Sam! You could lose it!"

He opened the rear door to the Cadillac and I spread the usual green towel across the backseat before the dog jumped in. "I didn't know how long I'd be living here," he replied, a little bit defensive, "so I thought cash is the best way to go."

"I guess," I relented. "But maybe you could open a checking account today. That should give you immediate access when you need it."

"I need it now." He opened the car door for me like a gentleman.

I sighed and got in. "I would worry about walking around with a lot of money."

"I won't be walking around for long; I'm going to spend it on a car," he said, getting in on the driver's side.

We would stop at the Galley first, where I would make sandwiches and pack them in a cooler for our lunch, then visit Town Hall to get a license for the dog, then drive to Wellfall, the nearest town—about forty-five minutes away—that had a car dealership. Sam was hoping for a good deal on a slightly used truck. A white one, he thought. Or silver-gray.

"All finished with pink?" I teased.

"Oh yes, ma'am," he replied emphatically. "Pink never really did much for me."

Shay was working hard in the Galley when we got there. There was a line of customers, Fleeties and tourists, all waiting for egg sandwiches or cold cuts or coffee to go, or to leave orders for my next batch of homemade bread. Shay rolled her eyes at me. "Great crowd this morning. I should have brought my roller skates."

"How are you feeling?" I whispered to her, slipping behind the counter and putting on my apron.

"Well, I didn't puke on any of the customers yet, so things are good."

"Well, hello, Aila." It always felt good to be greeted by customers who were locals. They were my family, of sorts, annoying, prying, demanding, and affectionate. Sam was standing at ease, hands clasped behind him, his back against a row of shelves while he faced the front door. They eyed him with curiosity. I knew his presence was going to unleash a barrage of questions. One Fleetie after another quietly apprised him as they walked out the door. They reminded me of the seagulls who patrol the beaches, swooping down, ready to snatch up any crumb of information available. I made sandwiches, poured coffee, sold T-shirts, stamps, newspapers, and eggs. Took several requests for my bread and made a dozen promises that I would start the summer off with my homemade iced tea/pomegranate juice drink. We finally managed to get everyone gone.

"I will be back here as soon as I'm finished," I promised Shay. "We're getting the dog a license and Sam a new car."

"Good idea," she said. "That dog is going to need a license before he borrows the car."

I grabbed a cooler, really a small insulated bag that we sell, filled it with ice, and set about making lunch, the Sandwich, one for each of us. Sam watched with great interest.

"I know," I said to him. "It's crazy. We speak of it with great respect. The Sandwich! It just kind of grew into this, but we love it, don't we, Shay?"

"Unh," Shay replied breathily, her face paling before she rushed off to the bathroom.

"She's pregnant," I explained to Sam. "I think the combination is too much for her."

"I think it's genius," Sam said. "But would you mind adding roasted red peppers?"

I lied to the town clerk.

Twice.

"Hello, Aila, thought you might be coming in," Mrs. Hummings greeted me as soon as I pushed through the glass doors into the License Office. "Heard from Mrs. Skipper you got a new dog."

I wasn't the least bit surprised that before the week was out dear old, feeble Mrs. Skipper had mustered the strength to pull on her little white orthopedic shoes and hustle herself down to Town Hall to lodge a complaint.

Mrs. Hummings reached toward a stack of blue papers and slipped one off the top. "DOG LICENSE," it read. She placed it on the glass-covered counter between us.

"Yeah, he sort of found me," I said. I had left the dog waiting in the car with Sam. "Is there a problem? I mean, we're allowed to own dogs, right?"

"Of course you are," she said. "It's just that Mrs. Skipper had voiced some concerns." She flashed me a sympathetic smile. "She mentioned something about passing an ordinance against allowing certain breeds within town limits. She was very worried about public safety."

"He's not any sort of a threat," I protested, putting the papers I had gotten from the veterinarian—his health certificate and confirmation of a rabies shot—on the counter.

She picked up a pen and wrote my name and address in capital letters on the top line of the application, then looked up at me. "Sex?"

"Male."

"Neutered?"

"We have an appointment."

She frowned. "The fee for a male who still has his . . . dangles is thirty-five dollars. If you get them cut off within two weeks, you get a rebate of fifteen dollars. So it's a bargain."

I smiled back, deciding not to comment that the surgery for dangle removal, though very necessary, probably cost over one hundred dollars, not quite the bargain.

"Age?" she asked.

"About eighteen months."

"Hmm," she said, glancing at my papers. "I see your veterinarian wrote 'mixed' on the breed line."

A chill ran through me. "Yep," I lied. "He's just an ordinary mixed breed."

"Odd. Mrs. Skipper suggested he might be a certain breed," she said. "And usually the vet can make a good guess just by looking. We like to keep statistics on our dog population."

I was sure the vet'd had very little trouble figuring out what breed of dog has a head shaped like a toolbox, with one triangle ear cut in half, a jackhammer muzzle, the body of a sumo wrestler, narrow, sad almond-shaped eyes, all of it topped off by a square red nose that perfectly matched his red fur, and I was grateful for her discretion. Once the breed was committed to paper, it could leave the dog open to all kinds of unfair rules and regulations. The sad thing about pit bulls is that people are never made aware that they are gentle, highly intelligent dogs, intensely loyal and faithful, and, despite having been the victims of some of the cruelest treatment a human could perpetuate upon another living creature, still find it in their hearts to trust and love.

"Does he look like a certain kind of dog?" Mrs. Hummings asked gently, pen poised.

"A lot of dogs look like a certain kind of dog," I said, my anxiety mounting, "but they can be total mixes of certain other kinds of dogs."

"But," she pointed out, "there are certain kinds of dogs that are . . . you know what, and certain other kinds of dogs that aren't." I knew we were talking in code about pit bulls.

"He's just a mixed kind of dog," I said. "How can anyone know what a stray dog's grandmother was?" I was hoping this wouldn't lead into grandma territory.

"Yes," she said, and sighed. "That's very true. Does he have a name?"

"Not yet," I said.

I think she was disappointed that I hadn't given away his breed by naming him the usual pit-bull name like Killer, or Slash, or Mongo.

"Thirty-five dollars, please," she said. "And he should have a name so we can register him."

I paid the fee.

"Don't forget, you get money back when he gets his dangles off," she said, stamping the license and handing it to me. "Dangles always cost more." I quickly stuffed the paper into my pocket and headed for the door. "But," she called after me, "I would be very careful, dear, keeping certain dogs around!"

"Yes, ma'am," I said, then decided to play the widow card. "But it's good to have a dog to protect me now that I live all alone. Sometimes I get nervous at night and certain dogs are good deterrents."

"Oh yes, indeed," she said. "Certain dogs make very good guardians. You have a lovely day now."

I was almost out the door when she hailed me again. "Oh, Aila!" I whirled around. What more could she possibly want?

"Please save me a loaf of that pecan-cranberry bread you make."

I promised her I would and left, practically vaulting down the Town Hall steps, using the tip of my crutch as the launch, to reach the waiting Cadillac. The dog was asleep, stretched across the backseat. Sam looked at me expectantly as I let myself into his car and sat down.

"So how did it go?" he asked. "Did you have any problems?"

"Nope," I crowed, taking the license from my pocket and waving it jubilantly in the air. "The dog is legal."

Chapter 10

They looked like a herd of cattle dozing quietly in the sun, the cars, new and used, docile, with big round, clear eyes, side-view mirror ears, patiently lined up in the parking lot of the Wellfall dealership waiting to be moved on out. Window signs promised fast deals, the best prices, easy loans, low interest rates, and the friendliest salespeople in town. Not wanting to intrude, I let Sam go ahead, into the gleaming showroom, while I stayed outside with the dog. Even though he was legal now, there was no point in testing his limits.

I watched through the glass doors as Sam entered the large window-lit room, checking it out before walking up to two lustrous new models parked in the center of the floor. He ran his hand over them appreciatively, opening doors to examine the interiors, smiling with appreciation. He looked happy and relaxed, his usual serious expression gone. It was a pivotal moment for him, I knew. He was buying his first car since he lost his leg. It bespoke of his first move toward independence and almost normalcy.

The salesman was over immediately. He was maybe in his

fifties, with thinning gray hair in a comb-over, and bushy white brows. He eyed Sam's cane, then grabbed Sam's hand and shook it firmly. They spoke, both of them gesturing and smiling. Sam touched his pocket and said something, which made the salesman's smile even broader, and I knew Sam was explaining about the money. They spoke some more; the salesman left for a moment and returned, holding up a set of keys. Then he led Sam out through the doors—I watched as Sam's eyes flicked left to right and back again while he barely moved his head before he stepped into the parking lot.

"We're going to look at some trucks!" Sam called over to me, his voice lilting with exhilaration. "Why don't you come?"

He introduced me as a good friend, and the salesman and I shook hands. The salesman gave the dog a questionable glance and I explained that he was well behaved. We all followed the salesman to a silver-gray truck, only two years old, parked four rows back.

The price seemed fair, and Sam spent some time exploring its features, looking more pleased with each passing minute. He was offered a test drive and left the lot driving slowly and carefully. He didn't need assistance to drive since the truck was an automatic and was easily operated by his good leg—I doubt if the salesman even knew that Sam had a prosthetic leg. The look on Sam's face when he returned told me it was a deal.

We were led back inside. Sam waved me in front of him, but the salesman hesitated for a moment.

"I don't know if we can have that dog in here," he said. "He looks sick."

"He's a rescue," I explained. "He's healing from some health issues."

"Oh!" the salesman replied. "Rescue? Does he work for the police department?"

"That's not—" I started, but Sam spoke over me with a loud, "Yes." We were ushered inside and offered bottles of water.

The paperwork was next. The salesman seated himself at a large wooden desk topped with a wedding photo and several pictures of smiling children. He gestured to a chair. Sam parked his cane against the desk and pulled the chair closer to the wall before sitting down, his prosthetic leg stretched out to the side. I took another chair. The dog lay down next to me. Sam cracked open the bottle of water and took an appreciative drink. The salesman reached into a drawer and withdrew a sheaf of papers. "We can do everything right from this showroom," he assured Sam. "License plates, registration. Just give me the name of your insurer. We can have you in that truck by tomorrow."

"Great!" Sam pulled the envelope of money from his pocket and a piece of paper with information from Miss Phyllis's insurance company. He started counting and sorting the money into piles. "Cash," he stated.

"We take anything," the salesman said jocularly. His pen was poised over the small pile of papers. "Name?"

"Sarim Ahmadi," Sam replied. It sounded musical.

The salesman looked up at him. "What?"

"Sarim Ahmadi," Sam spelled it out, then added, "But everyone calls me Sam."

"What kind of name is that?"

"My father is from Jordan, and I was raised there," Sam answered. "It's Muslim. I am Muslim."

The salesman studied the documents on his desk, his face suddenly gone grave. He shook his head, as though he had just discovered something in particular on one of the papers. "Oh. Well. I can't sell you the truck," he announced.

Sam leaned forward, confused. "Is it my credit?" he asked.

"You don't need credit to pay cash," I said to him, not sure what the salesman was getting at.

Sam sat straight up in his chair, a quizzical expression wrinkling his features. The dog sat up, too, just in case. "Why not?"

The salesman looked as though someone had pressed his pause button for a moment; his face went blank and his eyes fluttered. He stood up, his swivel chair rolling back a few feet from his effort. He seemed confused. He shot a questioning look across the floor to another salesman who was on the phone, then looked back at Sam. "We just can't sell you the truck, is all."

Sam stood, too. They were facing each other now, the desk between them. "You didn't give me a reason," Sam said evenly.

The salesman took a step back, allowing the fingers on his hands to flare open defensively. He took a deep breath. "Policy," he said, looking from Sam to the dog and back to Sam. "We don't sell to Muslims. What if you take the truck and send it overseas to ISIS? Especially a *truck!* It's like *I* potentially sold it to the enemy!"

Sam's large frame dwarfed the salesman; he leaned toward him a bit, his face flushed with fury. I could hear his lungs tightening with each ragged breath. I saw the rage in his eyes, a sudden glow, like the hint of a comet arriving in the sky, uncertain of its path just yet. "What?" he said in deadly, noisy breaths. "What?"

The dog was suddenly nervous, picking up on Sam's emotion and started whining. I felt him tug very lightly on his leash and I pulled him back.

Sam leaned over the desk, resting on his broad palms. "I am a veteran," he said loudly, his voice quivering with rage. "I fought for this country."

The salesman shrugged. "You know the political climate," he said. "You know how things are now. We have to be very careful about what we do and say." He pulled a drawer open and dropped the papers in. "I'm sorry. It's the manager's decision." He turned away as though the matter was closed. "Thank you for coming in." I could see that his hands were shaking.

"I am buying that truck!" Sam thundered, then was bent in half by a deep, rumbling cough.

"Get your manager," I said to the salesman. "This can't be legal." Sam pulled his shoulders straight, as though he were going to march across the desk. His lips were set in a grim line. I knew he was embarrassed, which was further fueling his anger.

"I am paying cash, and I am buying that truck!" Sam repeated. The dog glowered at the salesman.

"Listen, we don't even know where you got the cash from," the salesman said, sotto voce, as though the shameful deed of Sam having saved his money for years should be kept a secret. "My manager is out today. It's not my decision."

I stood up and took a deep breath. I was beginning to feel my scalp tingle. Sam had rolled his hands into two large, tight fists. The dog watched him intently. I worried that things could go south very quickly.

"Good boy," I quietly murmured. "Sit like a good boy." He ignored me. He knew.

I tried another tactic. "Sam, we can come back another time to talk to the manager." He ignored me, too.

"Please leave," the salesman asked. "We just don't serve Muslims here." He looked around the dealership as if for confirmation. "I can't do anything about it. I am trying to protect my country," he added stiffly. The dog was giving him the stink eye.

"I just want to buy the truck and then we'll leave," Sam said. I could see he was trying to control himself, trying to control his breathing and keep his lungs open, trying to be reasonable in a situation that was beyond reason. "Let's just get it done."

"Sorry. I can't," the salesman said. "It wouldn't be right." Sam slapped the desk hard in frustration and the dog released a cavernous pit-bull power bark.

"I am asking you to leave before I make a phone call," the salesman said.

"To the police?" I interjected. "You planning to file a complaint that a customer came in here to buy a truck?"

"We have to be very careful in this day and age," he replied loftily, putting his hand meaningfully on his desk phone. "They're all gonna get registered, those people, and the authorities will want to know where he got the truck from."

The veins were bulging in Sam's neck as he fought to control himself. His lips were set in a straight line and he was clenching his jaw so tightly I could hear his teeth grind together. The salesman backed up a few steps, looking worried. Suddenly Sam swept the phone off the desk; it landed on the floor with a half ring.

"I don't want a fight." The salesman put his hands up to his face.

"Damn you!" Sam grabbed the back of the chair he had been sitting in and pushed it hard. It flew across the floor, skidding

along the gleaming ice-like tile and slamming into a wastebas-
ket, tipping it over and disgorging its contents of shredded paper. The dog started barking wildly at it, his voice rolling deep
from his throat. I pulled on the leash; it was like pulling against
a cement wall.

I wrapped the leash around my hand, then grabbed Sam's
arm. It also felt like a cement wall. "Let's go," I said quietly. "We
need to get out of here. We need to protect you." He looked at
me and looked at the salesman. He stood for a long moment
like that, just staring at his opponent, before he took a breath.
I knew he was calculating risks.

"Sam," I said.

"Okay," he said, slowly unclenching his fists and letting me
lead him to the door. The dog followed, spinning at my side
and barking.

"Yeah! You better get that dog out of here!" the salesman
called after us, suddenly overcome with bravery. He bent over
to pick up the phone and replace it on his desk but kept his eyes
on the dog. "Threaten me with a fucking pit bull!"

"Don't worry; he doesn't eat garbage!" I called over my
shoulder.

Sam was standing in the parking lot, shaking. His face was
white, and he was coughing hard, fighting to pull air into his
constricted lungs.

"Are you okay?" I asked while the dog whirled circles around
the two of us, now barking at his reflection in the shiny glass
showroom doors.

Sam nodded, still coughing. "I could kill him," he choked
out. "I could kill him."

"I know," I said, putting my hand on his arm again. I knew
he could. "But you have to get a lawyer. Or contact some kind
of civil liberties group. You have to fight this."

He took a deep, shuddering breath and stood for a moment,
gathering himself, commanding his chest to rise and fall properly, trying to process what had happened. I recognized the
look, the confusion, the turmoil swirling through his mind

while he was trying to sort things out into their proper order. I know the struggle to make sense of an improbable event, in its entirety, grasping how it started and how it was playing out right now, so you can command it, draw a conclusion, get your emotional ducks in a row. I had done it when Dan and my father died. I stood then, on my back deck, enveloped by confusion, struggling to see through it, to hear through it, to understand their sudden deaths and find the reality of right now. I remember the Harbor Master standing at my back door and talking to me. "Do you hear me?" he kept saying. "Do you hear me?" But hearing and understanding are not the same. It was a huge wave, the Harbor Master said, a wave driven by a sudden strong squall. The full moon had pulled behind the clouds, betraying Dan and my father, abandoning them to the sudden black sea and the sudden black skies and maybe ten orcas, a pod working together, hungry and curious and opportunistic, thrusting about in the water until the boat was tipped and Dan and my father were gone. Just like that.

Sam's eyes were focused off in the distance. Maybe he had found his past; maybe he was at the explosion where his lungs were burned to shreds and he lost his leg. Maybe he was caught in the pain and the fire and the tearing of his limb from his body. Maybe he was hearing the arrogance of the salesman who felt he was protecting his country by turning its values on their head.

"Sam?" I tapped him on the arm. "Sam?"

"You know," he said softly. "I could have killed him. I wanted . . . I could have . . . killed . . . him."

"I know," I said.

His breath whistled from his broken lungs as he pulled open the door to the pink Eldorado, then eased himself in and started it up. The dog, now calm, jumped onto the backseat.

"We can fight this," I said to Sam after I sat down.

"No! I already fought. I fought fucking hard," Sam said bitterly. "I'm done. I lost too much. I'm not fighting anymore."

Chapter 11

I convinced Sam to drive us to the beach. We could sit by the water and catch our breath, I said. There is nothing like the sound of moving water to calm you, to claim away your thoughts, to empty your head of everything but its own rhythm and force. We could have lunch and talk and figure out what to do next. He grunted his assent, but his mood was somber.

The beach was almost vacant, except for a couple of teenagers running into the water while shrieking at it and then running out, still shrieking, pursued by the tide. We made our way to the pier with the dog and the cooler. We sat on a bench at the far end after Sam scanned the area and was satisfied. It was where the boats were tied up. Sam laid his cane against the rail. I opened the cooler and gave him a Sandwich and the dog his afternoon medicine wrapped in bologna. His skin was starting to heal; his shoulders had patches of handsome deep red fur and it seemed to me, he had fewer sharp crevices between his ribs. I pointed this out to Sam, who nodded while taking grim bites of his sandwich. The dog lay at our feet, watching us eat, his eyes rolling hopefully from one to the other until we were forced into giving him little pieces of our food. The boats rocked gently in the water; the sun sparkled and glanced off their cleats like laser shots. Right in the middle of them was a pink and white 1970 twenty-foot Chris-Craft cabin cruiser with the word *Follicles* painted in gold script on the side. I had to smile. Fluffy, if a boat could be called fluffy, it belonged, of course, to Miss Phyllis. She always liked having the best and her boat, despite its age, stood like a queen among the runabouts. An old queen.

"Your aunt's boat," I remarked to Sam, "matches her car."

He gave it a half smile. "Did you ever see the inside of her house?"

"No," I admitted.

"Well, she sure loves pink."

If you had walked past us, you would have thought it a tender scene. In truth, we were each locked into our own thoughts. The dog's ears perked with each shriek coming from the beach, Sam watched everything with vigilance, his eyes flickering from the boats, to the teens, then to the horizon and back again. I stared at the bay, watching sea foam caress the sand, leaving odd shells and stones and tendrils of seaweed like gifts from a lover. When I was a child, I spent my free days combing the beach for shells. The perfect ones were brought into the Galley and laid out on a piece of black velvet, so the tourists could buy them. That was my pocket money.

The gulls stood on the rail and mewed at us, begging for food. I tossed pieces of bread into the air and watched them catch it before it fell to the ground. The terns hovered and dove into the water, too proud to beg. The teenagers left, chattering and laughing and pushing one another along the water's edge, pretending they had spotted a great white. There had been local reports of an increase in great whites coming close to the beaches. The kids were joking, but it made me shudder.

"You ever go swimming?" Sam asked. He looked longingly at the water.

"I used to swim all the time," I said. I grew up swimming and had always considered myself pretty good at it, but now I resented the very water that I had once trusted to carry me on its shoulders.

"I lived to swim," Sam mused. "I'd give anything to do it again."

I looked at him, surprised. "Does the leg mean you can't?"

He shrugged. "It gets complicated."

"How?"

"Well, this leg isn't rated for swimming. It won't propel me if I swim; it just pulls me down. It has to be buoyant and let me push through the water." He tapped on the metal. "Plus it'll pit from the salt in the water." He sighed. "If I want to swim, first I have to drop this somewhere, and it's hard to take off. And then I have to hop over to the water and I could slip. I have to be helped in. And then after I'm done, I got to really dry my stump off so the sock doesn't get wet. It's a project."

"Is it your whole leg that's missing?" I asked.

"I have an above-knee amputation," he said. "It's—" He stopped abruptly. "Never mind. I don't like talking about it."

"I don't know anything about amputations," I said. "But I wouldn't mind learning."

He seemed reassured by this. "Maybe I'll show you . . . someday." He looked away, as though suddenly aware of how much his words left him vulnerable.

"Thank you," I said.

We fell into a silence. "There must be a way," I started, "for you to swim."

"I don't know." His voice became vague and he drifted back into silence. "Plus," he suddenly added, "I don't breathe so well, so I don't have the endurance anymore." The terns had flown out to sea and even the seagulls had lost their interest in us, leaving us alone. His mood was deep as the water.

"Can you operate a boat?" Sam suddenly asked, a tinge of anticipation lifting his words.

I didn't want to answer him. Of course I know how to operate a boat. I got my Boater Education Card before I was thirteen. Everyone on the Cape goes boating or kayaking or fishing. It

may even be in our collective genes. Miss Phyllis's boat was a
cabin cruiser and I had only driven runabouts, but I wasn't going to admit it.

"Hey. How about this?" he asked, his face brightening. "How
about if I ask my aunt if we can take her boat out? I can leave the
leg on the boat and just dive over the side. Would you mind?"

My heart sank. I couldn't answer him.

"Would you?" he pressed.

I hadn't stepped foot on a boat since the accident. I would
not give the bay the satisfaction of welcoming me back. I did
not want to coast along its water while it was offering me its false
hospitality while I wondered where Dan and my father died. I
did not want to think of a certain pod of orcas, wolves of the
sea, they are called, cruising the Chatham shoreline looking
for seals, dressed to kill in their formal black and white, eager
to make an easy meal of anything that fell into their path. Yet
how could I say no after he had been so kind to me?

"Oh." I jumped to my feet. "Please. I can't do it," I blurted.
"The bay—I haven't been in a boat since Dan and my father—I
couldn't possibly."

I felt bad for Sam, sorry for what he had to undergo every day.
We were becoming friends, but this was more than I could bear.
He didn't know, how could he know, what he was asking of me?

"I need to go," I gasped, grabbing my crutches and swinging
down from the pier, away from the beckoning, playful boats,
away from the murmuring seagulls and the coy, luring whispers
of the water, and, with Sam calling me to stop, calling wait, he
was sorry, sorry, and the dog following me, barking, I sobbed
and hobbled home as fast as I could.

I watched through the kitchen window as Sam got into that
damn pink car and drove away. Frustrated, I pulled off my soft
cast and walked carefully around the room for a few minutes,
to test my ankle. It felt weak and stiff, but the pain was almost
gone. I rewrapped it in an ACE bandage and pulled on my
sneaker, grabbed the dog and my car keys, and got into my little
red manual-shift Toyota and drove straight to the Galley.

"Hi!" Shay was surprised to see me. "I didn't think you were going to make it back anymore today," she said, turning off the flattop and grabbing the metal scraper to clean it. "Did you get everything done?"

"The dog got his license," I said, taking the scraper from her. She took it back from me.

"Just rest your foot," she said, "I can finish this. So, what kind of car did Sam pick out?"

I poured myself a cup of coffee, the last bit that was in the pot, added cream until it was pale beige, and gulped it. It was still bitter from sitting. "No car at all!" I exclaimed, starting to wash the pot out. "Nothing. They wouldn't sell him the truck he wanted."

She furrowed her brows and stopped working to look at me. "I thought he had the money on him."

"It was awful," I went on. "Because of his name. He's Muslim and the salesman is waiting for all the Muslims to get registered and deported or something. Sam was furious. Then the dog got upset. Can you believe this? Sam not allowed to buy a truck? Can you believe it? That people can think like this?"

Shay's eyes widened and her lips parted before she caught herself. Something flickered across her face—a micro-expression—that altered her features for only a moment, before it was shut down. Something she remembered and pushed away, something that had flooded her memory, had taken her back to a place where she had once struggled to understand what had just happened, a place where she had to learn to push her ducks back in their row. I recognized it.

"What?" I asked.

"Oh," she murmured. "It's just that I'm not surprised." She paused and I could see her retreating deeper into her thoughts, and for the first time a charge of bitterness ran through her voice. "That people can think like this?" she repeated, in a tone that I had never heard from her before. "Not surprised at all."

And then I thought, *Oh God, how could I have forgotten?*

Chapter 12

I had forgotten that Shay was black, although, of course, I *knew* she was. But I had forgotten, or maybe never gave it much thought, that we weren't *really* twins, not in color or experience. She had never spoken to me of her challenges; her always-present bright smile and joyful outlook were such a part of her that I guess I took them for granted. When she spoke those words, I was instantly ashamed.

I had forgotten an incident that had stayed with me a long time and then, somehow, got pushed from my mind while we were getting on with our lives.

We had been friends since kindergarten, maybe even before. We had each found something in the other that made us good and deep allies. Sisters, even then, when we had barely started kindergarten. She hadn't made a lot of friends yet, though she was outgoing and friendly, such a lovely little girl, and neither had I. I didn't know why she hadn't, but I had the crazy grandmother. Shay and I loved each other right away. We were together in every grade since, spending hours after school together, every summer together.

We were twelve years old and, as usual, walking home from school. One day, a boy named Tommy started following us. I remembered Tommy from second grade, when he had started taunting me about my crazy grandmother. How could I deny it, with her standing in the bay like a tourist attraction, singing her lungs out? I had run home in shame and he continued for the whole school year, until he got bored. I finally told my father, who whispered a secret to me about Tommy, which I was told to never use, but just so that I would know his life wasn't so perfect, either. But I thought of it as my secret weapon, just in case.

And now he was back. He had no reason to hate Shay; she was purely a good person, and her grandmother was normal as far as I could see. I didn't understand why he had chosen her. Yet he bedeviled her every day after school for weeks. Shay's mother gave us the usual advice: don't reply to him, don't razz him back, don't even look at him, but she was a busy dentist, Shay's father was a biology professor in Boston, and they couldn't do much more to help us. We tried it all and it wasn't working. One day, Tommy came with reinforcements. Maybe five other boys, known bullies, who apparently thought this was great entertainment and trailed us en masse. At first I didn't really understand what was happening. Shay was a good friend from a normal family; what could she possibly offer as bait? We kept walking until Tommy rushed past us and banged into Shay so hard, her books flew out of her hands; she fell to the ground and skinned her knee. There was a round of applause and encouraging shouts. I helped her up and we bent down to pick up her books, but Tommy stood on her notebook and spit on her. There was more approval from the ranks. They urged him on. I was terrified, while Shay stood next to me, shaking with fear. He used every ugly word he could think of, and finally even *that* word. And that's when I realized, so that's what it was all about. It sickened me.

"You're no better than she is, hanging around with her!" he yelled in my face, then spit on me, too.

Something stirred in my mind. Fortunately, I had by then built up a bit of muscle from years of helping my father carry in boxes and crates of Galley stock and then spending my afternoons loading all those items onto shelves. That day, as I listened to Tommy, a switch had been turned on. He had spent a whole school year torturing me and now he was hurting my friend. I'd had enough. He leaned toward her to unleash another barrage of words. I pulled my arm back and gave him the strongest roundhouse punch I could muster. It connected properly with his nose and he fell to the sidewalk. It nearly knocked him out. Being the ladies that we were, Shay and I pulled him to his feet, propped him, dizzy and bloodied, against a fence.

"Anyone else?" I asked, rage being the better part of my bravery. I held up my fist and then, my brain frying with fury, unleashed Tommy's secret. "You ought to treat me better," I shouted at him, holding on to that fence like he was on a boat in choppy waters, "since your family owes my father's store a ton of money for food!"

His retinue grew quiet, then looked at him with disdain. Cape Codders are a thrifty lot, penurious even, and keep their books in order, almost as a religion, right from childhood. They left him leaning against the fence and melted away in disgust.

The look on Tommy's face made me feel awful. He was mortified. And I was ashamed of myself for being no better than he. I had become cruel, too, and it horrified me.

He slunk into the school the next day with a royal shiner, a nose that was still trickling blood, and a big lump on the back of his head that showed through his buzz cut. He never bothered either one of us again.

It hadn't been her first experience, Shay confided to me later. It hadn't been the first time she had those words flung at her, nor the first senseless exchange that was meant to wound her. Apparently, that's where Tommy had disappeared to when he finally left me alone back in second grade. He had made his way to Shay's house and had started a career of taunting her before she left for school in the morning and had finished his day by continuing outside her house after she got home, with only her elderly grandmother to watch over things.

Why hadn't she ever told me? I demanded. She told me not to worry, she would handle her own problems, and refused to talk about it.

Of course, I realize now, she had handled the problem by not sharing any further incidents with me. I loved her with all my heart, she loved me, too, and it was, I think, her way of defining our relationship. She didn't *want* me to be her protector, just an equal in our friendship. And I suppose it worked, because we never mentioned it again.

Now this sudden revelation of pain from her, this hurtful secret that I hadn't been privy to, hurt me as well, even as I knew it hadn't been about me.

Of course, I knew she hadn't been born brimming with resolve and fortitude. She had made, at some point early in her childhood, when she was far too young to have to think of these things, a decision of courage, to carry herself through her wounds and come out better. I knew she was never invited to birthday parties, but neither was I. I knew something had made her mother open her dental practice in Provincetown, instead of Fleetbourne, but it was never discussed. She had left me out of it, or had I just developed a blind spot, happy to forget, embarrassed over the shameful way I had slipped from my own principles? Anyway, it had kept me from truly sharing her life.

"Shay," I told her now, "I would have wanted to know."

She gave me a sad smile. "No," she said. "It would have made it bigger, given it more power. It would have turned into a wedge between us and I wanted us to just be . . . *pure* . . . friends. You know, without all the crap." She put her hands on my shoulders. "I didn't want to be your mission, don't you see? I didn't want an avenging angel for a friend."

I didn't see. "We have to fight for each other," I told her. "Support and protect each other." She put a kiss on my cheek and said, "Leave it alone."

I had to think about that.

"You've always been there for me and I want to be there for you," I told her later. "I don't ever want to lose your friendship. I don't want things to change between us."

She stood in front of me and looked deep into my eyes.

"You won't ever lose me," she started slowly, "but, you know, after the baby comes, I won't be able to work here next summer. I want to spend my time off playing on the beach and raising my child. I plan to keep teaching in the winters, so I'll want to relax in the summers. Let's make this the best summer ever!"

Of course. She needed to spend time raising her new baby. It was reasonable. But it meant that everything was going to change. Actually, everything *had* changed, been changing for two years. There were things that I had lost and things that I had found. But there was nothing to grab on to; I just had to ride it all out.

We closed the Galley. I gave her a hug and she hugged me back. Then she got into her little yellow Fiat and I in my little red Toyota, with the dog in the backseat, and we both drove away home, in opposite directions.

Chapter 13

The dog and I ate a silent dinner together, chili for me, dog food for him. I picked at my food, pushing it around the bowl with my spoon while he gulped his down at record speed and then sat at my side, volunteering to help me finish. I declined his offer. Spicy foods do funny things to pit bulls; it turns them into lethal gas weapons.

The day, reflecting my mood, was graying around the edges. Of course things change. I know that. Shay was going to be a wonderful mother, and she needed to be with her family. I would have to make plans for someone to help run the Galley. I know that. I had always known that.

"Let's go for a walk," I said to the dog. "I am undone."

He ran to the door. I took a cane, just in case I was pushing my ankle faster than it liked, and we left the house.

The evening was breezy and there were clouds huddling together for comfort in a dreary sky. The freedom of walking on the sand barefoot, feeling cool water slide across my ankles, a light wind stroking my hair like my grandmother used to, my poor crazy grandmother. I realized my loneliness had always been bearable because Shay had been so much a part of my life. My mother and father worked long hours and spent very little time with me. There were purchase orders to be picked up and brought to the Galley, then inventoried and shelved. Everything had to be cleaned and cleaned again. Slicers and food cases and windows and doors and sinks and counters had to be immaculate. Deliveries signed for and double-checked, stock rotated. Food had to be prepared and wrapped and set up for the next day. People had to be served. The work never ended. Never ends now.

And my grandmother, oh, my crazy grandmother would stand in the bay and sing all day, and take me home and feed me warmed coffee-milk, sometimes leaving the milk out, wash and dry all her wet clothes, then nap before she started a late dinner for me. Sort of a dinner. My parents had worked long hours and usually ate at the Galley before they came home. My grandmother, thin as dune grass, sometimes forgot to eat and sometimes forgot to feed me. When she did manage, it was usually a piece of American cheese or a few slices of linguiça on a piece of bread. Sometimes, as a treat, she let me sneak a puff on her cigarillo. Sometimes she rolled her own, a sweet, cloying mixture that I recognized years later as weed. Sometimes I stole it from her ashtray when she napped and walked around the streets puffing on it. I had no sisters or brothers; I was always alone. Friends were very few. Kids in crazy families get shunned.

When I met Shay, we spent every minute together. Nobody in my family minded that I was never home unless it was summer, and then I was just expected to spend it working at the Galley.

When I met Dan, it was love and relief and joy. I had someone to love; I had someone who loved me, who noticed me, who loved being with me, who ate with me. It was such a happy time. I loved that I had a future with him.

I didn't know what I needed to do next. For Shay or for Sam or for anyone.

And so here we all were. Each of us standing on the precipice of an oddly spinning world, tilting off its tracks.

Crazy.
Black.
Muslim.
And a battered pit bull.

It was dark now and I was very tired, but the night called to me. I grabbed a jacket and opened the back door ready to walk to the pier. The dog rose from a light, anxious sleep to follow me. We walked together, down the back steps, to the sand; he pressed against my leg for guidance.

There was a rough chop to the water, a sign of bad weather to come. I am very keen on picking these things up now. Shells were being left on the beach from the ebbing water and shells were taken, the seaweed was flung against the sand, and pulled away. I could feel the temperature dropping.

The bay rushed to me like an old friend, then rushed out as we walked along, slowly, to give my ankle time to adjust to my weight with each step. Ahead, something on the pier had been upright, then moved, then dropped down, and I knew it had collapsed into a man cocooned in a heap of blankets. I knew who it was and I stopped. The dog stopped and sat, confused, and looked up at me.

"He's on the pier," I whispered, and knew right away I couldn't go there. Whatever Sam was mourning for, I knew he had to be left alone. There are things not to be intruded upon. I turned around to walk back.

"Aila?"

His voice startled me. He had obviously seen me and was pulling himself up, leaning against railings, now standing, wrapped in his blankets. He waved.

I hesitated, then waved back.

"Please, come sit with me!" he called. "I've just finished my prayers."

"Okay!" I called, and walked to the pier and climbed up to him.

"Let's sit here," he said, and held out his hand to lead me to a bench. "I see you are walking pretty good."

I sat down next to him, laying my cane down next to me. "My foot feels better." The dog jumped up squeezing between us like a chaperone. "You were praying?"

"Oh yes," he answered. "We pray five times a day." He started folding his blankets and put them, one by one, on the bench next to him. He sat pensively for a few moments before he started speaking.

"Listen, it's been a complicated day," he said. "I apologize. I shouldn't have brought you to the dealership and I didn't mean to pressure you into going boating. It's just that sometimes I don't feel I can do things alone yet."

"Don't apologize," I said. "And I'm sorry that whole car thing stunk."

"My aunt is going to take me to her dealer. Of course, she hasn't seen him since the seventies, but I should have a car in a few days."

"You should bring charges against that guy."

"I don't want to fight," he said dispiritedly. "I don't have the heart for it." A profound sadness crossed his features.

I patted his arm. "I'm sorry"—I didn't know how to finish—"that people are like that."

A breeze brushed against us, filled with soft mist, like tears. The air grew heavier, ripe with moisture and a sudden chill. There was a quick flicker of light across the bay that caught my eye. I could smell rain.

"It's going to pour," I said. "Do you want to come back to my house? I can make us tea or something." It was a hospitable offer, nothing more. Just as I said it, the rain started falling in big, loose drops.

"Thank you," he said, pulling himself up and extending his hand to help me. "I'd like that very much." We started for my house.

"Do you mind if I do this?" he asked, draping the blankets around my shoulders and his, to block the rain.

"No," I said truthfully, lifting them over our heads, too. "I appreciate it."

We made our way across the beach, a short walk made longer

by our swinging gaits and two canes. The rain, by now, was driving hard, pelting the beach, slapping into the water. Another flicker of lightning outlined the shore, accompanied by the soft thrum of thunder. Yellow flashes backlit the horizon, growing brighter and closer with each passing minute.

We hobbled faster, across the deepening sand, up the slippery deck steps, just making it into the kitchen as the sky grew pitiless, hurling the rain down in sweeping sheets. We stood safe, squeezing together to peer through the back door, watching the sky disappear into the bay.

We wiped ourselves and the dog off with dish towels, and I led Sam to the bathroom, so he could unfold his blankets over the shower rod to dry. Then I invited him into the living room, to sit on the couch and relax. It's a cozy room with a fireplace; there were white and yellow daffodils in a small jar on the hearth, leftover from the bounty at the store, just starting to look tired. Sam sat tentatively at first, his eyes swiveling left and right to check out the room before he threw his head back against the cushions and let out a long sigh. The dog rolled on the rug to finish drying off before curling up his thin frame for a nap in my reclining chair. I went into the kitchen and put on the kettle.

I placed two cups on the table. The sight of them put a catch in my throat. Two cups on the table, waiting for tea, looking so right; a man stretching across the couch looking so right, the rain falling outside, while we spoke in soft voices, it was all exactly right.

Except it wasn't really. I squeezed my eyes shut until the image of Dan left and the tears retreated.

The banana bread released its fragrance throughout the kitchen as I unwrapped and sliced it. *Oh, I remember too well how I used to do this.*

The kettle sputtered a soft whistle.

"Shall I bring the tea into the living room?" I called.

"Thank you!" he called back.

I grabbed a tray from a cabinet, put out two tea bags and two spoons, the two cups, sugar and cream, and carried it in to set down on the small coffee table in front of the sofa. A tea ceremony of old memories. He watched me go back for the kettle and return. He watched as I placed a tea bag in each cup, poured hot water, returned the kettle, and brought back two slices of banana bread on napkins. I sat on the floor next to the sofa, to eat from the table. I felt his eyes. Dan used to watch me, too.

Sam and I were awkward with each other. Sam took three sugars and let his tea steep very dark; then he sat forward and held the cup in his hands. I added cream to mine until it was the color of ivory. We drank in companionable silence. He delicately put his cup down on the tray and picked up a slice of bread and ate it in small, savoring bites. After finishing it, he turned to me.

"Thank you," he said, "that was awfully good."

"You're very welcome," I said. We were so polite.

There was a pause. I was going to make a silly remark about the dog, who hadn't stirred through all this, but Sam suddenly cleared his throat.

"So, do you want to see my leg?" he asked, his voice nervous. "It's okay, I have bathing trunks on."

My first impulse was to say no. It seemed an act of intimacy, too personal for us yet, we barely knew each other and it scared me a little. What might his leg look like? But he was staring at me, urgent and uncertain and so vulnerable.

I thought, *It's just his leg.*

And then, *It's his* leg.

"Okay," I said.

He pulled himself up and held on to the arm of the sofa. He unbuttoned his pants and unzipped his fly with shaking hands. The sight of him unzipping his pants startled me. What was happening here? It was the most intimate thing he could do. The pants slid to the floor.

And he stood there. A perfectly formed man. His beautifully muscled body, strong arms, one leg carved like a statue, from bone and sinew, one leg gleaming silver and blue, the mark of a warrior who had fallen and risen again, brilliant and strong and glorious. A leg that took nothing from him but added an extraordinary measure of strength and power. I couldn't stop myself; I reached out to touch it.

"I think . . . you look . . . perfect," I said.

He stood absolutely still; neither one of us knew what to do next.

"Should I take the leg off?" he finally asked. "There is nothing but a stump underneath."

I knew he wanted me to see. I knew he wanted to bare himself, leave himself exposed to whatever my reaction was, as though it were a test, not for me—but for him. I nodded mutely. He sat down on the sofa again and slid his hand down to the bottom of the leg and pressed a button on the side. Something clicked and released and he started sliding the leg off, leaving his remaining half thigh, encompassed in a white silicon fabric sleeve.

"No one except my mom and the nurses at the VA has seen my stump before," he said, trying to slide the sleeve down. His face was full of concentration and worry, as though he was waiting for something awful to overcome both of us.

"Do you need help taking that off?" I asked, reaching for the sleeve.

Relief fell across his face. "Thank you." He guided my hand and together we slowly and carefully slid the leg off.

"Is it okay?" he asked when his bare half thigh was finally revealed. "Are you okay with it?" His eyes never left my face.

I touched the leg gently. It was scarred, the end neatly stitched into a flap, as though the making of a leg had been started and left uncompleted, right there, in the middle of his thigh. It was still swollen, still had a certain rawness, still needed to heal.

"It needs the sun and the sea," I said, realizing what I was offering. Tears slid down his face and he swallowed hard, then nodded. My heart opened for a moment. There are many ways to love; I knew this. To love a new friend would be okay. I reached out to touch his hand, to tell him it was all right. To thank him for trusting me with this. His injury, painful and sacred, broke my heart. I wanted him to know, but there were no words.

I wanted to thank him for his sacrifice. More than that, I wanted to acknowledge its terribleness, its finality that bestowed upon him a certain nobility. I wanted to acknowledge his suffering. My fingers, instead, touched his thigh, lingering on his warm flesh for a moment.

Touching his skin, tracing the scars. Mourning for him, his lost limb.

And then I leaned forward and kissed it.

Chapter 14

It rained all night.

It poured like a baptism, the heavens trying to wash away our fear and pain and leave us both reborn with acceptance and compassion and relief. I'm not sure it was successful. Sam stayed another hour, sitting on my couch, while I sat on the floor next to him, my head leaning against his good leg. We spoke of nothing. He had tears in his eyes after I had kissed him, but he said nothing. It hadn't been awkward, and I hadn't meant it to be sexual, and he understood that. It was actually very ordinary, and it was comforting because it was ordinary. We said nothing, just sat in the dim light of a small lamp watching the bold rhythm of lightning and thunder and the quiet insistence of the rain, and it was peaceful.

After a while, the rain let up and he showed me how he put his leg back on. I needed to help him smooth the sock. There could be no air pockets, no folds, no wrinkles; it had to be perfectly, perfectly smooth. Then he snapped the limb into place and pulled on his pants and stood up.

I wanted him to stay, for safety's sake in case there were

downed lines, but I didn't tell him and let him go. I rose to my feet, fetched his blankets, and followed him to the door and held it open. The dog ran into the night—I knew he'd be back—while Sam stood for a moment on the threshold, glancing apprehensively at the slick deck and stairs ahead. He took a tentative step outside, walked to the stairs, then stopped, nervous about descending.

I joined him. "Let me help you down," I said. "Sometimes they can get slippery."

He shook his head. "No, I'm good." He gestured to the still-open kitchen door. "Get out of the rain; I got this." The rain was sluicing through his hair and slicking it down.

"Be careful," I said.

Suddenly he turned and enfolded me into his arms and kissed me with rain-wet lips. We pressed together for a moment, only for a moment, and it was unbearably sweet.

"Good night, Aila," he said, into my hair. "You don't know what you've done for me. I'll never forget you. I'm just so lost."

I watched as he made his way down the stairs, first step, second step, cane down, leg swinging out and set down, third step, slowly, carefully. He was so careful. Actually, we had both been careful. There had been no commitments, no declarations. I was merely being kind; and he, grateful.

But I was struck. My heart felt motionless, like a deer frozen in the headlights of memories. I couldn't move from the top of the steps. It had been two years since I felt someone's arms around me. This had been so effortless, so natural, as though it had never been taken from me. He made it safely to the bottom and I ducked into the kitchen, out of the rain, still feeling the strength in his arms.

A few minutes later, I saw his car light up and pull away. The dog returned; I gently wiped his body dry with a towel, feeling bones and spine under his skin, a mere outline of a dog. I put out the lights and we went to bed.

The room was dark—there was no moon; it was behind clouds. The dog was curled on my blankets sleeping peacefully.

I was left alone to think. Sam and I had reached for each other and comforted each other, this one time. It meant I still had a working heart, didn't it? I felt a spark of hope—I wanted to keep my heart.

In the end, we were only a man and a woman, both of us bruised and broken, yet it seemed we had also found a small piece of grace.

And, ha!—we had done it behind the moon's back.

He called early the next morning; it was barely dawn. Maybe we could spend the day, he asked. I reminded him I had to work. "Okay," he said, "maybe dinner?"

"I don't date," I reminded him.

He was just going to get some dinner for himself, he explained. He didn't want to eat alone. Would I mind just coming along?

I laughed at this iteration but managed not to give him a definite answer.

Then I called Shay. It had occurred to me she might not be up to working anymore, and I wanted her to have a good pregnancy. I asked her if she wanted to stay home and rest.

"I don't mind working," she insisted. "I feel great really, except for when I have to puke."

The dog and I got into my car and I drove to the Galley. Exactly five blocks down Mainsail Road and a right turn onto Beach Six, passing all those houses I knew since childhood, so pink or yellow or blue or sea foam, so perfectly trimmed in white, painted in harmony, with their cerise beach roses and orange daylilies growing like a paschal meditation on life. Now they seemed corrupted, more in rigid lockstep than picturesque agreement. I used to take such pleasure imagining what was happening behind each pastel façade, who was eating breakfast, who was getting ready for work, who would be coming into the Galley for milk and eggs later. I thought I knew them, knew what they ate, and how they thought and what they cared about. My surrogate family, benign, friendly—all of them—visiting the Galley every day. I didn't have much family, but I had them.

And now I am thinking how naïve I was. How disappointed I am. For all my silly imaginings about being a part of my town, a part of one big extended family, I am thinking of Tommy, how his behavior had to be learned from somewhere, and how I never really knew my town at all.

Shay came through the door an hour later, holding a home-made bouquet of pink and purple hyacinth and red tulips to replace the wilting daffodils from a few days before. She was in her usual tee with jeans, her black curls tied up in a dozen tiny happy plaid ribbons, like a party. I couldn't help but notice that her jeans were getting a little snug.

"Promise you'll let me know when you get too uncomfortable to work," I said.

"I promise," she said, "but I'm happy to come here."

She grabbed the old flowers from the mayonnaise jar. "Always throw out dying flowers," she announced, rinsing the jar. "They emit negative energy—it's a feng shui thing."

"I should be giving *you* flowers," I said, admiring the new ones, looking so fresh and cheerful.

"Don't worry about me," she said. "My heart is filled with flowers."

The day flew by. The usual sales, the usual requests, the usual scrutiny from Mrs. Skipper, who warned me that she had heard things about my dog.

"What things?" I asked her, smiling at her empty statement.

"Things," she said, nodding. "Just things."

Shay had yogurt for lunch while I had the Sandwich. The dog was on his best behavior, and before we knew it, it was closing time.

My cell phone rang. I had left it next to the cash register.

"It's Sam!" Shay called out, grabbing the phone to hand it to me.

"Leave it." I didn't want to talk to him yet.

Shay raised her eyebrows. "I thought you kind of liked him," she said, putting the phone back down.

"I do," I said. "We're friends. I want us to just be friends. I think I might have made a mistake."

I told her about the previous night. She listened with pursed lips, then giggled. "Yep," she said. "You kissed the wrong spot, honey. That kiss was a standard sex invitation. Big mistake. Your second one this month—the dog being your first."

My hand flew over my mouth, over my offending lips. "Oh God," I said. "Now I'm mortified. What is wrong with me?"

She shook her finger at me. "I don't know. You don't want to get involved, but you keep acting straight from your heart."

Sam stopped by before I could close the store. Shay had left a little early; the dog, cued by the sight of my keys, was sitting by the door, and waiting. He leapt to his feet at the sound of the Cadillac pulling up.

Sam was shining. His thick dark hair was combed and styled, and he had new brown slacks and a yellow shirt that set off his olive skin. Even his cane was polished. He looked happy as I exited the store. I locked the door before pulling the creaking old gate across the front of it and locked that, too.

"I am taking myself to dinner," he said with a shy grin. "Maybe you'd like some, too?"

He followed my car, smiling at me in my rearview mirror, parked at my house, and waited in the kitchen, closely monitored by the dog, while I scooted around grabbing up a simple blue dress and sandals, took a quick shower, and emerged from the bathroom, still slightly damp, with makeup more or less in place. He beamed as soon as I entered the kitchen.

"Wow—you look terrific," he said.

"Thank you," I said, wishing it didn't mean so much to hear that. "So, have you been to Provincetown? I suppose we could go there to eat. It's about six miles from here."

"Haven't been anywhere yet," he said. "Except your beach."

I grabbed a light jacket and my purse. I never liked eating

alone, and was looking forward to the evening. He stepped across the floor to open the back door for us, moving close to me. The dog ran to the door, and I realized that, for the first time, I would have to leave him behind. Alone.

"Maybe we should take the dog," I said. "Everybody walks their dog in Provincetown. And there are lots of places we can eat outside."

"I would like to spend the evening with *you*," Sam replied softly.

"He's never been alone," I worried, staring down at the dog who was now wagging his tail in a slow arc and expectantly staring up at me with compelling almond-shaped pit-bull eyes.

"He'll be fine," Sam reassured me. "He'll settle in and go to sleep."

Sam was probably right. The dog had just eaten a good dinner and had the choice of sleeping on any piece of furniture. He was safe and well cared for. *And besides,* I thought, *what is a pit bull for, if not for protecting an empty house?*

Chapter 15

Provincetown comes to life at night. P-town, as it is called, is a playful place filled with fun and mischief. The streets are alive with tourists and locals, with families of all colors and combinations. Couples stroll by, men with men, women with women, straight couples, all of them welcome, and almost all walking dogs of every size and breed, some of them quite au courant in dog fashion. Though everyone uses the sidewalks, it's practically a tradition to walk down the middle of the narrow streets while cars roll slowly and patiently behind you. The police are always smiling.

All right, almost always.

I have loved going there since I was a child. And because of the Galley, my family was known by almost everyone. When I was a child, it was fun to play the pianos left out on the streets, watch the street magicians perform, or listen to talented musicians jam in the open courtyards outside the clubs.

Sam and I had to take a brief walk from a lucky-find nearby parking spot to the small dumpling shop that I chose, just around the corner from the wharf. We were walking slowly, he holding my hand and taking in the dazzling atmosphere as we passed through the one-block theater district that always reminded me of a carnival.

"Dahling!" I am greeted affectionately by an old friend, Lynne Guini, a drag queen in hot pink feathers that adorned her long sequined cape and tight, skimpy bikini. She was wearing her usual heavy makeup, a big blond wig, and impossibly high hot pink satin platform shoes and dancing in the street hoping to draw people upstairs to the performances. "What are you doing tonight?" She gave me a perfume-drenched hug and Sam a smoldering once-over. "We have new material!" I promised I would attend, not tonight but soon, and before Sam and I had taken a few more steps, her co-dancers, Summer Clearance and Starr Trek, greeted me effusively, with air kisses and finger hugs, while shedding glitter and feathers all over the street. Carmen Dioxide, in red body paint and strategic sparkles, handed Sam a flyer and gave him a long, lingering glance. Sam looked panicked and I just managed to pull him away before Carmen could make her usual offer.

While Sam and I walked, I pointed out every quaint store tucked up and down the cozy side streets that branched off Commercial Street, which ran through the center of town. I know who sells the real jewelry, the best homemade ice cream, where the fudge samples are generous, the locations of the funkiest head shops—courtesy of my grandmother—and where to get free Dramamine for the whale watches. And everywhere we went, I received a warm greeting, a hug, an invitation. And sympathy.

Sam and I entered the small dumpling shop, inconspicuously tucked in the corner made by two diagonal streets, and were immediately bathed in a cloud of fragrant spices. I come here once in a while to take home a white cardboard box of favorites and bring them home, to sit alone on my deck and eat. The store is rarely crowded and I thought Sam might like that.

He followed me in, first pausing at the door to quickly glance around. There were only four tiny tables on one side and a high counter with barstools on the other, now occupied by two young men holding hands. Sam chose a table against the wall, hooked his cane over the back of his chair, and sat down.

I sat across from him. "Why do you do that?" I asked him. "You know, check the room out before you walk in?"

"Do I?" He looked caught unawares. "I didn't know I was still doing that."

Ling, the owner, interrupted us, greeting me by name. "Aila! So good to see you again," she said, leaning over to give me a quick kiss on my cheek, then bowing politely at Sam before putting a handwritten menu on the table. We ordered tea and told her we needed a few minutes. I waited for her to leave before I spoke again.

"You didn't answer me," I reminded Sam.

He stared down at his menu without reading it, reluctant, it seemed, to speak.

"You do it every time. Even in my house," I pressed. "Check everything out."

Ling brought us a pot of tea and two cups. He waited until she left before he spoke again.

"You got to have eyes on your surroundings at all times," he answered slowly. "You got to make sure. Precautionary measures. I can't stop myself."

"In a war zone," I pointed out. "Which this is not."

He shrugged and stirred three packets of sugar into his tea. "That's how I lost my leg," he said, so low I could hardly hear him. "They didn't clear the building and I thought they did. We all overlooked an IED. I gave the signal to leave the building and pick up the wounded." He stopped abruptly. "So I made a mistake and paid for it. I lost a man, too. We should have stayed in the building, but we got ambushed. I waited with him to be evacuated. He died in my arms. I think about him all the time."

"But you're safe *here*."

"Yeah?" he said, a touch of something—irony—in his voice. "You think so?"

He picked up his tea, and his sleeve slid back. I noticed the thin silver metal band on his wrist, etched with faded black letters. I couldn't read it. "What is that?" I asked, reaching out to gingerly touch the worn engraving. "What does it say? KI . . . ?"

"Corporal Mike Edison—KIA," he said. "Killed in action. That's the guy I told you about." He ran his thumb over the letters, rubbing a circle, then another, then another. "I always wear it. I even have a couple of challenge coins I was going to give him." He grew somber. His eyes lost their focus, lost in the past.

"That must be so hard for you," I finally said.

"He was twenty-two," he replied. "He was a kid. Too young."

Ah, yes. Too young.

"I would swap myself for him in a minute," he said. "Because there's nothing left of me."

I know about having nothing left. I know about death. I know about being too young, though, really, death has no preferences for age or plans or dreams. It harvests without prejudice, without strategy, without care. And it is greedy, always greedy for more, like the killer whales that roam the sea to devour whatever they come upon in their path just because they are hungry deep into their souls and the bait is there.

Ling returned and Sam and I ordered all kinds of dumplings except pork, because Muslims don't eat pork. The dough was tender and delicately fried, and the fillings were a spicy mixture of chopped chives and meat, mixed with vegetables. Sam stared at his meal, no, past it, no, through it, for a few minutes until I touched his hand.

"Why don't you eat before they get cold?" I reminded him. His face snapped awake and he looked down at his plate.

"Oh," he said. "Right." He took a pair of chopsticks from the table, picked up a dumpling, and dipped it into the little bowl of pungent black broth. A few bites and he grinned.

"Good food," he agreed.

We ate in silence. He was enjoying his food but seemed removed. He ate, he commented on its quality, he sipped his tea between bites, but he was absent. His eyes were watching some remote action unfolding in the past, far removed from the little table in the dumpling shop.

Ling made us a special dessert, little dumplings with sweet red bean paste, and Sam's attention returned. He ate a few and I was pleased that he liked them.

"Terrific," he said. "We are definitely coming back."

I smiled indulgently and thought that's what people say on dates, but we weren't dating.

We finished our meal—he insisted on paying, even though I had taken out my wallet—then he pulled himself to his feet, picking up his cane and gently guiding me out the door with his hand on the small of my back. "We have to slow down a little," he said. "But I'm ready for you to show me the rest of your town."

The sun was setting, washing the sky and the air and the streets pale pink, like the inside of a rose. MacMillan Wharf meets Commercial Street at an odd angle and we crossed together in his now familiar rocking gait, the metallic click of his cane accompanying his every step, as we headed to the pier.

The ferries and fishing boats were tethered along the wharf, each one next to its own gangplank, a kindergarten of smaller boats tied at one end, rocking gently in their slips, to some unheard lullaby from the bay. Gulls sat in neat lines on the gunwales and crowded along the boat cabin roofs calling hoarse good nights to one another. A few fishermen had dropped anchor for the day and were traipsing down the ramps carrying coolers. Sam and I stood under the yellow lights of the pier, side by side, to watch as couples leisurely walked by, hand in hand, eating ice cream, bits of their conversation floating behind them like butterflies.

Sam took my hand and I allowed him. How hungry I had been for the feel of a hand in mine to make me part of a couple. How much I craved someone to eat with me, walk beside me, to hear a voice next to my ear. We stared across the bay for a while, listening to the music coming from the clubs. Sam pointed to the ice-cream shop and raised his eyebrows. I nodded in response. We walked there slowly—the rhythm of his cane, *click, click,* growing slower and slower. He was tiring and starting to drag his leg. We bought double scoops of homemade pistachio ice cream in sugar cones. I led him across the street to the large courtyard called Portuguese Square in the very center of town, surrounded with red flowering bushes and wrought-iron benches, and we sat and rested and licked our cones in the perfect night.

"So, you like running the Galley?" he asked.

I shrugged. "It's always been my life," I said. "For a time I ran the science department in a private school in Boston, but I seem to have come full circle."

"You were a science teacher?" he asked. I nodded. "You're a smart girl," he said approvingly, and it irritated me for the moment that he called me a girl.

"What about you?" I asked. "What did you do before you went into the navy?"

He looked across the court.

"You don't want me to ask you?"

"I was a cop," he finally said. "A *cop.* I can't be a cop anymore. I'm nothing."

"But you can do other things," I said. "What else do you like?"

"What difference does it make?" He suddenly pushed to his feet using his cane and extended his hand to me. "My plans are to take each day as it comes, if it comes. Let's walk."

We walked only a few minutes more before he began stumbling, struggling to swing his leg forward, after which he put it down tenderly. I knew he was in pain.

"Why don't we leave?" I suggested. "I'm getting tired, and I'll bet you are, too."

"Oh," he said, sounding disappointed. "I wanted to get you a little gift to remind you of tonight. Of me."

I smiled up at him. "Another time. It'll give me something to look forward to."

"Maybe we can spend tomorrow together," he said hesitantly.

"Tomorrow after work, I have to see my mother," I replied. "She's in a nursing home and I missed her this week because of my ankle."

"Soon then," he said. "Time is short."

I glanced sideways at him. His face was bleak and there was something ominous in his words. I linked my arm through his very lightly, so that I didn't throw off his walk; and then, acting like any other ordinary couple, which we were and which we weren't, we made our way to the pink Cadillac.

My house was waiting up for me, like a good parent, a soft reassuring glow coming from the kitchen. He walked me to my back steps. I knew he was in too much pain to climb them, so I thanked him while we stood at the bottom. He took my hand in his and attempted to say something, then stopped, searching for the right words.

"You made this a really nice evening," he finally said. He was facing me directly, his eyes searching mine, dark and serious, always serious. "I haven't dated since"—he paused, then looked down—"since, you know, my leg. I hope you didn't mind that I took up your time."

"Sam," I said. "I really enjoyed myself."

"Thank you," he whispered, not sure what to do next. "I hope I see you again." He tightened his grip on my hands. "Good night."

"Good night," I said. "You will. I promise."

He leaned over and gave me a light kiss on my cheek, then stood awkwardly for a moment before pulling me hard against him and kissing me urgently. I almost pulled away—it wasn't right; it wasn't with the right man—but then I kissed him back. His lips took everything from me that I offered and our blood stirred like the waves, our hearts floating up together against the tiny stars that welcomed us.

He said good night a second time and turned to walk slowly away. I climbed the steps and watched him from the deck, struggling through the sand, wincing now with each step. I listened to the cane clicking, until he reached his car and turned to salute me. I saluted back and waited until he got in and started the engine.

Hundreds of stars and one slim crescent moon sparkled like a chest full of medals. *How precocious,* I thought, glancing up. A moon is born, grows to fullness, and dies in one month's time, its whole lifetime spent in one month. And friendships? Only time would tell.

I unlocked the door and entered the kitchen. The small night-light gave off a dim glow and I stood for a moment, enjoying the intimacy and quiet to reflect on the evening. I know something isn't right with Sam. It was obvious that he was burdened with guilt and pain, but I didn't know what I could do to help him. No wonder he checked out every room before he walked into it. Precautionary measures, he said. I understood that. I had been employing some of my own. They protect you from harm; they keep you safe.

But sometimes they just get in the way.

The dog was nowhere to be seen. I thought he might run and greet me as soon as I came in, but the house remained quiet. I *wanted* him to greet me; it was such a customary, normal thing for a dog to do and I suddenly craved it. I was tired of an empty house, tired of being haunted by memories, tired of my heart craving things that it couldn't have. I was finding it harder and harder to be alone. Dan and his touch and our conversations were becoming distant. Maybe some of it could be completed by a dog who missed me when I was away.

"Here, boy!" I called out. He still didn't come. I thought it strange until I turned the kitchen light on.

The house had been turned into a debris field. The kitchen floor had disappeared under a snowfall of chewed paper towels; the living room had festoons of toilet paper draped over the furniture; the laundry basket had been raided and dirty towels and socks and undies were strewn decoratively across the floor. He had apparently spent the evening in reconnaissance mode before mounting a successful attack on the trash pail. Two days' worth of coffee grounds were blended into the rug, topped with food wrappers, vegetable peelings, and moldy bread, all of it liberally sprinkled with eggshells.

"Oh my god! What happened?" I gasped out loud. Then I stopped, wondering if I should scold him. This behavior was one I would not tolerate, yet I was acutely mindful of his brutal past. He had been starved and here was a pail filled with remnants of food just like the garbage he had lived on for months before I found him. How could he not eat it? He was worrying where his next meal would come from. How could he know that I would always make sure he had food? He was a dog haunted by hunger and rejection and fear. Eating garbage was a precautionary measure.

"Where are you?" I called.

I was answered by a very soft woof. I could make out a set of eyes following me from under my bed.

"You can come out," I said to him. "Come on."

He slid out very slowly on his stomach, his face filled with guilt and remorse, and sat down in front of me with his head hanging.

"This wasn't your best idea," I said gently. He reached over to lick my hand but sat glued to the spot, his eyes cast down.

"It's okay," I reassured him. "It's all okay."

And then, because I understood so well how important it is to have precautionary measures, I said nothing more, just grabbed a fresh trash bag and a broom, sighed loudly, and started cleaning it all up.

Chapter 16

I am very faithful. I never miss a visit to my mother. I see her every week at the Royale Pavilion, her nursing home, an old three-story white—what else?—Cape Cod that sits on a bluff overlooking the Atlantic Ocean. It's practical and plain, the wraparound porch surrounded by sturdy white balustrades and big bay windows. The landscape is typical, Irish moss and yellow coreopsis entangled with straggly pink beach roses struggling to fill two sandy acres.

It's only a ten-minute distance from me, but I drive there dreading what new deficit my mother will reveal this week. In a bag next to me is a small container of her favorite chocolate ice cream from the Galley. I always bring her chocolate ice cream.

The residents sit out on the porches in almost any kind of weather, wrapped in heavy jackets and yellow wool caps and plaid blankets, all of them facing out to sea like old wooden figureheads guarding their ship against the relentless waves and thrashing tides of the ocean. These are fierce old Cape Codders, with weather-beaten skin and snow-white hair. They are

strong and opinionated; even now, they still understand the red
skies at night and pale blue milk skies, and black-smoke clouds,
and ice rings around the moon. They know all about the sea-
driven weather as intimately as they once knew their families.

Aides bring them hot tea and apple slices. Sometimes they
are pushed in their wheelchairs down the weathered wooden
ramps, to sun in the craggy Memory Garden lined with wood
benches and little gnome statues and bird feeders and a running fountain for the cardinals that attend. But mostly the residents stay on the porches.

A dozen pairs of pale eyes turned to me as I made my way up
the brick walk and climbed the porch steps. I greeted each one.
I saw past the wrinkled skin, the cloud white hair, the blank
faces. I see them young, dancing at their wedding, making
dinner for their family, scolding a naughty child, dressing for
work, worrying about a repair bill for the car, opening gifts on
Christmas. I know their minds were busy now with the work of
grasping at old memories, longing for a brief replay, and they
looked at me with hope that I belonged to them, that I can find
them in the spaces they are lost in and bring them back for a
moment. I smiled and greeted them and then I looked away,
because I am terrified. A full moon, for all its brilliance, has
only a month of life; it goes so fast.

The front hall was cool, even though the sun was streaming
in through the bay windows and making bright patterns across
the yellow upholstered chairs and the black-and-white checker-
board floors. This was an old mansion that, like its residents,
had been restructured to accommodate old age.

I ran for the elevator and almost didn't even have to wait.
Totally modern and silvery sleek, it glided open almost right
away accompanied by a soft ping. My mother was on the second
floor, to the left, administrative offices on the third.

She looked like an angel wrapped in clouds, a big white pillow under her head and white puffy blankets tucked up to her
armpits revealing Hello Kitty pajamas, which, since I had never

bought them for her, had obviously come through the byzan-
tine laundry service intent on exchanging clothing between
the residents on a regular basis. Someone had put a pink bow
in her wild, white hair—how, I can't imagine, as she gets com-
bative if anyone tries to comb it. And she'd had a manicure; her
nails were the color of poppies. She had always been vain about
her nails, even when she worked at the Galley, and I was glad to
see she was being well cared for. I worry about her being well
cared for, and I was glad that there was someone there to do the
things I could no longer do for her. I kissed her forehead and
sat in the floral chair next to her bed.

"Hi, Mom," I said gently. "How are you feeling today?"

She mumbled something I couldn't understand, then made
an effort to rise.

"You need to rest, Mom, until your hip heals," I told her, leaning over to find the button to raise her head a little. "I have your
favorite ice cream." I took the spoon and the container out of
the bag.

She picked up her hand to push it away. "Have to get out of
here," she said clearly, and pulled at the side rails. "Out of here.
I have to get out. I have to get back." She was getting agitated,
pushing away her covers and upsetting her pillows, and before
I could get to the door to summon a nurse one suddenly appeared. I recognized her as the nurse who usually took care of
my mother.

She walked over to the bed. "Miss Winnie! Is that you making
all that noise?" She put her hand on my mother's head, a laying
on of hands, and my mother fell back against her pillows.

"You want some juice, sweetie?" She kept up the conversation and my mother, distracted, calmed down. "We have apple
juice and orange juice. I know you like apple. Shall I get some
for you?"

My mother nodded. The nurse turned to me as she cranked
the bed up a little more. "You want some juice, too?"

"I'm good, thanks."

She gave me a smile and left, returning with a juice box and
straw.

"Here you go, sweetie." She held the box while my mother sipped, childlike. "Miss Winnie had two hours of rehab today," she said to me while keeping her eyes on my mother. "Didn't you, Miss Winnie? She fights doing her rehab, you know, but we got her to do some of it, and then we brought her into the cafeteria for lunch—a tuna fish sandwich—but she didn't want it, so we brought her to the sun-room for a bit, just to give her a change of scenery. She didn't want to stay there. So we brought her back to bed to rest until her dinner. She liked dinner— tonight she had the broiled chicken and mashed potatoes and peas, ate almost all of it." The day's history and the juice box were finished simultaneously and she wiped my mother's lips. "If you need anything else, just call me," she said, fluffing every-thing back together before leaving.

My mother had been either in her bed or in a wheelchair for three weeks now. She had broken her hip falling after trying to wheel her walker through a solid wall and she had to have surgery to replace it. She is sixty-two and has early onset Al-zheimer's. I visit her every week and stand on the pier of sanity watching her mind recede like a boat drifting off into the ho-rizon. Every week another memory fades, another member of her family is erased, another cluster of words disappears, never to return.

I took her hand. "You have to do your rehab, Mom," I told her. "You want to walk again, right? And then you can go out-side. You always like going outside."

"I went there," she said urgently, her words tumbling out and barely comprehensible. "I had to find them."

"Where did you go, Mom?" I asked.

She suddenly spoke. "To the house," she said. "I went back to the house. You know—the *house*."

I am used to these conversations that are half fantasy and half remembered events mixed together, a thousand-piece puz-zle with no solution. Sometimes I am almost able to make sense of them, and sometimes I am just baffled.

She grabbed her blankets. "You've got to put the heat on," she said. "It was very cold."

"The heat is on at the house, Mom," I reassured her. "It's toasty warm."

Tears started from her eyes and left rivulets down her pale cheeks. "It was empty," she insisted, oblivious to them. "I went there to look for my mother and my father, and Uncle Jake, but the house was empty. They were all gone. I couldn't find anyone."

"I know," I agreed with her. "They aren't there anymore."

She looked up at me. "You have to find them," she said sharply. "You have to find them and tell them to come home."

"I will," I said, stroking her hand.

"Tell them," she said again. "Tell them to come back, because the house is empty."

"The house has me," I replied. "It's not empty. *I'm* there."

She peered up at my face. "Who are you? What do you want?"

"Aila. I'm Aila. Your daughter."

She scanned my face, puzzled, then looked away, blank, disinterested, and suddenly I understood that my time had come; she had lost me, too.

She started another conversation, this one totally incomprehensible. Half muttered, half uttered aloud, a compendium of vowels and consonants, sounds without meaning. She gestured to the window, I guessed a thousand guesses, all wrong, until she stopped, depleted, drowsy. Whatever part of the brain that turns sensibility into conversation was spent.

I thought about this, sitting in the floral chair. I thought about it as I watched her fall asleep, her snores coming in soft purrs. The last member of my family lay before me. My presence didn't matter. My love didn't matter. Though she was right there, she was unreachable and not there at all.

A slow hour hung in the air, then finally passed away. I thought I might as well leave. Another visit was over.

I pulled the covers up over her shoulders and tucked them around her so she'd feel warm and safe and then I threw the melted chocolate ice cream into the trash container next to her heavenly white, fluffy bed.

"Don't leave me," I pleaded softly.

She mumbled something that I couldn't understand. I patted her head and she turned her face away.

"Good-bye, Mom," I whispered now, not sure, entirely, what I meant by this.

Chapter 17

Even though I knew the dog would be waiting for me at home with a bag of garbage hanging from his mouth, I took the winding coastal road that ran along the ocean, following miles of brownish green compass grass punctuated by snowy egrets. It's a little longer, more scenic, driving along the dunes before the road veers five miles inward, across Truro, toward the bay. It would give me the opportunity to watch the sky fill with the rose colors of early evening while the clouds backlit with gold. I think about how my mother loved roses. She would bring home bags of topsoil and peat moss to cover the naturally sandy soil in the garden, and plant dozens of roses. They never lasted more than a year or two—the winds from the bay were too harsh for them, the soil too barren—but she never gave up. Sometimes they were all pink, sometimes scarlet, sometimes every shade of yellow, sometimes mixed together as she replaced the dying plants with new ones halfway through the summer.

I had always felt guilty that I couldn't duplicate her efforts. My garden this summer would have some hardy geraniums and a few other things that are rated for salt air. And this year they will have to contend with a dog who will dig holes and carry rocks into the house and pull the leaves from bushes and curl up for a nap on my best flowers.

The dog.

He was probably beside himself with anxiety, but I needed this drive to reflect on the visit to my mother. If I ever had children, she would never know them. The knowledge of love and sense of family that winds through generation after generation, like a climbing rose, ends with me. I decided to plant a rose-bush for her and work very hard to keep it alive.

There is a Burger King on the way home and I planned a quick stop. I was hungry and fast-food burgers were my guilty pleasure. Sometimes I eat them in the car and pretend the other people in the parking lot are having dinner with me. This time, I would bring one home for me and one for the dog. He was my dinner companion now.

There was no line, not surprising for a small town just past dinnertime. Families were home, sitting around the table, finishing dessert and setting off to read the evening paper or watching the news or putting the kitchen back to order. Now was the time that singles grab quick bites before they spend their evenings alone. I put in my order. As I watched the girl behind the counter wrap the burgers, then skillfully scoop up the fries into a cup, I was acutely aware of how alone I was.

I wasn't an orphan, exactly. I know there are technicalities about things like that. You had to have lost both parents, and though I had, sort of, it still didn't make me an orphan. I had lost my father. Was my mother considered lost? My crazy grandmother went to bed one day and never got up again. Terrified, I had run into the bay and screamed for her for hours. We had been a family of singletons; neither of my parents had siblings, and I didn't, either. And once I lost my husband, Dan's family had gotten back to the business of living their own lives.

I hadn't set out to be single; it just came upon me.

* * *

Two people behind me were holding a distracting conversation. An older woman with a red sweater and a younger one in a blue jacket.

"Right in Wellfall," the red sweater was saying. "Got attacked in the showroom."

"Arab," replied the blue jacket. "Someone said he was an Arab."

"You know what they are," the red sweater added.

"Muslim," the blue jacket agreed. "Came in and ordered a couple of trucks to ship to ISIS."

My heart stopped beating and I half-turned to hear better. I knew right away who they were discussing.

"The salesman refused—" Red Sweater started.

"Smart guy," Blue Jacket interrupted. "He sure caught on fast—"

"I heard he threw the guy out and then the guy's pit bull attacked him!" Red Sweater finished with a flourish.

My heart was pounding. There was no question it was about Sam, and it was all wrong, all horribly wrong. I turned to face them.

"No, no," I said, "I was there. The guy was an American—a vet, a soldier who just wanted to buy a car. The salesman didn't want to sell to him because he was Muslim. The dog just barked. It wasn't like that at all."

"Your order is ready." The girl behind the counter held my food out to me.

"I heard it was one of those homegrown terrorists," said the red sweater adamantly.

"I heard it, too," agreed the blue jacket. "And we come from Wellfall, so we would know."

They stepped up to the counter to order. I stared at their backs. How did you fix that? Heartsick, I took my bag and left.

Two words kept repeating in my mind as I drove home. *Dune fire.* This story was going to spread like a dune fire. Nothing moves faster. It races along the shore, ravaging everything it touches, decimating the tall, dry beach grasses with their delicate pink plumes, nesting birds, turtles, taking it all, taking everything; everything in its path is consumed without mercy until nothing is left but ashes.

I wanted to call Sam immediately, drive to the dealership and pound the big glass show windows until they shattered. I wanted to summon the gods and the newspapers and straighten it all out with the truth. But I had to think things through.

First of all, I wasn't sure Sam was up to handling such news; he seemed so troubled during dinner the night before. I needed to have some kind of solution in place before I spoke to him. And I needed to protect the dog.

There had to be witnesses; we hadn't been the only ones in the showroom, though I doubted that the other salesmen would back us up. Maybe there were video cameras in place, but getting access to them before they were tampered with would be a major problem. What could I do? I wished I had family. I wished I had my father, who was so pragmatic, or Dan, who was always calm and sensible. Even my mother, when she was my mother, was full of good advice and common sense.

I opened my kitchen door and slipped inside. The dog came to me with an air of apology. There was trash on the kitchen floor again, but I didn't care. I dropped to my knees and threw my arms around his neck.

"Life is so tricky," I said, burying my face against him. "I don't know how to fix it. I don't know what to do." I burst into tears; my stomach was in knots. He just sat patiently, wrapped in my arms, sniffing hopefully at the hamburgers, his eyes on the bag. He knew I would never let him come to harm, even if I didn't know how to manage it right now. I promised I would keep him safe, poor orphan that he was, and asked him to keep me safe. He licked my face. He loved me, I knew that. And he was trying so hard to be my family.

"What a good boy," I murmured. Then I opened the bag of burgers and fed both of them to him. He gulped them down and gave me a pickle-scented kiss. Maybe I wasn't an orphan as long as I had him.

I guess that's what pit bulls are really for.

* * *

There were already three messages on my answering machine.

The first two were from Shay. "Exactly what went on when you and Sam were shopping for a car?" she asked calmly from the phone before her voice rose. "I think maybe you left out the best part of the story. A *big* part. You better call me."

The second one was from Sam. "I know you're with your mother tonight, but my aunt Phyllis just told me the craziest thing. We got to talk. I'm so sorry. I didn't mean to get your dog in trouble."

The third call was also from Shay. "Okay, okay. Terrell knows a lawyer. His name is Lawrence LaSalle, LLD. He plays the banjo and he sings a little flat, but he said he would help you. I know you're with your mom, so if you can't call me back tonight I'll talk to you at the Galley tomorrow."

"Calm down," Shay said to me first thing as we opened the Galley the next morning. "Calm down." I hadn't said anything yet, but she was bristling with nerves. "It's going to be business as usual. We're not going to let on that anything is wrong."

"Okay," I agreed.

"Just stay calm. It's a stupid rumor," she went on. "We're not going to say anything, and if anyone mentions it we'll just laugh it off."

"Okay."

"And maybe we should keep the dog—damn, why don't you give him a name already?—keep him under wraps."

"Okay." Of course I had brought the dog with me; he was now behind the counter eating his breakfast. "How do I do that?"

"One idea he might like a lot," she mused.

"Which is?"

"Lock him in the back kitchen with a box of snacks."

Mrs. Skipper was, as usual, the first customer of the day. She took a shopping basket from the stack and headed for the back of the store.

"Go make bread," Shay whispered to me, shooing me out from behind the front counter. "I'll take care of Mrs. Skipper." I headed for the little kitchen, joining the dog. I would keep myself busy and not worry. Okay, maybe I stood in the kitchen door with my eye pressed to the crack, peering out, staring at the back of Mrs. Skipper's blue sweater.

She seemed to take an inordinately long amount of time to select her groceries. She pondered over a small box of spaghetti as though purchasing it would affect the future of Italy. Then she picked up a box of cornflakes and shook it hard to determine whether it was full. Next came a can of tomato soup; yes, she seemed to decide, it would go great on the spaghetti with butter and cheese, a recipe she had once shared with me. She selected a few more items before finally standing at the front counter. I switched from my eye to my ear.

"Two cherry Danishes," she ordered. "You know, the fresh ones."

"Everything is fresh here," Shay replied politely, taking a piece of white bakery tissue and picking up the Danishes.

Mrs. Skipper watched her carefully, then sighed loudly. "I don't know if I'll be coming here anymore," she said. "I heard about that dog and I'm not surprised. Attacking that poor car salesman. Who would ever want to bite a car salesman? You know, he growled at me last time I was in. And then he tried to jump over the counter, if you remember. He's very dangerous."

"Car salesmen can get very aggressive," Shay replied coolly.

"The dog," said Mrs. Skipper. "I told you the last time I was in that he was dangerous. He almost bit me when I started to pay for my groceries."

I was next to her in a flash. "What day was that, Mrs. Skipper?" I asked with faux concern.

"Last time I was in," she repeated, whirling around to face me. "He was growling viciously. I even complained about it."

"It never happened," Shay said firmly.

Mrs. Skipper looked from Shay to me. "Did so," she said.

"Maybe you can tell us what specific day it was, since I only just got him last week," I said.

"Tuesday," she answered firmly. "I remember because I picked up my mail and got a letter from my niece. Her granddaughter just graduated college and wanted to—"

I interrupted her. "He was at the vet on Tuesday," I said. "Went for his shots."

"Then it was Thursday," Mrs. Skipper said.

"That's the day I took him to the town clerk to get his license," I replied calmly.

"I'm sure it was last week," she said.

"We have video cameras set up, Mrs. Skipper," I said. "Just for our customers' protection. All over the store." I paused to let it sink in. "Outside, too."

Shay was right on it. "We'll take some time tonight, after we close, and go over all the videos," she said. "Since he was here only three days last week and you don't come on the weekends, the video should be easy to find."

"I'll have to think on this," Mrs. Skipper murmured, taking out her little gold beaded purse to pay for her groceries. "Maybe it was Mr. Castro's big dog at the gas station. He can be mean."

"That dog is fifteen years old and blind in one eye," I reminded her.

"Could be Miss Phyllis's pink poodle," she reflected. "Had my hair done on Friday."

"He doesn't have teeth," I said. "Just an old toothless pink poodle."

"Gums can do a lot of damage," she said, "but now that I think, I'm certain it was your dog." She left without a glance back at us, slamming the door behind her hard enough that the hanging bell hit the glass and rang loudly.

Shay turned to me "Video cameras?" she asked, a half smile playing on her lips. "Inside and out?"

"Not a one," I admitted, "but guess what I'm buying this afternoon."

"Am I going to have to start wearing makeup again?" She sighed. "I'm pregnant. I don't have the energy to even look in the mirror."

* * *

At the end of the day, I bought two video cameras and dropped them off at the Galley. Even in the dark, I knew where everything was, the store was so comfortingly familiar. I stood by the front counter and peered through the darkness, seeing more from memory than anything. My store. There were ghosts here. My father stirring a big pile of home fries on the flattop. My mother making change at the register. My grandmother sneaking a pack of rolling papers into her pocket. Customers. Friends. Recollections. I didn't want things to change, I loved the old white marble counters worn from years of being wiped down, the food cases, the whiteboard with Marine Conditions hanging on the wall with the day's forecast in Shay's handwriting. My heart was here. The Galley was a member of my family.

But I had a prickling feeling that things were going to change and that I wasn't going to like it.

Chapter 18

It was the usual morning. Fleeties and tourists piling in, orders coming fast, good-natured conversation swirling around us, discussions about the weather and the prospect of seeing a great white in local waters, which they had been frequenting. When we had a break, Shay wrote the Marine Conditions for the day.

Small waves, south-southeast 4 sec, high tide 1:18 p.m. low tide 7:06 a.m. calm winds

"I love doing this!" she called over her shoulder. "I feel like I'm influencing the weather."

"We need a place to sit!" yelled one man waving his egg sandwich in the air. He was in a lime green *Welcome to Fleetbourne* shirt, size triple X, which I remembered selling to him the day before.

"Would be nice if there was a breakfast place in town," a second man, tall and slim, agreed. I listened in while juggling a dozen ham and egg sandwiches.

"Somebody should open a little café in this town!" called out a woman in a pink seagull *Fleetbourne* tee.

I caught Shay raising her eyebrows at me and flashing me the look that said, *"I've been telling you the same thing."*

"Hear that? A place to *sit*," she murmured to me as we crossed paths in front of the Portuguese muffins.

I was about to reply with something snarky when the store suddenly grew quiet for just an instant before the chatter started up again. I turned around, curious, and saw that a woman had made her way to the counter. She was wearing slacks, a pale blue blouse, her head covered with a pale blue hijab.

"Hi." I smiled at her. "Can I help you?"

"Yes," she said softly. "I'd like a muffin with butter and jam, and a coffee, light and sweet."

I knew right away she was related to Sam, most likely his mother. They shared the same round eyes—though her eyes were lighter—and had the same pleasantly generous mouth.

"Toasted muffin?" I asked. She nodded. I knew she was watching me. I could feel her studying my back when I turned away to slice the muffin and slip it into the toaster, and my face as I buttered it and fixed her coffee. She was closely scrutinizing my every move.

"Light and sweet, please," she repeated, revealing there was a definite sweet tooth in the family genes as well. I added two more sugars.

"I remember your father, Aila," she said, and it surprised me, though it shouldn't have. After all, she was Miss Phyllis's sister and a Reyes daughter, from one of the original settler families, who had lived here since forever. I could see her resemblance to her sister right away. "He was such a nice man," she added.

My dad was *a nice man,* I thought with an ache.

"I've been living in Jordan," she said. "So I didn't know that he passed until my sister told me. I'm sorry for your loss."

"Yes," I answered breathily, holding back sudden tears. "Thank you." She paid me and left.

I turned to Shay. "I just met Sam's mother."

She gave me a good-natured poke. "Well, things must be getting serious, meeting the parent."

But the mood was different among our customers. "Now we got *them* in town?" Tall and Slim muttered to no one.

"They're everywhere," agreed Triple X. "Like roaches. All over Boston—with the rags on their heads."

I stopped dead in my tracks. Shay and I had had many discussions about how to handle bigoted remarks that occasionally came across the counter. What to say? We both wanted to respect our customers and not jeopardize business, but not to say something was to give the idea that we might condone it. It was like walking along the edge of a cliff. The solution, we decided, was to remain neutral and educational, to hold ourselves above our anger but be firm in our rebuttal.

"Excuse me," I said to Triple X. "I won't have you talk like that in my store. That woman grew up right here in Fleetbourne, not that it matters."

"Dressed like that?" Triple X asked sharply.

"I thought we were free to dress any way we want in this country," I replied, trying not to eye his lime green triple X *Fleetbourne* shirt with the whale swimming across his stomach, for which I do take responsibility. I added in a regretful but kindly tone, "I'm afraid I'm going to have to ask you to leave if you continue."

"Sure, honey." He pushed close to the counter and leaned in. "Let's see how your little business does when you start losing your *American* customers." He paid for his sandwich and left. A few people silently made their purchases and followed.

"I don't like what I'm hearing," I said to Shay when we had a moment.

She made a face. "Times are changing," she agreed. "The loonies have been given permission to crawl out of the woodwork. We are regressing from bigotry to officially condoned hatred."

The phone rang almost as soon as the dog and I got home from work. It was Mrs. Hummings, the town clerk.

"Aila," she said, "I got an inquiry about your dog."

"What kind of inquiry?" I asked. "He's not up for adoption. Yet."

"The lawyer for a car salesman over in Wellfall called me and asked how many pit bulls were in the dog license registry," she said. "I told him we have only two. Yours and Bill Castro's, who owns the gas station."

"I never said that my dog was a pit bull!" I exclaimed. "I said he was a mixed breed. We're not sure at all what he is. He could be a boxer mix or Great Dane—they all have the same kind of head."

"Well, no matter what he is, the lawyer says he has a video from the store of your dog biting his client."

It was a struggle to remain calm. A video of it was impossible, I knew, but I feared that something might have been tampered with. "It's just not true," I said.

"Aila, I don't know who is right, but I suggest you get a lawyer," Mrs. Hummings replied sympathetically. "You don't want Animal Control to impound your dog."

The words shocked me. "I didn't even know we have Animal Control."

"Well, actually we don't," she said. "It's the police. They take on the job if there are any complaints."

"Thank you for the warning, Mrs. Hummings," I said. "The whole thing is a terrible lie, but I will get to the bottom of it."

"And one more thing," she said. "The deadline for getting his dangles removed was a few days ago, but I will give you extra time. I know how busy you get at the Galley in the summer."

"Thank you, Mrs. Hummings."

"Good luck, dear."

I hung up the phone and sat down on a kitchen chair. The dog immediately sat next to me and stared up questioningly into my eyes. He looked healthy now since he had put on a little weight and his coat had grown in, filling the gaps across his skin like a jigsaw puzzle getting solved. His face had lost its haunted look, replaced now with an expression of tranquility, and typical of his breed, he seemed to happily anticipate my every move so that he could leap to his feet and be of service, even though most of the time he wound up either tripping me or body slamming me into the nearest wall.

He was still staring up at me, and I thought I saw the smallest glimmer of a smile.

"Good boy," I said, rubbing his head. "I'm going to make an appointment to get your dangles off."

He licked my hand and blinked his eyes a few times, full of affection and pure trust backed up by the purest of dog hearts. I leaned over to kiss him on his head, blinking back tears. Why was I getting so emotional over a routine neuter surgery? It doesn't take long, and he'd be home for dinner.

"You're the best boy," I said. "Don't worry; I'll make sure you're okay." He wagged his tail and reached up to lick my face, paying special attention to the water coming from my eyes. I felt lucky to have him. I had caught a blessing—for to have earned the trust of a beaten dog is to own the heavens.

Sam thought it only fitting to accompany me to the vet for the surgery. I had called him after I made an appointment for the following afternoon.

"Of course I want to support him through this," he said. "I know how I'd feel if that were—oh, right, never mind."

The pink Cadillac pulled into my driveway right on time. There is only one vet in Fleetbourne, Dr. Susan Greenberg, Dr. Susan, as she is called by Fleeties prone to reducing the names of fellow citizens to characters who sound like they are in children's books. Her office—converted from a weathered white beach house—was only a few blocks away.

Once in the examining room, she greeted me with a quick hug, then took a long look at the dog, running her fingers over his body, checking his eyes and ears.

"He looks wonderful," she declared. "His skin is healing; his fur has a shine to it—he's quite a handsome dog, isn't he!"

Sam and I beamed with pleasure as she made notes in his chart. "So what did you name him?"

"I haven't named him yet," I said.

"I suppose you're waiting for the perfect name to come along," she said. I didn't want to tell her that actually I had been waiting for the perfect home to come along and then have his new owner name him, so he didn't get confused.

After a thorough examination, Dr. Susan was satisfied he was finally healthy enough for surgery.

"I'll do it this afternoon—you didn't feed him, right?" I nodded. "Good, so we'll go ahead and then keep him overnight on painkillers, and you can pick him up first thing in the morning," she said.

I turned to leave and noticed that Sam had a funny look on his face. "Is something wrong?" I asked him.

"Just the thought of it," he said, shuddering.

"Oh, all the guys get squeamish like that," the vet said, laughing. "They take it so personally."

I had grabbed my purse, ready to leave, when someone knocked on the exam room door.

"Come in!" Dr. Susan called out.

It was the receptionist. "Officer Joe Miranda—you know, Animal Control—is here to talk to you," she said to Dr. Susan.

"Animal Control?" the vet repeated, surprised.

"Well, actually, he followed the pink car here. He has some sort of alert on both the car and Aila's dog," the receptionist said.

We all went outside to talk to them. The dog was being impounded, Officer Joe apologetically explained to us, and since the animal hospital was where all impounded dogs were boarded, he had come straight here to save time. I was appalled.

"They can't do this," I insisted. "He's having surgery and he needs a clear mind and besides, he's . . . he's innocent."

Officer Joe, a regular at the Galley, was sympathetic. "I have to do it," he said. "I've seen him at the store and he seems like a great dog, but until this is straightened out I have to follow the law. I have a complaint that he viciously attacked a man and I have to impound him until we straighten it out."

"That's crazy," Sam interjected. "Don't you need proof? I was there. He just barked."

Officer Joe pulled a white summons from a clipboard and handed it to me. "I'm really sorry."

I stuffed it into my handbag. "I won't let you take him away," I said angrily.

"He's already here," Dr. Susan pointed out.

Officer Joe studied his clipboard. "Male dog. Rust-colored fur. Is he neutered?"

"In about an hour," Dr. Susan said.

Officer Joe checked it off. "His name?" he asked.

"He doesn't have—" Sam started.

"Yes, he does," I interrupted him. "Of course he has a name," I said indignantly, and looked around at the small crowd of people in the waiting room—Sam, Dr. Susan, the receptionist, Officer Joe—and the dog.

"What is it?" everyone asked at the same time.

I had to think. It had to be a perfect name because he was the perfect dog. Despite how he had suffered, he turned out to be gentle, dignified, smart, and affectionate. He was always well behaved at the Galley. If we were apart for the evening, I could look forward to his joyful greeting when I got home, even if it was accompanied by a sprinkling of garbage. He was the best company when we sat on the pier together. And when I reached across the bed at night, he was always there, large and warm and snoring and comforting, keeping my nightmares at bay.

All of a sudden, I couldn't conceive—didn't want—a life without him.

I . . . *loved* . . . him.

I looked at his scarred and broken skin struggling to grow new, fresh fur, met his eyes as he looked up at me with love and trust. I ran my hand over his square box head, his powerful jaws that carefully took treats from my hand with such tenderness, his powerful, muscular body, even more bulked up from running on the beach every day. And his ears, oh, his poor ears, one ear ripped off . . . one ear cruelly cut in half. *One ear* . . . *one ear* . . . And then I knew. I knew his name as clearly as if he had whispered it to me.

"*Vincent!*" I exclaimed with finality. "His name is Vincent."

Chapter 19

Vincent spent a week in jail.

Even though the first thing I did after I left Dr. Susan's office was call Lawrence LaSalle, LLD, the lawyer Shay had mentioned, Vincent and his new name spent their first week together incarcerated.

But I was lucky. Even though impounded dogs are usually kept in isolation, Dr. Susan did me a favor by allowing me to visit Vincent, who, newly neutered and groggy from painkillers, sleepily greeted me with a thorough licking every day.

"I can't remember the last time they impounded an animal," Dr. Susan said to me over lunch, a modified version—no anchovies—of the Sandwich that I brought her from the Galley. "Though I seem to remember a potbellied pig that escaped into someone's backyard last year and ate all their cherry tomatoes. He was caught running down the middle of Beach Five with red stains all over his body, like a serial killer."

"Doesn't there have to be a bite mark?" I asked, wondering if the salesman had somehow faked one from Vincent.

"No bite marks," she replied. "He just ate them all. Two whole bushes."

Despite several frantic phone calls from me, it took the lawyer several days to call me back. He spoke in a deep, measured voice that immediately made me feel reassured.

"Did Shay tell you anything about me?" he asked.

"Yes," I replied. "She said your name was Lawrence LaSalle, LLD, and that you sang flat."

He laughed. "My reputation precedes me. But they needed a baritone, so they got what they got."

He explained that he was a Boston trial lawyer, had actually been thinking of a long-overdue visit to Shay and Terrell, and so decided to combine a business and pleasure trip into his crammed schedule that coming weekend. "Shay gave me a vague idea of what's happening," he said. "Now, who was supposed to be the terrorist? You or your dog?"

"A friend of mine," I answered. "He's a wounded vet. He just wanted to buy a truck."

"Why would that create a problem?" he asked.

"His family is from Jordan, so he has a Muslim name," I explained. "And then he told the salesman he was Muslim. The salesman accused him of buying trucks for ISIS."

"Wow. I see." He then gave me a list of things he needed: a full narrative with the date and time, Sam's version, a copy of Vincent's dog license and health history, a copy of Sam's driver's license, and anything else I wanted to add. In the meantime, he would have an assistant do some investigating.

"We can meet as soon as I get a hole in my schedule and go over your options," he said. "It's obviously a ploy to scare you off from filing a civil suit over that salesman's behavior."

"We should discuss fees first," I said, worried.

"Ah, yes, fees." He paused for a moment. "Shay once told me your specialty is some kind of weird sandwich. I love weird sandwiches, so, if you are in agreement, we can negotiate a few of those."

* * *

It was a slow-moving week. I missed Vincent terribly and worried constantly about what he was thinking.

"I don't want him to feel I abandoned him," I told Shay while we were setting the Galley up for the day.

"Listen, you're doing the best you can," she reminded me. "Vincent is in good hands, in a safe place with someone you totally trust. It's not like he's eating cold gruel every day and making license plates."

Little consolation. My nightmares came back. Boats slipping under the water, venomous sharks circling the pier, Dan and my father swimming out to sea under a full moon that suddenly disappears. I would bolt from my bed and throw on a jacket and race down the beach to sit on the pier. I felt safer there than in my own bed. It was like sitting with an old friend; the creaky, swaying wooden boards stretching across the moving water brought me back to myself. I watched the moon wax gibbous, night after night, watching it grow increasingly ominous, becoming a presence in the sky, menacing, stronger, turning the beguiling, winking crescent it once was into a traitorous full moon.

Mrs. Skipper came in not long after Vincent was impounded, a satisfied smile playing on her lips as she picked out her groceries and returned to the front of the store to order her morning Danish.

"Good thing you got rid of that dog," she said approvingly, tugging her old blue sweater across her shoulders as though it were going to shield her from danger. She set down her shopping basket.

"He's just on vacation," I said airily. "He'll be back soon." I picked up a bakery tissue and put two cherry Danishes into a white bakery bag.

"He was vicious," she added, emptying her groceries onto the counter.

"I've known people who were more vicious than he could ever be, Mrs. Skipper," I retorted, looking her straight in the eye.

She raised her eyebrows at this. My remark didn't sit well with her at all. Shay was writing the Marine Conditions on the white-board and turned around to give me a surprised look.

"Are you implying that I'm vicious?" Mrs. Skipper raised her chin, ready for combat.

"Just saying that I know people who are." And then I couldn't help myself. "By the way, I checked those videos and there wasn't one second that you and he were together." I raised my chin, too. "He was behind the counter the whole time." It was a lie—I had just gotten the cameras installed by a local handy-man the day before—but she had no way to know that.

She squinted her eyes just a tiny bit. Then she cleared her throat. "You know," she started, "I knew your family right down to your great-grandparents."

I stopped checking out her groceries. "Yes, you did," I replied evenly.

"And," she added, "I know your grandmother was crazy as a loon. In fact, all the DeCastros were crazy."

DeCastro had been my grandmother's maiden name. Though I felt a rush of anger, I shrugged and smiled. "She just liked to sing, Mrs. Skipper. Like some people like to gossip. It made her feel fulfilled." I finished totaling her order and started bagging it.

"Aaand," she continued, her voice rising to make sure I could hear her over the crinkle of paper, "you're crazy, just like her. You were a crazy little kid, and you've never outgrown it." She leaned forward so I would get the full effect of her next words. "Tell me, do you still stand in the bay and scream for her? How long did that go on? Two, three months?" She counted out the exact change, took her packages, and headed for the door, pausing in front of it. "Everyone knows you sit on the pier all night. Who are you waiting for?" She opened the door and the bell tinkled wildly. "Crazy is crazy," she ended. "It never goes away. Good day, dear."

How right she was. You don't outgrow crazy. It has followed me like the tail on a dog. After I beat up Tommy his revenge was to tell anyone in school who would listen that I was crazy like my grandmother. Every social gaffe I made after that was seen through the filter of madness. Of course, my grandmother, toking away her days and nights, submerged in water up to her hips, while her white hair blew wildly in the wind, only added to my reputation.

If I were superstitious, I would have stayed indoors that night. You are not supposed to talk about the dead, it summons them, but I didn't know that then. I had barely eaten dinner; it had become such a habit to share it with Vincent that it didn't seem worthwhile to even prepare. The house felt hollow without him, how could I once ever have thought to give him up! I loved him so. I left the kitchen and went outside. The moon was robustly full, and though I didn't really have the courage to endure it alone, I sat in the rocker on the deck and faced the bay.

The moon was leering over the still, black water. There were dark smoke clouds clustering together like a conspiracy before drifting across the sky, reaching toward the moon, in order to cloak its murderous luminescence. I sat very still in my chair, very alone, looking up, unable to turn my face away. The moon became a Cyclopean eye peering into my soul. It knew I was there. It had been a night such as this, still, calm, that the moon drew my father and Dan out to sea, reassuring them, making promises that it would be the perfect night to boat and fish before it betrayed them to the oncoming storm.

How I missed them all, my grandmother, my father, my mother, my husband. Yes, I wanted them all returned. I loved them, crazy or foolish as they were. I closed my eyes and thought if I concentrated, if I wished hard enough, maybe I could call them in. Maybe they could ride the waves to the beach and just come home.

A wind started up and I could see the white-fringed waves coming toward the shore, then leaving their lace prints behind as the water retreated. It was hypnotic to hear their rhythmic lapping against the sand and see the slow, inexorable rising of the bay as it crept toward me, starting its journey to high tide. And then, in the cloud-broken moonlight, a visage, a dark figure, its head and shoulders rising slowly as the water streamed off, leaving it slick and ominous, before it disappeared, only to appear again, even closer to the shore.

I stood, transfixed. My tongue was frozen to the roof of my mouth. The figure, substantial and solid, stopped, now standing staunch against the waves, the white foam swirling circles around it. The moon was tormenting me, barely allowing me to see. A dim figure, head and shoulders. Then suddenly joined by another. And another. My heart was pounding with apprehension as three, then four, rose from the sea, wavering for a moment before disappearing into the water, only to rise again, water streaming from their bodies as they faced me. A crevice of moonlight caught something and four pairs of eyes gleamed at me. Just for a moment. Just long enough for me to realize they had faces.

Oh! I knew. I knew who they were.

Oh God.

The ghosts of my family, finally returning to me.

Chapter 20

Sam's voice sounded sleepy. "Aila?"

"I need to talk," I gasped. "Please. Just talk to me."

He was awake in an instant, on full alert. "What's wrong?"

My voice betrayed my fear. "It's just such a bad night. I can't—"

"I'll be right there," he cut me off. "Hang on. I'm coming over."

I was sitting in the kitchen now, the back door open, waiting. I had to talk to someone and didn't want to wake Shay. I knew she went to sleep early, and there was no one else. I used to call my mother.

A car pulled up, I didn't even rise from my chair; I knew who it was. No one comes to the beach at night, except the very lonely. Everyone sleeps; everyone else is content enough to leave the moon and the tides and the water alone to do whatever business is necessary for their survival. I am the only one who sits on the pier. Except for Sam.

He didn't bother to knock; he just let himself in. I stood up to greet him, but he swept me into his arms before I could utter a word.

"You're all right," he said, breathing his relief against my face, stroking my hair, my back. "Thank God you're all right. I didn't know what to think."

He stood back to look at me more carefully. "What's wrong?"

I instantly felt foolish. "There was something out there—in the bay. Coming close to shore," I said. "Several of them. I don't know who they are."

"You have a flashlight?" He was a soldier. Instantly ready to patrol. And protect.

I pulled one out of a kitchen drawer and he took it and, without another word, left through the back door, snapping it shut behind him.

I am not the type to pace the floor and wring my hands in useless emotion. I grabbed a knife and followed him.

"I see them!" he called to me as he headed toward the water, his cane clicking against the wet, hardpacked sand. "I see four of them."

I couldn't breathe. "Sam. Wait!" My mouth was so dry, I could barely call to him. I didn't want him to stand there and face them alone. I raced down the steps and across the sand to his side. He had placed himself on the gravel, away from the water—I realized the water would damage his leg—and he was holding his cane unsteadily under his arm, fumbling with the flashlight, until it suddenly snapped on. The beam fell across the black figures. They turned to him, in unison, their large, blank sea eyes glowing in the light.

"Seals!" he shouted. "Seals! They're just seals!"

And they were. I had never seen grey seals come so far into this part of the bay, but tonight they had. Rising and slipping back into the black water and rising again, their true selves veiled by the clouds, there were four of them, silently watching me, heads and shoulders—if you can call them shoulders—sticking up from the surface, watching this crazy woman stare back at them.

Sam grabbed me. "Let's go home," he said into my ear, but I fell to my knees in the sand, gasping with relief. The clouds moved away, unveiling the bright moon. I could see them as the sky cleared and glowed from moonlight. "Seals!" was all I could choke out. "Seals!"

Sam pulled me to my feet with one arm and we walked back to my house, leaning against each other, under a now bright silver full moon.

Sam closed the door behind us and locked it. He took the knife from my hand and dropped it into the kitchen sink. I stood there for a moment, shaking with relief, waiting for my heart and my breath to even out. How foolish. How very foolish of me.

"Hey," Sam said, reaching out to take me into his arms.

I gave him a shaky smile. "Thank you."

His fingers rubbed across my cheek. "Hey," he said again, softly. We stared at each other, and I suddenly understood what he wanted. I could allow myself to want this, too. I could try to put my memories on the back burner and allow myself this one night. There was no one here but Sam and me and my memories. I could allow myself this.

Sam led me into my bedroom and, with shaking hands, slid off my wet, sandy clothes.

"It's okay," he whispered. "It'll be good."

He pulled his shirt over his head and dropped it to the floor. On his back, just below his neck, was a tattoo. A moody, dark blue, American eagle superimposed across an anchor, holding a trident in his claw and a cocked pistol in the other, fierce and dark and sharp, poised and angry, ready to protect him.

"You have a tattoo," I said.

"Navy SEAL." He smiled, shrugging. I traced it across his back with my fingers. He stopped my hand with his, then fumbled with the zipper of his fly before allowing his jeans to slip down.

"Help me," he asked softly. "I need you to help me." He sat down to guide me as I helped him with his leg. It was so natural and right, the smooth, eager rhythm of working together as we eased his leg to the floor, like we had done it a thousand times before. He kissed me, and held his mouth against my lips while pulling me down to sit next to him, to pull me close to him, closer, lying back against the bed until we fell together. I could hear the usual struggle of his breath.

"Hold me," he said hoarsely. "It'll be okay. Just hold me." I relaxed into his arms. They had such strength. We held each other for a long time, while he methodically covered my face and body with a thousand kisses. More than a thousand. His face felt rough, but his skin was warm and smooth. He touched every part of my body with great gentleness and pulled my hand to him. I pulled away at first, suddenly filled with guilt and reservations, but he took my hand again.

"Do you really want to stop?" he whispered.

No, I didn't. I touched him willingly, caressed him. I remembered all these things from a life before, even though it was our first time. I remembered what to do, and how to hold him, and even though his leg was gone, I wouldn't have known. He remembered everything he had ever learned about a woman. He pressed on top of me, and I wouldn't allow myself to think of anything but him.

There was no past, no cares about a future, no promises, just joy that we had found this moment.

I dozed off in his arms, waking to the sound of his voice. Startled, I looked around. He was in the corner of the room, on his knees, praying.

We spent the night making love and sleeping, and holding each other and falling back to sleep again in peace. I turned onto my side to face him—he was sleeping—and ran my hand across his body, his chest, his arms, his legs. I felt such sympathy for him; he had suffered such losses. His breathing was noisy from damaged lungs; the blanket outlined his good leg and what remained of the one torn from his body, and I leaned over and kissed his face. He smiled in his sleep and I put my head against his shoulder and allowed myself to sleep, too. We opened our eyes to the blue morning light, repaired.

He pulled himself over me to wake me and his dark hair fell into his eyes. He took my hand and ran it across the stubble on his cheek. "This is how I look in the morning," he said. "A bit untamed. Is that okay?"

My hair was standing up in the back and I raked it down with my fingers. "Me too," I said, without apology.

"I have an idea," he said as I showered. He was standing in the bathroom watching; the night had entitled him to new familiarities.

"Did you pray again this morning?" I asked him. I liked that he prayed. That he kept in constant touch with God.

"Always," he said, then "I have an idea. Maybe you can take the day off and we can go somewhere. Anywhere you want."

I poked my head through the shower curtain. "I'm a working girl," I said. "There is only one place I can go."

"Right," he said, disappointment in his face.

We dressed and I made him scrambled eggs for breakfast and insisted that he eat them. I had coffee and added a lot of cream until it looked beige while he put three sugars in his. I toasted my last muffin for him and he buttered it, then split it in half for us to both eat. It was so good to have him sitting at the table with me. The day was just awakening, but it was awakening to something lovely.

Then he said, "Listen, why don't you come to dinner? My aunt Phyllis has been asking me to invite you. And my mother, too."

My heart dropped. I knew what that meant. Meet the family, except I had known his aunt since forever and his mother had been introducing herself slowly at the Galley every morning.

"I don't want to bother anyone," I replied, a standard no in these parts. Normally, I would be thrilled to eat dinner with a whole family, but I was afraid this would send the wrong message.

"No worries," he said. "Tomorrow night. I'll tell them that you're coming tomorrow night."

"I don't want them to think anything," I cautioned. "Because we don't know anything ourselves."

He gave me a teasing smile. "We don't?" he asked.

I didn't answer him.

He changed the subject. "I am picking up my new truck today," he said. "My aunt made the arrangements. I already paid for it. And then I am going to help you get Vincent back."

"I just got a lawyer," I told him. "He said he would do it."

"Let me pay for him," he said. "It was all my fault."

"It wasn't your fault at all," I said.

He took my hand across the table and we fell into silence, contemplating the day ahead. There were things we needed to do to straighten out our lives.

He pushed himself to his feet and while I tidied the kitchen, he slipped into the living room to pray again. I finished the dishes to turn around into his open arms. He pulled me into an embrace by the door that ended in a million kisses.

"We can spend our nights together," he said between kisses. "There was nothing special about nights until I met you."

"Wait a bit. There's a lunar eclipse coming soon," I said, only half-joking.

"We'll spend that together, too," he said. "Until tomorrow." He sealed his words with a dozen more kisses around my face.

I took my car keys from a silver dragonfly hook that Dan had hung by the door, then stared at it as it hung in place. A dragonfly symbolized change, Dan had told me when he hung it on the doorframe. Change was good, he said. It meant we were moving forward. Then he had solemnly promised that his feelings for me would never change and I promised him the same.

I sighed and threw open the door to the morning.

The sky was refracting gold-white sunlight against the house and glinting dapples in the bay like gold coins. The air was filled with flowers starting to open themselves to the sun; everything was fresh and clean and original, all of it waiting patiently out there beyond the house to start us on our day.

"It's time," I said.

"I know," he replied.

And we left the house with great reluctance.

Chapter 21

Miss Phyllis's house was the pinkest one on Beach Six Street, the pinkest in the entire village, highlighted, of course, by her pink car screaming *Follicles,* parked in the driveway. Sam was waiting outside when I pulled up. I grabbed the bottle of wine I had brought while he eagerly opened the car door for me and then stood there, grinning happily.

"Thank you for coming," he said, and almost leaned over to kiss my cheek as I got out, but stopped himself. I knew why as soon as I heard Miss Phyllis's voice.

"Yoo-hoo." She was already descending the porch steps waving a pink spatula. "Right on time!" she called. "Of course you would be punctual, having to open your store so early every morning." She was wearing a light pink pantsuit, as she always did, with a white lace blouse and rose corsage on her wrist. Her curly hair was cropped close in its usual tight curls and dyed a light brown. She always dyed her hair for special occasions—red for Valentine's Day, green for St. Patrick's, pink and yellow for Easter, but I had no idea why she chose light brown today—maybe she was trying to match my cranberry-pecan loaves. Her dog, a standard poodle, dyed a light pink to match her clothes, was behind her, prancing in circles.

"You know my aunt, of course," Sam said, guiding me toward her with his hand on the small of my back.

Miss Phyllis may have been a bad hairstylist, but she was a cordial hostess and gave me a big lung-impairing hug, beating out her dog, who was next in line to jump me.

"Darling!" she boomed into my ear. "We don't get many people visiting. This is wonderful! I even wore flowers to mark the occasion." She held up her wrist. "Are you hungry? We have so much food! Dorothea and I have been cooking all day." She released me and I caught my breath just as the poodle stood on his hind legs trying to lick my face before ominously sliding down my leg to humping position.

"Isn't that cute!" Miss Phyllis said, pulling him away. "Carnation loves you, too. Well, come in, what are we waiting for? Come in." Carnation led the way, followed by Miss Phyllis and Sam and me.

Stepping into Miss Phyllis's house was a bit like stepping into someone's stomach lining. Pink walls blended into the pink furniture, drapes, and rose floral prints on the walls.

Carnation continued to lead us ahead into the dining room, Miss Phyllis behind him, Sam and I behind her single file. We passed a black motorized wheelchair parked in the corner of the dining room with several canes hanging over the back.

Sam noticed that the wheelchair caught my eye.

"Mine," he said softly. "Sometimes I need to use it."

The dining room table was set with pink and green dishes and pink glass cups. A short vase squatted in the middle of the table, resembling a bulldog or a Martian, depending on the angle, holding a bunch of purple and orange flowers.

"Don't you love it?" Miss Phyllis gestured to the table. "I decided on that centerpiece because, you know, the rules of good decorating say that you should strive for the unexpected."

"It really was," I murmured, and held out the bottle of wine. "Thank you for inviting me."

"Thank you for a lovely gift," she said, accepting it. "I won't serve it tonight, but I'll look forward to you coming over one night and we can have a glass or two together." She tucked it under her arm and ducked into the kitchen.

"Sorry about that." Sam turned to me when she left; he took my hand between both of his. "You know, wine is haram, forbidden to Muslims."

"I didn't know," I gasped. "I'm so sorry!"

"No worries." Miss Phyllis reappeared from the kitchen. "I'm not Muslim, so you and I can definitely enjoy your wine another time." Sam's mother was behind her looking festive and bright in a red and white dress and a matching red floral hijab. She was carrying a small tray of very dark coffee in thimble-size cups. Miss Phyllis presented her. "This is Sam's mother, my sister, Dorothea Ahmadi."

"So nice to meet you again, Mrs. Ahmadi."

"Welcome to my table," she said with a little bow of her head. She was polite, very polite, but there was a warmth missing. "Please make yourself comfortable." She handed each one of us a cup, and following her lead, we gulped the coffee down. It was very bitter.

"That is to honor you and welcome you to a meal," Sam explained. "Please sit."

I chose a chair and Sam sat next to me. Miss Phyllis and Sam's mother made small talk while bringing in heaping platters of tempting and colorful food and placing them around the table before settling themselves across from us.

"This is so nice, to have you in my home," Miss Phyllis said, putting down a bowl of fragrant rice and lentils. "This is called *mujaddara*. My sister made it."

It was all interesting and delicious. Mrs. Ahmadi carefully explained the contents of each dish and how it was prepared. Tabbouleh was a salad of chopped cucumbers and tomatoes and peppers in yogurt sauce. There were stewed tomatoes called *galayet,* and what was obviously Sam's favorite, *mansaf,* a stewed lamb, vegetable, and rice dish, along with a pile of hot flatbread that we used to scoop up the food.

"*Sahtanya,*" Mrs. Ahmadi declared as she started passing the food. "May you eat with two appetites."

A glass teapot filled with black tea, fragrant with sage, was passed around and I filled the little glass cup in front of me and added a lump of brown sugar. I watched, smiling inwardly, as Sam and his mother simultaneously added three sugars each to their tea. Sam heaped piles of food on his plate and then laughingly apologized for being so keen. He looked like an eager little boy, he was enjoying it so.

We ate a lot of food and chatted easily with one another, Miss Phyllis doing most of the talking. She told me how Sam and his brother had been born in the States but spent their childhood in Jordan because their Jordanian grandparents were elderly and had to be cared for. Sam had come back to attend high school, staying with his aunt Margaret, a third Reyes sister, on Long Island. His mother returned from living in Jordan after many years of taking care of her in-laws, to be by Sam's side while he recuperated from his injuries. His father and brother had visas to return but had been stopped at the airport. It was a terrible problem. Sam and his mother talked about politics and war and policy and borders, and their fears of how things might change for them, when Sam's cell phone suddenly rang. He took it from his pocket and looked at the number.

"Wow—it's the leg," he said, pulling himself up from his chair. "Let me take this; I'll be right back."

Miss Phyllis looked delighted and his mother smiled easily for the first time that evening. "It's his new leg," Sam's mother remarked from across the table. "It just came on the market. It's buoyant, so he can swim with it."

"We chipped in together to buy it," Miss Phyllis explained. "It was very expensive."

"Oh, I am sure that Miss Aila isn't interested in all the financial details," Mrs. Ahmadi said.

"Well, it will make a big difference to him," I agreed, remembering what he had told me about his problems swimming.

"We are so appreciative that you have taken an interest in him," said Miss Phyllis. "He always loved the water—"

"He misses the water very much," said his mother. She passed me more food and I started to protest, but she insisted. "We have a saying in Jordan, There is always room for forty bites more." She added more food to my plate.

"Sam even asked me about my old boat last week," said Miss Phyllis, picking up another serving dish and refilling my plate with rice. "Do you remember me taking my boat out, Aila?"

"A little bit," I said, thinking back to my childhood. "I did spend a lot of time in the water when I was young."

She smiled at me, and I thought I saw sympathy in her face. "Yes, your grandmother took you to the beach every day. Even if the weather was terrible. I worried for your health, sometimes."

Her concern surprised and annoyed me a little. "I grew up fine," I said softly.

"Yes, you did."

She took a sip of her tea and leaned back in her chair. "He's so excited to get the leg. It's been very hard for him. His injuries were so severe."

"I know," I said.

"He just gave up," Miss Phyllis continued. "That's why he spent all that time in the psych—"

"Phyllis," Mrs. Ahmadi sharply interrupted her sister, "why don't you pass Miss Aila some more bread. Family business is private."

"Oh, poo, Dottie, we can talk," Miss Phyllis said, handing me the bread. "I've known Aila since she was a little girl and she is a good person. We *want* him to make friends."

Mrs. Ahmadi pursed her lips. "It's my job to protect him. I *understand* him."

"Aila understands him," Miss Phyllis countered. "Don't you, dear?"

"I think so," I answered.

"He's very sensitive," Mrs. Ahmadi said.

Miss Phyllis gave a dismissive flap of her hand. "He just went through some mental troubles. Aila knows what that is—her own grandmother went through mental troubles because of you know what."

"O-oh," I stammered, wondering just how popular a topic my grandmother had been in her day and exactly who knew what.

"Of course, Sam's problems were a lot worse," Miss Phyllis added, "but I hope that doesn't change your opinion of him."

My mind was spinning, quickly putting all the pieces together from earlier conversations with Sam. "I think he's a . . . great guy."

"I used to sit with him all night," his mother said softly. "His nightmares were terrible."

"Everyone is afraid of people who have been in the psych unit, you know," Miss Phyllis mused. She piled more stew on my plate. "Especially a vet. They think that something is going to happen—that he might just snap and attack them for no reason. 'The psych unit' has bad connotations."

My heart jumped. "Psych unit," I repeated dumbly, adding another piece to the puzzle. "Right."

Miss Phyllis sighed loudly. "We're so thankful they were finally able to release him."

The conversation ended when we heard the click of Sam's cane approaching from the other room. "My apologies," he announced, his face glowing. "My new leg is ready. Final fitting this week and then that's it. I can use it."

"Congratulations!" I exclaimed, raising my glass of tea.

His mother and aunt cheered and then refilled his plate. His appetite renewed by the good news, he sat down and dug in. I tried to eat my own food with gusto, but I was bursting.

"We'll be in the water before you know it," he said, and clinked his glass against mine.

Dinner was over and Sam escorted me to the front porch. A gentle breeze caressed our faces and the full moon blazed sterling silver in the dark sky. We stood at the top of the steps.

"Thank you for coming," he said. "It meant the world to me."

"I had a great time," I said. "Your mother is a good person. And you are very important to her."

"She stayed with me," he said. "She stayed with me the whole time I was recovering. Even slept in the hospital next to my bed. I owe her everything."

"You're lucky to have her," I agreed. "And now, with your new leg, you will be able to do almost anything."

"May I do this?" he asked, tipping my chin up with his free hand and leaning over to kiss me. It was sweet and languid, but from the corner of my eye I could see a shadow, like an eclipse, quickly pass across the living room window.

Chapter 22

"Go pick up your dog." Lawrence LaSalle called me on my cell phone while I was busy at the Galley serving breakfast.

"What?"

"He's been released," he said.

"How is that possible?" I shouted with joy. "That's the best news!"

"We did some preliminary work," he replied. "The salesman has been let go from his job, but that doesn't preclude us from filing a civil suit against him and his employer. I want to get together with you as soon as I get a hole in my schedule. Is a weekend good?"

"*Yes!*" I screamed. "*Thank you!*"

"Great," he replied. "Now go order those sandwich fixin's."

Vincent was waiting for me, appropriately, in the waiting room, his tail nearly flying out of its socket when I stepped inside. Dr. Susan could barely hold on to him.

"I got the release order just half an hour ago," she said. "He did miss you, he just sat in his crate and howled all day, but it didn't seem to affect his appetite."

Indeed, he looked like he hadn't dropped an ounce. I knelt down and hugged him while he slathered my face with adoring wet kisses.

"He's very friendly," she said. "And a really nice dog. If you need a statement from me, I'll be glad to write something." I gave her a hug and we left.

Vincent eagerly jumped into my car and we drove all the way back to the Galley with his head hanging out the front window.

I called Sam to let him know.

"Please let me take care of your expenses," he said.

"No," I said. "I can pay my own expenses. Just because we—" I was going to say *slept together,* but Shay was right behind me writing the Marine Conditions—

"Slept together," Shay finished. "I know what you were going to say."

Sam and I ended our conversation and I turned to Shay. "—are good friends; that's what I was going to say."

"Right," she said. "Just because you invited him in for a cup of tea and then kissed him. On his thigh, no less, which is a tricky spot to show your moral support and then think you're going to get away with just being pals." She leaned forward and stared into my eyes. "Ha! You already slept with him, didn't you?"

"No."

"Lying eyes," she hooted. "I can smell them a mile away."

Vincent settled right into his old spot behind the counter while Shay and I carried on with the day's work.

Our regulars usually come in at the same time, as though the whole town awakens, showers, and gets hungry together. Martha Winston, who owns the floral shop, came in for her usual breakfast, a fried-egg sandwich with bacon, though she always swore she was a vegetarian and that bacon was just a topping.

She leaned over the counter conspiratorially. "I heard you were dating a Muslim, Aila. How could you?"

"Did you want that roll toasted?" I asked coolly.

"Yes, but not dark," she said. She rocked back on her heels. "Now, Aila, I know you since you were a baby. I worry for you." She slapped two plump hands on the counter. "They beat their wives, you know. And hide them in the cellar. They do terrible things."

"How do you know any of this?" I asked.

She blinked. "People read things."

"Stupid things," I said. "I am very fond of you, Miss Martha, but shame on you for talking like that." I handed over her breakfast. "You know he's an American, right? An American *soldier?*"

"Be very careful anyway," she said, paid for her food, and left.

She was followed by several other Fleeties, who seemed unusually reserved. Or maybe I was looking for something that wasn't there.

"What's become of this town?" I asked Shay when we had some time to eat lunch together. "Why is everything changing?"

She gave me a sympathetic look. "There is nothing changed," she said evenly. "Things are now just bobbing to the surface."

Sam met me with a big grin on his face after I closed the Galley for the night. "My aunt is signing that big old boat over to me. I'm going to get it running again. How's that for good news?"

"I'm happy for you," I said, checking the motion detector lights and cameras and rolling up the awnings. Next, I locked the front door and finished by setting the alarm and quickly sliding the little wooden scissor gate closed, locking it in place. "You must be getting used to pink."

He laughed. "Gonna paint it," he said. He was always so introspective, I was glad to see his face brighten with anticipation. I finished locking up.

"You got some fancy equipment there," he observed.

"Yes," I agreed. "But I don't even know why I bought it."

He patted my shoulder. "Things will be okay. Listen, I have fried chicken in the car. Let's go to the beach and admire my boat."

Vincent and I followed him—Sam was still driving the pink

Cadillac—and we sat on our usual bench facing the bay. He had a cooler packed with two lemon sodas, chicken—more chicken than two people could eat in a month—and a big salad and served me with great ceremony. A dinner napkin for my lap and another for my hands. He was excited about his new project and apparently had decided to include me—and Vincent—in all his plans.

"I thought sometime this summer we could boat over to Boston, or along the coast," he said. "Maybe eventually I could trade it up and do some traveling."

But I had no intention of going boating and the assumption that I would just do it bothered me.

"Sam, I don't trust boats anymore," I finally told him, picking chicken from a bone and feeding it to Vincent. "So don't include me."

"I'll help you get over it," he said, placing his hand gently over mine. "I promise. Just trust me."

"I do trust you," I said. "But I don't trust the water."

"You have to let go at some point," he said. He took a biscuit from the cooler and flipped it to the gulls, which were parading up and down on the pier and mewing like cats.

I studied his face. It was filled with concern, but he was asking the impossible. "You can't let the past rule your life," he added.

"Are you able to do that, Sam?" I asked sharply. "Are you letting go of the past?"

He sighed. "I'm trying. I carry my past below my waist," he said, pain etching his features. "Every minute of the day. How do I let go of that?"

I was in bed, curled against Vincent, whispering his name and holding him close to me. I had missed him terribly the whole time he was gone. I realized how much I had depended on him to comfort me when we went to bed at night, the sound of his snoring, the feel of his soft, patchy fur under my arm, the shape of his silly, boxy head against my shoulder. He was always at my side, always waiting for our next move. My life had been set to rights when he came back home. "Vincent, have I told you that I love you?" I whispered over and over into his tattered ear. Now that I had allowed myself to love him, I wanted him to hear it all the time. He opened one eye and gave me a lazy lick across my chin.

"Thank you," I whispered. He meant everything to me.

But still, I couldn't sleep.

There were new things to worry about. Sam, for one. I didn't want to disappoint him, but there was no way I would get in a boat again. And then there were the remarks from my customers at the Galley. These were people I had known and loved for years. Security equipment? Why had I even installed it? What was it going to prevent in this little village? My thoughts were scattering like wild birds.

The dog, driven by my restlessness, finally went from my bed to the floor to get some sleep. I sat up, wide awake. I needed to sit next to something bigger, more unruly than the thoughts that troubled me. I left my bed and pulled on a jacket and slipped outside. Vincent immediately followed. We headed for our old spot.

"Now, don't get scared," I said to him as we walked along the beach. It wasn't high tide yet, so the sand was filled with the detritus of the bay, sharp-edged shells and thick seaweed and smooth-washed stones and things that glittered in the moonlight but turned out to be nothing at all. "The seals just started coming in this week."

And there they were. Sentries watching in eerie silence, the moonlight highlighting their round heads as they lifted above the water, watching as we walked past them, watching without expression or concern. There was just the sound of the water, until a hoarse call made Vincent stop and face the water, his ears pricked. He raised his muzzle and sniffed at the air before answering the seal with a low growl.

"Remember what I told you," I said. "We leave them alone."

Now that they had established a new territory, they had been getting more vocal, hooting at me when I walked along the beach at night, making long, eerie calls that echoed softly across the sand. A few glided through the water as smoothly as if they were made of glass, coming closer to the shoreline, peering at me from the water, heads and necks shining in the moonlight. They turned their heads to follow us with their large, round, glistening dark eyes. I shuddered as we passed them, and led Vincent to the end of the dock.

I sat there, letting my legs dangle over the edge, my jacket collar pulled close to my neck while Vincent trotted back to the beach to sniff around. A few minutes later, he returned, with something in his mouth. He had done this many times before, finding himself a piece of driftwood or some dead and decomposing sea creature. Usually he dropped it on the pier and rolled all over it, then hid it until later, bringing it out just in time for us to go home, where he would eventually sneak it into my bed. I ignored him this time and listened to the hard chop of the bay making tough little waves while the doleful horns from the boats coming back into the P-town harbor provided a counterpoint to the calls of the seals.

After a while, Vincent dropped what was in his mouth onto the wooden boards. I leaned over to pick it up. All around us was full moonlight, its luminescence allowing me to see that Vincent had found a shell, the color of sand and clouds, its tiny, intricate convolutions reflecting the gleaming light, and, for all the dog's mouthing, still in nearly perfect condition. It was a wentletrap, much like the shell necklace Dan had given me, the one I had worn on my wedding day and faithfully every day after that until it broke.

"Oh," I said to the dog, holding the shell up to examine it, to run my fingers lightly across its spirals, pressing my thumb against the point at its top. Such an intricate shell, like life itself, filled with twists and turns, coiling round and round, reaching for some kind of pinnacle. I had felt awful when my necklace broke. I tried to remember when it happened—it was sometime after Dan died. Had I been sleeping with it under my pillow? Or in my hand while I slept? It was so delicate, why would I have done that?

I closed my eyes to picture Dan's face when he gave it to me, his eyes shining with love. They were hazel. Green-hazel. I pictured the shape of his face, his jaw; he had a nice nose, thin and aquiline, with just the suggestion of a bump. He had the most disarming smile; I could never stay mad at him. His chin had a cleft that was a little bit off center—and his voice . . . I tried to hear his voice in my head; why couldn't I hear his voice? He was from the South and had a silky South Carolina accent. I tried to grab it from my memory. He had sung to me so many times, why couldn't I hear his voice? Then the shape of his face grew dim . . . his features started fading. I tried to summon him, how it was all put together, his dear face—*Don't leave me.* I strained for a vision of his face, fought to think . . . *Dan—*

And then, and then, for a few horrible moments, I couldn't remember what he looked like at all.

Chapter 23

"Curious," Shay said the next day when I showed her the shell.

"That's all?" I asked. "Just 'curious'? Dan gave me one before we were married. And now Vincent found one. What do you think it *means*?"

She had just turned on the flattop and was setting things up for breakfast while I ground the coffee beans. Though she was wearing a loose top over sweats that had been cut off at the knees, her baby bump was now quite apparent. She turned around to give me an exasperated look. "You want me to forecast your future from a shell?"

"Yes. Do you think it means something?" I pressed. "When I was a kid I always looked for perfect shells." I turned the shell over and over, feeling its ridges against my fingers. "I always wanted a shell collection, but my father made me sell them in the store. He always kept a basket of perfect shells on the counter. Tourists like buying shells," I said, "and the store made some extra money. Everything was for the store."

"You want to sell it?" she asked, surprised.

I rolled it around in my hand. "I don't think so." I wrapped it in a napkin and tucked it into my jeans pocket. "It's so odd to find such a perfect shell. Vincent was so gentle. What am I supposed to do with it?"

She sighed. "I don't do shells; I don't read palms. When the time comes, I suspect you'll know what to do with it. In the meantime, I don't have a clue."

"Tea leaves?" I joked. "Can you do tea leaves?"

"No."

"How about casting runes?"

She rolled her eyes. "How about casting a few eggs upon the griddle," she said. "We've got customers."

But not as many customers that day as we would have liked.

"Is it slow?" I asked Shay late morning. "Or am I imagining it?"

"It's slow," she said. "We usually finish the bacon before this."

I knew it. I always semi-fry about ten pounds of bacon the night before and refrigerate it, finishing it off as people order bacon and eggs. It makes for fast cooking when we need it. We never have any left over, but it was already near noon and we still had nearly half of it wrapped on the flattop. Shay always referred to whatever bacon was left over as the Baconometer. It was definitely reading too high this morning.

It had been a week now, since Sam's mother had been in, and I wondered if that was the problem. Of course we still got the tourists, but it seemed to me a fair number of Fleeties were slipping in quietly to pick up their mail and leave. There is a supermarket a few miles out of town, which I suspected was now the destination of some of our formerly loyal customers.

"Why?" I asked Shay. "It can't be because one person came in here with a head scarf and ordered a muffin."

"Of course not," she said in a way that I knew she meant the opposite.

But Mrs. Skipper could still be lured in by our cherry Danishes. Today she came in accompanied by The Skipper himself. Their real last name is Healey, but they've always been The Skipper and Mrs. Skipper. He used to come in alone, almost every afternoon, to pick up the mail when it was delivered late. He was always courteous, courtly, even, with a blue fisherman's cap perched on top of his thick white hair. He was a tall man, lean and weather-beaten. His arms were ropy from muscles, betraying a life spent as a commercial fisherman. All I knew was that he had his own boat years ago and kept it docked at the wharf in P-town. We guessed him to be in his early nineties now; he had been the mayor ever since I could remember. He seemed in good health and always ordered Earl Grey tea with honey and lemon, and imported kippered herrings on toasted rye with two tomato slices. We always made sure to order a case of kippered herrings every so often to keep it in stock in the back room, just for him. "It's the Skipper's kippers," Shay always made it into a little ditty that she thought was immensely funny.

"Don't tell Florence I'm eating this," he would say. "She doesn't like me to have so much salt."

And we kept our word. But it had been a while since The Skipper had been in for his kippered herring. We still had three cases in the store room. I don't think anyone else even knew what they were.

Now The Skipper was helping his wife shop, apparently adding a few unplanned-for items to the grocery basket and making frequent suggestions.

"We don't need dog food," I could hear Mrs. Skipper tell him from the next aisle. "We don't have a dog."

"Katy!" he snapped. "So who's Katy if we don't have a dog! We have an Irish setter."

"Katy died eleven years ago, Donald." Mrs. Skipper was sounding exasperated. "Don't argue with me." She took the dog food from the basket and plopped it back on the shelf.

"She's waiting at home; you don't know what you're talking about," The Skipper argued back. "I just paid the vet bill for her. Dr. Amsher wants to see her again on Monday."

"You're just an old fool. Dr. Amsher is dead, too. Dr. Susan bought out his practice after he passed." Mrs. Skipper left him standing in the aisle and made her way to the front counter.

He followed her and they continued bickering. I knew exactly what was going on. I had gone through practically the same thing with my mother. I suddenly felt sorry for Mrs. Skipper.

She stood in front of me and pulled the groceries from her basket, making two piles. One pile she declared she was paying for; the other, she apologized, we would have to return to the shelves after she got The Skipper out of the store.

"It's not a problem," I said, pushing the second pile aside. "I totally understand." Of course I did, suddenly realizing something—why hadn't I figured it all out before? My grandmother singing her heart out, standing in the bay—insisting "he" was waiting to hear her. Feeding five-year-old me cups of strong coffee for lunch. Letting me puff on my own cigarillos for fun. Sometimes she forgot to dress me and I went to school in my pajamas and Mrs. Farnham, my teacher through second grade, would have to bring me home to get properly dressed. Sometimes she would buy me boy shirts and dress me in them, much to the amusement of my classmates. Sweatshirts, jeans, ugly sneakers. My mother was caught between needing to work, needing a babysitter, and needing to keep her mother safe.

Mrs. Skipper looked up at me. Our eyes met.

"You remember my grandmother, of course," I said pointedly.

Her mouth opened slightly for a moment in surprise. "Yes," she said. "How was I supposed to forget her?" There was a tone of—what? Sarcasm?—in her voice. But now she knew her secret about The Skipper's state of mind was out. She knew I knew. She had been protecting him all this time and I would certainly not violate that, but I suddenly knew that her pronouncements about my grandmother had been put to an end. She blinked her pale eyes a few times and suddenly reached across the counter and took my hand in hers. Her hand was shaking. She wanted to say something, I could see words starting, but they were stuck behind her pride.

I went back to ringing up her order as though we hadn't spoken at all. She watched me.

"I'm sorry," she said. "None of it was your fault."

"No worries." I started bagging her groceries before I realized that I had no idea what she meant. She took out her gold purse and stared down, as though she couldn't figure out what to do with it. She finally opened it and took out a few bills, paid me, and snapped it shut.

"Make sure you give the girl a tip," The Skipper said behind her. "The waitress is very nice here."

She turned around to take his arm. "Let's go home, Donald," she said.

"I'll carry these out for you." I came out from behind the counter.

Such an elderly couple they were, walking slowly to the door together. I hadn't noticed how hunched over she had become or how frail she looked. Hadn't noticed before the prominent blue veins that crisscrossed the thin skin on the back of her hands. How much her white hair had gone patchy. She looked over at me and stuck her chin in the air and led him through the door. *Yes*, I thought, *go with dignity, side by side. Both of you. At lease you have that.* I grabbed their bags and followed them.

"Stay well, Skipper," I said to him, as though everything were normal. I put their order in the backseat of their old faded green Ford. "Have a nice day, Mrs. Skipper. Hope to see you tomorrow."

"Yes," she replied. "Tomorrow."

I waited outside for a moment, watching as the car burped up a small puff of white smoke just before she drove away, Mrs. Skipper at the wheel, leaning forward to peer through the windshield, The Skipper already starting to nap. I thought how my mother had gone through all this with my grandmother. I didn't realize it, growing up. I suppose families in the past just took care of their loved ones all by themselves, the work falling to the daughters, a sad duty passed down, quietly keeping the parents at home in familiar surroundings, loving them, protecting them, serving them. My grandmother had been able to spend her life, up to her last moments, thanks to my mother, secure and happy and totally demented. The duties get passed on, almost always in matrilineal descent, the obligation, the responsibility of caring and hard work and breaking hearts falling to the daughters. It was now my turn to care for my mother. Crazy was slithering through my family genes like a snake in a field. Slithering through parts of my community. Taking the elderly as hostages. You can't help crazy, crazy is involuntary, but you can treat it with compassion.

Shay came outside to see what was keeping me. I turned to her. "Who will take care of me?" I wailed.

She knew what I meant and scolded me. "Don't you worry. You will marry again and have children, and when you go crazy *they* will take care of you and when I go crazy my kids will bring me over and we'll sit together in front of the Galley and cackle like geese and chew on Sandwiches until our dentures fall out and scare away the customers." We hugged each other.

I didn't believe her for one minute, but it felt good to be loved like that.

Chapter 24

The moon, once full of arrogance and light, was slowly quitting us, retreating into its waning gibbous phase, slowly returning the night sky to its feral state. Once again we could sit on the pier anonymously in the semidarkness, Vincent and I, tucked together to get through the ending of the day.

My arm was around him and we were listening to the barks and yips of the seals as they swam in the bay, sliding in on the high tide to sleep on the beach. Some of them had learned to climb onto the boats, sleeping one next to the other, laid out like logs, their collective weight putting the boats in peril of sinking. Boats that were moored well sat obediently, safely resting within their fenders made from used tires, tugging gently against their lines and rocking back and forth on the waves. Boats that had been neglected and badly secured bumped and poked their neighbors, banging and thumping against one another like restless children. Sam didn't come this night and that was all right with me. Vincent and I went home to bed.

Later, I peeked out my bedroom window and there was the

familiar blanket-bound figure on the pier. It comforted me more than I wanted to admit. He was there; he was out there. What could happen to me if he was out there to watch over me, he and his proud, powerful tattoo? I wanted this from him, and I wanted to give him the same comfort, but I was worried about our friendship accelerating only because we were both too vulnerable. We had become companions, but like the loosely moored boats we were bumping against each other, trying to find our places.

The next morning opened with a blaze of sun that glittered across the bay, a million sequins riding the tide out. I opened the Galley alone; Shay needed to sleep in. She hadn't been feeling well the past two weeks. Every so often, she would grab the folding chair we kept behind the counter and sit down. Sometimes her face would pale and she would rub her stomach.

"What's wrong?" I would immediately be at her side. "Maybe you should go home. Let me call Terrell so you can go to the doctor."

She was adamant about staying and insisted she was just fine. And then, whatever it was would dissipate, and she rallied, but I always kept a watchful eye on her. She and Terrell had been waiting for her eighteenth-week mark to find out what the gender was.

She came in today while the impatient and hungry breakfast crowd was at its peak. I was scurrying from counter to deli case to the grill, helping everyone at once, when she suddenly appeared.

"Looks like you need me," she said, poking her head through the top of an apron and then tying the sash into a big bow behind her back.

"Are you sure you're up to it?" I cautioned, packing an order of five sandwiches into a cardboard box and adding containers of salad around them.

"No worries." She smoothly took on the next customer as if she had been there all day.

But by noon, she had sunk wearily onto the chair. I offered her water, tea, coffee, juice, a doughnut, and half my Sandwich. She didn't want anything.

"I'm calling Terrell, and if I can't get him then I'm going to close the Galley and take you to your doctor," I said firmly. "You don't look so good."

This time she didn't argue, which worried me even more. I called and Terrell was at the Galley in a flash.

"I can take it from here, Aila," he said to me as he led her out to the car. "I already notified the doctor that we were on our way."

I loved how he put his arm around her waist while gently guiding her to his car. I loved the look on his face, the concern, the pride, the complete adoration. I knew he made her dinner every night, and gave great back rubs and called her honey girl and sometimes played his fiddle until she fell asleep, and that she knew, *appreciated,* how good things were between them. I had to turn away and take a deep breath. It was everything I wanted. It was everything I once had. I stood next to his car while he pulled the seat belt across her waist and handed her a bottle of water.

I moved to the doorway of the Galley and stared after them. "We'll call you and let you know what's going on!" he yelled through the window. I nodded and waved as he drove down the road; I stood in the doorway until they were out of sight, waving, waving, waving. I wanted to get in the car with them. Or follow in my car. I wanted to be part of it all, but it wasn't my life and it wasn't my turn. I returned inside the store to wait.

A late-model silver-gray pickup truck pulled into the Galley's small parking lot and stopped abruptly with a little screech of the brakes and a bounce. The door opened and Mrs. Ahmadi, Sam's mother, jumped down from the cab. Today she was wearing a black-and-white print blouse over jeans, and a black hijab. A few customers paused for a second or two to look at her as she grabbed her purse from the front seat, slammed the heavy door, and entered the Galley.

"Is that Sam's new truck?" I asked when she came in.

"Yes," she replied, adjusting her head covering. "I dropped him off at the beach so he could work on the boat. My sister needed her car back."

I peered at the truck through the store window; it looked to be in perfect condition, even to its fancy hubcaps. "Send him my congratulations."

"He knew you were too busy working, so Phyllis and I went with him to pick it up."

"I'm so glad he found something he liked," I said, only a little bit glad that I didn't need to go with him.

Mrs. Ahmadi waited on line to order her usual toasted muffin with butter and jelly, and a coffee, light and sweet. The lunch crowd was in and I was flying around behind the counter, racing to make sandwiches and ring up orders while apologizing a dozen times to everyone for taking so long. There was a weekend coming up and the day before is always a hectic time because of extra houseguests and special outings.

"You're really busy, aren't you?" Mrs. Ahmadi commented softly. "Where is that lovely lady who helps you?"

"Oh, Shay is off," I said, handing her the coffee.

"Will she be gone for long?" she asked. "Because I noticed she was pregnant. I can help you, if you're looking for an assistant. I could use the work." I looked up at her in surprise. It had occurred to me that at some point Shay would not be able to work anymore, and though I couldn't bear the thought of having someone else by my side, I might need help sooner than I expected.

Mrs. Ahmadi tilted her head and made a wry face. "Would this be a problem?" Her hand went up to her hijab and she touched it gently.

"Not at all," I said. "In fact, I'm glad you offered." She jotted down her phone number and left it on the counter and I put it in my pocket.

It was a long day. Every time my cell phone rang I thought it might be Shay, but when closing time finally came I still hadn't heard from her or Terrell.

I was more than ready to go home, but even closing the Galley was filled with chores. I had to pre-cook ten pounds of bacon, clean the flattop, wipe down the counters, doors, and windows, mop the floors, leave orders out for the muffin and bread man, as well as the milk and egg man, set the alarm, turn on the cameras and the motion detector lights, and finally lock the front door, pull the little scissor gate across it, and lock that as well. Vincent accompanied me as I did each chore and then, sighing heavily with fatigue, followed me out the door.

My plans for the night consisted of a big, comforting bowl of homemade vegetable barley soup and a glass of my special brew of iced tea and pomegranate juice.

We both had soup for dinner—Vincent's followed by a biscuit, mine by my iced tea and two cookies. I put the bowls and the tea on a platter and carried them outside to the back deck so we could sit at the little table and watch the seals. I made sure to bring my cell phone, too, in case Terrell called.

It was a quiet night, getting enclosed by twilight. Smoke gray clouds smudged the sky; darker clouds turned it into base metal. A breeze suddenly played with the leaves on the garden plants, making them dip and bow in an obedient dance, and the tide started rippling with small fringes of foam. I liked having Vincent by my side to talk to, as though he understood my words.

"See the sky? I bet it's going to rain," I said to him. "We'd better finish our dinners and plan to stay in this evening." He didn't need to be prompted to lap up his soup.

"You're the best boy," I said, and then a sudden lump in my throat warned me that tears were imminent. "You know I love you." I watched as he licked his bowl clean and then sniffed the biscuit before taking it from my hand, then lying down to eat it leisurely. "You're my family now."

Who was I kidding?

As the moistened air lingered against my face, it was dampening my spirit. I was kidding no one. The dog wasn't Dan's replacement, or my real child, or even a blood member of my family. I loved him. Yes, I loved him, but I wanted more.

He stood up and looked at the bay. The seals were waddling across the beach to find their favorite spots and Vincent's tattered half ear perked up, the muscles tensing in his neck as he watched them. He sniffed the air and whined ever so softly.

"No running on the beach," I said. "Just stay with me." He must have heard something in my voice and sat down again, turning his face up to lick my chin. "Thank you," I whispered.

The house phone suddenly rang and I rushed inside to answer it.

It was Shay.

"I'm so glad to hear from you," I gushed. "Are you okay? How's the baby?"

She sighed. "I have to keep off my feet," she said regretfully. "Everything should be fine, but I do have to stay off my feet for a while."

"Oh, Shay, I'm so sorry!"

"I'm basically okay. Just need to rest," she said. "I'm not high risk, but I'm not twenty years old, either. We just have to be watchful."

"You do everything you need to," I replied. "Listen to your doctor."

"I know it leaves you in a spot."

"Don't worry about me. Taking care of yourself and the baby is the most important thing. Did you get your sonogram done?"

There was a long pause. She giggled. "Yes. I'm further along than we thought."

"So aren't you going to tell me what it is?"

"Well, we were going to call our parents to tell them," she said, "but since you were so worried, and you're practically family, I'll tell you first. It's twins! Twin boys! We're going to need more names!"

Chapter 25

It is never the same water. My grandmother told me that once when I was upset about a bad day in school.

I guess I had forgotten that. Even when the bay looks like it did yesterday, every molecule has been altered by some alchemy of time and space and movement. Of course Shay has her own life and was only working summers more as a tribute to old times than economic need. We both knew the day would come when she would leave for New Jersey one winter and not return the following summer because there were other things she wanted or needed to do. I knew this from the beginning, but I didn't want it to be now, or next week, or next year. Or ever, so I had put it out of my mind.

Now I had to be pragmatic. Summer is a very busy time for the store, and there was no way I could handle it alone. I was thankful Sam's mother appeared when she did and I called her first thing the next day to ask her to come in for an interview, though I had already decided that I would hire her. She was mature; she knew how to handle food; it would be just a matter of showing her how the Galley functioned. I was sure I would be able to depend on her and hoped we could work well together, even though she had given me the distinct feeling that she didn't quite approve of me.

Mrs. Ahmadi was very polite on the phone, but she wanted to discuss salary first. She wanted much more than minimum wage because she felt maturity brings benefits. She wanted to arrive at eight thirty in the morning and leave at three. She didn't especially care to work weekends and would not sell beer. And she didn't like working the meat slicer, because she had cultivated long nails and, well, the slicer *slices*. But I needed help right away and thought it prudent to just agree to her terms. She arrived half an hour later.

"I don't mind helping you out," she said, tying on an apron, *Shay's* apron, and taking her place behind the counter. "I'll have this place pulled together in short order."

Though I wasn't entirely sure that the Galley needed to be pulled together, I was relieved I had found someone to help me who was over seventeen and didn't have a cell phone growing out of the palm of her hand. I did wonder how those customers who had a problem with a woman standing on line buying a cup of coffee while wearing a hijab would adjust to actually having one helping them from behind the counter.

But the day went smoothly. Customers were in and out, not one negative comment—perhaps the bigots were just not coming into the store anymore—and I began to think that my worries were for nothing. After all, Sam's mother had grown up in Fleetbourne, had attended the local schools, and knew a lot of people, all of which made her perfect for giving directions and sailing tips and weather predictions. She was outgoing, liked to chat, and was happy to see people she knew from years ago. She had common sense and was good at fielding questions.

One lady wanted to order four pair of eclipse glasses for the forthcoming eclipse.

"No glasses," Mrs. Ahmadi said firmly.

"I need four pair," the customer insisted.

"It's a partial lunar eclipse," Mrs. Ahamadi explained. "You don't need glasses at night to look at the moon."

I was pleased she was able to take care of things. She even took care of Mrs. Skipper, who had come in alone and stopped in her tracks when she reached the counter. "Where's Miss Shay?" she asked, surprised.

"She'll be out for a while," I replied. "This is Mrs. Ahamadi."

She knew Sam's mother right away. "Of course! You're one of the Reyes girls!" Mrs. Skipper immediately exclaimed. "There were three of you. Phyllis stayed on; Margaret got married and moved to Long Island; you're . . . Dorothea! My, you've been gone a long time."

"Almost fifteen years," said Sam's mother.

"Well, it's very nice to see you again," said Mrs. Skipper. "I remember you when you were a sweet little girl."

"Actually, I was the smart and pretty one, Mrs. Skipper. My sister Phyllis was the sweet one and Margaret was the athletic one who juggled oranges in the high school talent show."

"Wonderful, dear. I'll have two cherry Danishes, please, and make sure they're the freshest." Mrs. Skipper pushed her day's grocery items across the counter. She paid no attention to Vincent, who was sitting up in his doggie bed, staring at her and wagging his tail. She didn't pay much attention to me, either, though I had also been a sweet—albeit crazy—little girl.

Mrs. Ahamadi finished the transaction and I was pleased that it had gone well. She turned to me after Mrs. Skipper left the store. "I'm surprised that she comes in here, Aila. Especially after all that business with your grandmother." She put her hand on my arm. "I'm pleased she knows that forgiveness is the best path to a good life."

"Forgiveness?"

She wagged her finger at me. "I'm not one to gossip," she said. "So I'd rather not say, but it involved your grandmother and The Skipper."

I was shocked. "What involved them?"

"I don't spread gossip," she said, "but maybe you should ask

Lorna Hummings. She's much older than I am and she always gets all the good details."

"The town clerk?"

She nodded. "Lorna knows everything."

It seemed Mrs. Ahmadi wouldn't spread gossip but didn't seem to have an aversion to listening to it.

It was mid-afternoon when Shay called. After many questions and reassurances about how she was feeling, how well she was resting, and how many baby names she had gone through, we got to her reason for calling.

"Larry just called. He's coming over tonight, if you want to meet him before you meet him. We plan to walk around P-town, because if I don't get out of the house I will go crazy from boredom. Terrell rented a wheelchair for me."

"You've only been home one day; how can you be bored?"

"I don't know. I might have to make a few dozen bacon and egg sandwiches to feel normal," she replied. "I can't imagine staying home with two babies. I think I'll go crazy."

"Well, I can take one since you're going to have extra," I offered. "That might make it easier."

"Never mind," she replied. "I have a funny feeling Terrell might object."

Mrs. Ahmadi stayed until closing time, standing patiently next to Vincent so I could show her how to lock up the Galley for the night, just in case. The cameras were turned on as well as the motion detector lights; the front door was locked and the gate pulled across and locked, too.

"I think you have more security than we had in Jordan," she said after watching the whole routine. She pulled the keys to Sam's truck from her purse. "Well, Sam is at the beach. He's been working on the boat all day. I'm going to pick him up and bring him home for dinner."

"Tell him I said hello. And that I have an appointment tomorrow with the attorney. He's still welcome to come."

She paused and turned to face me. "You don't understand," she said, her voice deadly quiet. "He's fragile. He's not strong enough to fight. I have to protect him and I don't want him to get involved with an attorney. It could set him back."

"I do understand," I said, though I really wasn't all that certain where it was going to set him back to.

Vincent and I left for home. I hated leaving him alone for the evening and he sensed it. As I showered and dressed, he followed me around carrying his favorite toy, a big blue stuffed elephant—former elephant, actually, due to the fact that its trunk had been chewed off and its body leaked white fluffy foam entrails everywhere. I gave him a quick pat, wishing I were the one hosting; then we could all be together, me and Vincent and Shay and Terrell and their guest, Lawrence LaSalle, LLD, and sit on my back deck and watch the bay and eat. I had hosted Shay and Terrell a thousand times over the years, but with Dan gone, it felt lopsided.

Maybe I was the one changing. Does it matter if a boat slowly drifts in the water, gently riding the tides to a new location, or if it stays in place barely moving and everything around it is transformed?

Either way you can get lost.

Chapter 26

The scent of flowers was so strong, I probably could have driven to their house on Beach Fourteen with my eyes closed. Every summer Shay and Terrell move back into her late grandmother's house, having brought it back from disrepair, and Shay turns her combination of ambition, high metabolism, and flower worship into a one-woman beautification program by placing pots of color-coordinated petunias and carnations next to every mailbox, street lamp, and traffic sign on her street. Of course, her own house gets extra-special treatment. She practically smothers it in brilliant red roses and white geraniums. They line the brick walkway, hang from crevices, and fill the gardens, along with a generous helping of basil, mint, and oregano that punctuate the air with a nice vegetal base.

Her yellow Fiat was in the driveway; Terrell had pulled his own car right up to the garage door to allow room for what I guessed was Lawrence LaSalle's car, an old blue Chevy that hosted more dings than a doorbell. I was surprised that a Boston lawyer drove such an unprepossessing vehicle; I had expected something more posh. I crept my car into place next to it and got out. Their cat, Dude, ginger striped and overweight, was sitting on the front step meowing hello. He stood up and stretched his front toes as I rang the doorbell, then raced inside as soon as Terrell answered.

"Hey!" Terrell said as we gave each other hugs. "So glad you could make it. Shay is afraid she's getting fat from sitting around for one day. Come on in." He led me through the living room and into the kitchen. Shay was sitting at the table with a glass of lemonade.

It had been less than forty-eight hours since I'd seen her, but something had changed. The lines around her mouth had softened; her brow was relaxed; her face was filled with peace and contentment. In one day, the imprint of work and pressure from the Galley had been erased.

"Wow, Shay," I said. "You look positively radiant. How are you feeling?"

"Much better," she said, turning her face up as I bent over to kiss her cheek. Sitting across from her was a pleasant-looking man smiling at us. He was dressed casually, jeans and a white polo. I guessed he was Lawrence LaSalle, LLD.

She waved her hand to include him. "Aila, this is our friend Larry. I know you've been talking."

He stood up to greet me, leaning across the table and extending his arm. "It's great to finally meet you, Aila," he said in a rich baritone that took over the kitchen. He was tall and chunky with a thin mustache, a handsome man, darker than Terrell, with penetrating, mischievous eyes and a warm, gentle smile. He took my hand in his and though he gave it a brief, formal squeeze, his demeanor was cordial.

"He's the man," Terrell added.

"That's only because he lets me sing with him," Larry said.

"My best friend." Shay nodded toward me.

"That's only because she will eat my crazy Sandwiches," I said.

Larry nodded. "Ah, yes," he said. "The Sandwiches. I hope to partake of one soon." He was so completely confident and self-possessed that I suddenly felt shy. Terrell put a glass of lemonade on the table in front of me.

"To best friends." Larry raised his glass to mine and we clinked.

"Hope you don't mind; the boys feel like walking around P-town," Shay said. "They promised an evening of fun food. Terry rented a wheelchair for the duration of my pregnancy, so I can get around."

"Great," I said as Terrell left the kitchen and returned, pushing a wheelchair. It was smaller and lighter than the one I saw at Sam's house. "Get in the chair, woman," he said to Shay.

Shay stood up carefully. "Let's roll."

Terrell drove and Shay sat next to him while Larry and I sat in the back of their car.

"So, the Galley," Larry said to me. "Tell me about the Galley." His demeanor was probing and intense, which I supposed made him a very good lawyer.

"It's just a little general store that was passed down from my grandparents. My parents ran it for years until—" I stopped. I had led myself right into a place I didn't want to go. "My father . . . left it to me."

"Oh yes, I'm sorry," he said gently. "Shay told me. That must have been very hard for you." I gave him an appreciative smile. "I hope to visit your place tomorrow," he added, "if that's all right."

"Absolutely," I replied. "It's the home of the Sandwich. I'll even make you one."

"Deal!" he said, extending his hand again to me. We touched fingers, and when his gaze lingered on my face I didn't look away.

Terrell and Larry had made dinner plans of a sort. We wandered up and down the streets of P-town, taking turns pushing Shay and eating, in no particular order, cups of clam chowder, clams on the half shell, fried clams, minced clams and onion rings, French fries with clam dip, stuffed clams, clams casino with bacon, and, for a change of menu, hot dogs.

We were greeted effusively by the drag queens on Commercial Street and invited to their new show, "It's the best one since our last show!" a green-feathered Pam Cakes exclaimed, draping herself across Larry. We were serenaded by a street band and amazed by a magician. It was P-town up to its old wonderful tricks.

Larry tried on and bought red sneakers at a shoe shop, which he immediately wore, tossing his old ones in the trash. Terrell bought a light blue jacket with the usual humpback whale logo on the front, and when Shay admired a pair of small, flower-shaped amethyst earrings Terrell bought them for her as a pregnancy thank-you gift, which brought a lump to my throat.

"On to the last course!" Larry led the way to a small street shack that featured lobster tails.

"This is what you get when you let the guys choose the dinner menu," Shay sighed happily, swallowing the last of her butter-drenched lobster. "I hope my babies aren't born looking like crustaceans."

"Speaking of shells." Larry pointed to The Blue Cowry, a little shell shop tucked away in one of the colorful buildings. "Ever been in there?"

I had, when I was younger, but not recently. Terrell folded up Shay's chair and led us all inside.

There were dozens of large wooden barrels filled to the brims with shells. Every shell imaginable, of every color, with neat signs overhead that identified them. Boxes of shells were stacked on glass shelving, and jars of shells were stored in the big front window. There were wind chimes and crystals and wreaths made of shells and pinecones.

"Fascinating," Larry said, running his fingers carefully through the iridescent and fragile structures as he gazed around at the displays. "So this is where the shells go after we eat."

"Hardly," I said. I put my hand down gently on a pile of shells in a cardboard box labeled RARE. They felt cool and glassy smooth, some covered with the thinnest filament-shaped channels, some with rounded swirls. Shells from exotic locations far from Cape Cod, a few dozen delicate, flat white baby ears that resembled their name, a handful of long white angel wings that could have graced the smallest of sea angels, and next to that several rare Antilles Glassy Bubble shells that were so transparent I could see my fingers on the other side.

I stood there, transfixed. These were the most exquisite of shells, hundreds of variations; what was wrong? I couldn't find the heart to admire them, though they were graceful and polished, with the most subtle pinks and yellows, some that darkened into the deepest rose, or glowing golden browns, mysterious ambers, burnished ebony black cowry shells, some midnight blue, a dozen or so paper white fig shells in perfect copy of the fruit.

And then I realized, with a sickening feeling, that this was a graveyard. The whole shop was a graveyard. There was no way these shells could have been collected naturally. They had been scooped up by trawlers dropping huge nets along the ocean floors and ripping them from their homes, hoisting them into giant vats where they were steamed and stripped of their creatures. Not for sustenance, but because they were pretty. Because they would fill a collection. Trophy hunting from the seas. I had a sudden sense of death. Of pain. Had Dan and my father suffered? I had never allowed myself to think of it, but here, surrounded by a million reminders of senseless death, I was overwhelmed.

"I am going outside," I mumbled to Terrell. "I can't bear this." Shay, who was holding a shell in her hand to examine it, turned around and looked over at me questioningly.

"It's not right," I said to her. "It's all death."

"Oh God, I never thought about it," she said softly. "You're right. There's so many."

We looked at each other for a moment, and she followed me out. I opened up the wheelchair for her and she sat down.

"We used to keep a box on the counter," I murmured, thinking back. "My father always kept a box to sell. I think he bought them from here, except I sometimes added the ones I found on the beach."

"I remember," she said quietly.

You can't fix the things you used to do wrong, except to stop doing them.

"I didn't realize," I said, and she nodded in agreement, "but I'm not going to sell shells anymore."

Larry and Terrell were still hungry. "These fools want pizza," Shay announced, and in honor of junk night they found a nearby shop and, over our protests, ordered two large pies. "One for each of us"—Larry jokingly pointed to himself and Terrell—"since the girls appear to be full." We seated ourselves at a table outside to wait for our order.

The evening slowly enfolded us and I leaned back in my chair, enjoying the conversation. Of course Shay and I had pizza. It was all as easy as floating on a raft in the bay. No direction, no special topics, no destination. Just good food, a glass of wine, rolling with the tide, letting it carry us from thought to thought, stopping just long enough for one of us to contribute something, a comment, a corny joke, a remembrance. I felt an ease I hadn't felt for a long time. I knew where the water had been and where it was going; we were suspended on a gentle tide of friendship. Every once in a while, I caught Larry staring at me. Sometimes our eyes met and he gave me a quick wink. He was brash and booming and fascinating.

I learned that Terrell and Larry had been roommates at college and played in the Chess Club, mostly against each other. That Larry had broken his leg skiing five years in a row and let Terrell talk him out of a sixth ski trip for safety's sake but managed to slip on ice in front of his office that winter, resulting in a broken leg anyway, and was so incensed that he closed his office and moved to New Orleans for years, married, divorced, and moved back only recently. Shay and I smiled at each other as the two men laughed heartily at the memories.

We ordered ice cream for dessert.

Larry turned to me, between spoonfuls of his pineapple sundae, and proudly announced, "So I heard our two best friends are going to use our names for the babies."

"I didn't know that," I said, startled. "I'm thrilled."

"Lawrence will be a *middle* name," Terrell corrected him. "We have a whole bunch of people we have to honor."

"And we still have to find a masculine version of 'Aila,'" Shay added.

"Don't try very hard." I laughed. "I never liked my name."

"Well, I want my name used for the best-looking baby," Larry directed. "I never had kids, so somebody's got to name a kid after me. I can't imagine the work involved raising two of them! But as your attorney, I should warn you to get your ducks in a row."

"What kind of ducks are you talking about?" Shay asked, puzzled.

"Well, for one thing, guardianship," he replied, "just in case of emergency."

I raised my hand. "I volunteer," I said. "I would be honored to take care of your children."

Terrell laughed. "Larry, you are really getting lawyerly now, jumping the gun."

Larry ignored him and turned to Shay. "Shay, your parents are retired and Terrell only has his mother and she has very bad arthritis. I hope you never need to choose a guardian, but you don't have siblings and his one brother lives in London and, the youngest, isn't even married."

Shay glanced over at Terrell and raised her eyebrows. "Well, actually," she started, "we were going to ask my cousin Joralynn to be guardian if we ever needed one."

The raft jerked to a halt. "I didn't know you had a cousin Joralynn," I said. "I thought I knew all your cousins." I suddenly felt hurt. We were so close that I had automatically assumed I would be included as some kind of baby official, if needed.

"She's her mother's first cousin," Terrell explained. "She lives in Maine, though we hope we never need her."

Shay stared into her melting ice cream as though suddenly fascinated by its loss of structure.

"It's because they're boys," Terrell added. Shay nodded, still saying nothing.

"I don't understand," I said. "What does being a boy have to do with being a guardian, hoping again you never need one."

"It's not the guardian part," Shay said quietly. "It's the . . . the—"

"White girl part," Larry finished.

"Oh," I said, then, "What?"

Terrell sat up in his chair and leaned toward me. "You have to understand—these are going to be two black boys growing up in a mostly hostile culture. You have to know how to navigate things. You can't send them out in society like white boys, thinking it's all okay."

I instantly thought back to Tommy, though he was a universal bigot. "I get that," I said. "But why couldn't I teach them whatever they need?"

Terrell laughed, but there was no mirth in it. "It's something you have to live to understand," he said. "We live in different worlds. Man, I've been stopped just for driving through my own neighborhood."

"DWB," Larry said knowingly. "Me too, many times."

I looked at them, puzzled.

"Driving While Black," Larry explained.

"Try Jogging While Black. We've all experienced that," Terrell said quietly. "Some cop stops you because you're *running*."

"But you got to do the dance," Larry added. "You know what I mean?"

"I guess so," I replied.

"You have got to be not just respectful—okay—that's the right thing to do anyway," Larry continued, "but you've got to be extra, extra, *extra* respectful. 'Yes, sir,' 'no, sir,' 'yes, *sir*.' And be careful as shit."

"And you still can get killed," Terrell finished. "That's the way it is."

I looked at Shay, nodding her head, her face filled with fear and sadness, knowing something that I had no real knowledge of, even though I had read it a million times in the newspapers and seen sickening incidents on television that had enraged me. Still, I had never *worried* about it on a personal level. I lived insulated. White people do. I never worried if I could rent a vacant apartment when I was in college and didn't want to live in the dorm anymore or suddenly found someone tailing me in a fancy department store. I had never watched a patrol car in my rearview mirror with dread and wondered if this was going to be my last day on earth, for a flickering brake light. I couldn't imagine a black mother waiting by her window for her son to come back from the store with a loaf of bread, and hear sirens and worry that he's late.

I took a deep breath. "I never realized, Shay, that it was something that worried you!"

"I love you," Shay said. "But you're not equipped to raise black boys to be safe." She looked down at her hands, and clenched and unclenched them, and said very, very softly, "I don't even know if I can."

"Oh, Shay." I got up to go over and give her a kiss on the top of her head. "I love you, too. I will always be there if you need me, hoping you never do."

She grabbed my hand and kissed it. "Thank you. Hope I never do."

I returned to my ice cream. The table was quiet for a moment. Maybe we were all realizing, sadly, it will always be the same bay, but very different water.

Chapter 27

Lawrence LaSalle was already waiting for me at the Galley when I arrived to open the doors at six a.m. He was wearing white slacks, the red sneakers, a Red Sox baseball cap, and a French sailor striped blue shirt in what I guessed was a city-boy attempt to look like he was at home on the seas. I had to smile.

"What took you so long?" he asked in mock impatience. "I've been waiting here for half an hour."

I started to explain that he was way too early, but he interrupted me, laughing. "Just teasing, I got here about two minutes ago! I'm going fishing with Terrell this afternoon, so I thought I'd get our interview finished in the morning before we both got busy."

He helped me open the gate and followed me into the store, waiting while I shut off the alarm and cameras. Then I introduced him to Vincent, who started sniffing Larry's new red sneakers with great interest.

Larry bent over to pet his head and Vincent licked his hand in friendship. "I think he likes me," Larry said. "You know, I wouldn't mind having a dog like this."

I turned on the lights and ducked behind the counter to start heating up the flattop.

"You want breakfast?" I asked.

"I already ha—wow—yes, thank you," he replied, slowly turning on his heels, looking around the store like a kid in a candy shop. "Could I have anything I want?" I nodded and he rubbed his hands together in anticipation. "What shall we make?"

"Anything you like," I replied. The front doorbell tinkled and Mrs. Ahmadi arrived, looking like a large daffodil in green and white, with a yellow head covering.

"Good morning," she said cheerily, and headed to the back door to bring in the bakery goods.

"I can't decide what I want," Larry said, his eyes glowing with anticipation. "There's too much to choose from."

"How about bacon and eggs?"

His face lit up. "Yes, yes! I love bacon and eggs. Just the thing." I started his breakfast while he poked around behind the counter.

"We have one of these in my office," he announced after examining the coffeepot. "I'll make the coffee." He expertly filled the grinder with fresh beans, added water, and started it up. Mrs. Ahmadi returned with her arms full of newspapers and bags of muffins and took her place behind the counter.

"Do you want something to eat?" I asked her.

"Oh, no thank you," she replied. "I pray before and after breakfast, so it's easier for me to eat at home."

The early morning crowd starting coming in, some of them pausing in surprise at the sight of a trio working behind the counter. But the orders came fast, as they usually do, and though we were working hard, Larry, who had now just finished his second breakfast, smoothly started helping without my even asking. He was ebullient, whistling show tunes and singing as he served the customers, making cup after cup of coffee while I made the sandwiches and Mrs. Ahmadi rang them all up.

"I guess Miss Shay worked so hard she needed two people to

replace her," one customer joked as Sam's mother bagged her groceries.

Mrs. Skipper worried aloud when her turn came and she saw that Larry was serving her. "Does he know how to pick out fresh cherry Danishes? I only want the freshest ones," she warned.

"Yes, ma'am, they're so fresh, I had to smack them," Larry said as he handed her the little white bakery bag. Mrs. Skipper smiled despite herself. I groaned and rolled my eyes.

The morning passed quickly and I was surprised how helpful Larry had actually been. He seemed to like the work and his easy, joking manner had everyone, even Mrs. Ahmadi, smiling. Everyone except for Sam.

The bell on the door tinkled and Sam stepped into the store. He stopped in surprise when he saw the three of us crowded behind the counter.

"Sam!" I summoned him to come and meet Larry.

"Thank you for serving our country." Larry extended his hand to Sam. Sam flushed and shook it and mumbled something I couldn't hear.

"Larry is the lawyer I was telling you about," I explained. "He says that you have a strong lawsuit against the dealership. You two should really talk."

"Anytime you want," Larry agreed. He moved to the flattop. "So, dude! Food before business, right?" He held up a spatula. "I always wanted to do this. How do you like your eggs? You want a bacon and egg sandwich?"

"No pork," Sam replied dourly. "And no lawsuit." He turned around abruptly and left without saying good-bye.

"I guess no sandwich, either," Larry said.

"Please excuse my son," Sam's mother said to Larry after Sam left. "He needs to be alone, sometimes. He's fighting other battles."

Lunch orders came fast but we were on top of them all.

"You need vegetarian bacon," Larry boomed out after a customer ordered a bacon substitute for his sandwich. "The world is filling up with vegetarians! Where's the grocery list? Put in on the list!" To my consternation, he wrote *FAKON* in big letters on my Marine Conditions Board. "Come back tomorrow, friend," he told the customer. "We'll give you a sandwich half-price for your trouble." The customer practically bowed his way out the door. "I'll pay for his sandwich," Larry said to me. "It's worth building good relationships.

"It would be easier if everyone who came in made their own coffee," Larry advised another time after a rush of coffee orders. "You know, give them a cup and a pod and let them brew it themselves, any flavor, keep the pot and the cream and sugar on a table over there. It'll cut the crowding at the counter." He wrote *new coffeepot and pods* on the Marine Conditions Board, as well.

And Boston Crème Doughnuts, because they were his favorites.

And *New! Chicken-Fried Steak Sandwiches* because his late mother used to make them and he missed her.

When the crowd thinned out, Larry grabbed me by the elbow. "Where can we talk?" he asked.

"The kitchen," I said, then gestured to Sam's mother. "She's new. She's never worked the counter alone before."

He looked over at her. "Stop worrying. She's a grown-up," he pronounced. "She can figure it out. The counter's not going to blow up if she makes a mistake."

His remark had a few people suddenly eye Mrs. Ahmadi's hijab. "Take care of things for a few minutes, Mrs. A!" he shouted over to her. "We love you, but we have some important business to conduct. The store is in your capable hands."

She gave Larry a thumbs-up and the people in line smiled at her while she smoothly returned to her next customer.

Larry already had a plan outlined. I had sent him all the information two weeks before and he was ready with papers for me to sign. He had already filed against the dealership and the parent car manufacturer. Now he was planning to announce it to the newspapers, make it go viral on the Internet, arrange for radio interviews. He was also going to embarrass the dealership and push for a public apology and financial damages. I signed.

"We're dealing with assholes," he said. "The best cure is to hit them in their pocketbooks. Your dog was innocent and was seized on false testimony. A rescue dog traumatized again! They claim they have no security tape of the day you came in, but we're going to question it. There was no hospital report, no wounds, no scars, no corroboration at all. Time to fight back."

I already had my fists clenched.

"Your friend has an even stronger case, too," he added as he put the papers back in a folder. "An important one. What happened to him was blatantly against the law. Tell him he's making a big mistake."

"It's not up to me," I explained, peeking out at Mrs. Ahmadi. "And I have a feeling it's not up to him, either."

Terrell came in and announced it was time to leave. "We'll pick up some pizza on the way," he said to Larry. "Shay was going to make us sandwiches, but she couldn't look at food."

I didn't point out that he was quite capable of making sandwiches, too, but then felt sorry for him. "How would you like me to make you two my special Sandwiches?" I offered. "I do owe Larry payment for his advice."

Larry practically salivated on my shoulder as I worked and I hoped that he would like them. I had promised him an extraordinary sandwich, or had I said "weird"?—I couldn't remember—but I very carefully layered the ingredients, making sure to color-coordinate them, then wrapped the final product, a Sandwich of massive size and eclectic mixture, in aluminum foil and handed one to Terrell and one to Larry. Terrell thanked me as he tucked his into a small thermal carrier, but Larry said nothing. He opened the foil to carefully examine the Sandwich, his lips pursed in concentration. He pulled back the bread, which had been upgraded from rye bread to a more structurally substantial ciabatta, and lifted the contents gingerly with a toothpick.

"Hmmmm."

"What's wrong?" I asked.

He said nothing. Now he was sniffing it.

"What?" I asked again.

"Be patient," he said. "Let me check this thing out. What did you call this?"

"A Sandwich. But you have to say it with a capital *S*."

"Okay," he finally said. "Is there room for negotiation?"

"Oh God," I groaned. "What's wrong?"

"It needs marinated artichoke hearts."

"Deal," I said, relieved, and we shook hands. He handed the Sandwich over to Terrell, who put it in the thermal bag, and they headed for the door. Once they were gone, I marveled at how much energy and good humor Larry generated and how, when he left, the store felt like the air had gone out of it.

Chapter 28

My curiosity was getting the better of me. I hate people who imply they have a secret that they couldn't possibly share but really want to tell you, which is the only reason they mentioned it in the first place. Mrs. Ahmadi had hinted that she had gossip about my family and I wanted to know what it was.

Business had slowed down and now Mrs. A, as Larry had addressed her, was stocking the shelves. "I noticed that somebody likes Cheerios!" she called out, lining the boxes in a neat row on the shelf.

"I do," I replied. "And so does Mrs. Skipper. That's why I order so many."

"You're very kind to her, considering that she's sometimes rude to you." She started setting up the potato chip rack. "Family history and all."

That did it. Another reference to her "secret." "You have to tell me what family history you're referring to," I told her. "It's not fair to keep talking about it without talking about it."

She smiled at me. "I was wondering how long it was going to take you to get curious."

"My grandmother was very important to me," I said. "So either explain all these mysterious comments or don't mention it again."

"The town clerk knows everything," she said. "She's the best source of anything that concerns anyone in town. She knows everything, and she doesn't mind gossiping one bit. She can tell you whatever you want to know. About anybody."

Lorna Hummings, the town clerk, was surprised to see me. She came out from behind her desk and trundled over to the window to talk. "How's that dog of yours?" she asked right away. "He's had a bit of an exciting life."

I had to agree that he did.

"I understand your lawyer sprung him from jail," she said.

"Dogs don't go to jail," I said. "Someone lied and reported that he bit them and I had to leave him with the vet."

"I heard Animal Control seized him," she said. "That's what happens with dogs that look a certain way. They get arrested."

"He's a good dog," I said.

"I'm a fish person myself," she said. "You'll never see a fish get incarcerated."

"May I ask you something? I'm hoping you can help me," I started. "I had heard something about my family that was from years ago and someone said to ask you."

"Who said to ask me?"

"Dorothea Reyes. Ahmadi," I replied.

"Oh yes, Dottie," she said. "She's back from Jordan with her son. I heard he got badly wounded and had some kind of breakdown and they're living with Phyllis. They're sisters, Dottie and Phyllis, and another one, though they didn't become Muslims like Dottie did."

"Yes," I said. "I know. But I'm curious about something I heard about my family."

"I don't know if I know," she said. "Besides, I'm not one to gossip."

I wondered how stories got around if no one was the one to gossip but pressed further. "Well, actually, it was about my grandmother and The Skipper."

"Oh my, yes," she said. "Now there's an interesting story. But I don't like to goss—"

"It's not gossip," I interrupted her. "It's family history. And since it's my family, I would *really* appreciate it if you could tell me what you know."

She stood in front of me for a moment, pondering my request.

"Please," I said.

"I only know what I heard. I was very young. Everyone was talking about it then; the whole town was talking about it."

I nodded my head. "My family seems to provide a great deal of entertainment for this town."

"Not as much as some, dear." She stepped away and opened the door to her office. "Come have a seat," she summoned me. "We'll have some privacy in here."

The walls of her office were glass from the middle of the walls and up. Privacy was the last thing it provided. But I sat in the chair in front of her desk as she plopped down in the cushiony leather chair behind it. She leaned back and cleared her throat.

"Now, I'm not telling tales, but from what I understand," she said, plunging right into it, "your grandmother was single and The Skipper was engaged to Mrs. Skipper who was just Florence at the time, and they had an affair, your grandmother and Donald, Donald being The Skipper. I'm not sure he was The Skipper at the time, but he was still Donald." She put her finger to the side of her nose to help her remember. "I think she— your grandmother, not Florence—got pregnant and everyone was shocked. You know, it was a long time ago and things were different back then. Now you got every movie star getting pregnant without getting married—and personally, I think it's crazy to bring a baby into the world just because you starred in a movie with its father. In fact—"

"Yes," I interrupted her. "What happened after that?"

"I heard he, Donald, took Ida, your grandmother, on his boat and he brought her somewhere and when they came back she wasn't pregnant anymore."

"Oh," I said, appalled. "How horrible."

"So, Donald went on to marry his wife, you know, Florence, and about a year later Ida, your grandmother, married your grandfather, Joseph."

I had never heard any of this. I was sitting close to her desk, my elbow resting on it and my head resting in my hand, trying to imagine it all. "Wow," I said. "If he, The Skipper, loved my grandmother that much, why didn't he just marry her?"

Mrs. Hummings sighed. "I heard she was very much in love with him, but he didn't want to break his engagement to Florence. Her father owned the biggest fishing fleet on the Cape and Donald wanted his own boat."

"I guess my grandmother had nothing to offer him," I said. "I know her family was poor. I think my great-grandfather was the custodian of a church in P-town until he became the postmaster in Fleetbourne."

"Your grandmother was supposed to have been very pretty," Mrs. Hummings said. "Some people said she bewitched him. Donald."

She *was* pretty. I remembered her with her long hair braided up in a bun. It used to be chestnut when I was very young, flecked with white before it turned totally white like a young moon becoming full. And she had sea-worthy green eyes, my grandmother, that used to look longingly across the bay. "He took her on his fishing boat?" I asked softly.

"Oh yes," she said. "He had been given a large fishing boat from his prospective father-in-law. He kept it at the dock in P-town and they sailed in secret, except it can't be a secret when it has a crew." She paused, thinking about it. "The boat anchored in the harbor for years. I believe it was called *The Man in the Moon*."

Oh, how I knew that name.

I returned to the Galley and found an expectant Mrs. A. "Did you get the information you wanted from Lorna?" she asked.

I nodded, not answering her, still processing it all.

"Anything I don't know?"

I smiled at her. "You never told me what you knew so I don't know what you don't know. It was all fascinating, but, you know, I'm not one to gossip."

It was closing time. Mrs. A watched me as I turned on the cameras and the security lights from inside the store, then followed me outside as I locked the front door and pulled the gate across. I handed her the spare key to the Galley. "If you need to close up," I explained.

"Well," she said. "I guess I can tell you everything I know—the whole story about your grandmother. Did Lorna tell you the *whole* story?"

I stopped. "I don't know. She said my grandmother was pregnant and she came back on the boat not pregnant."

Mrs. A nodded. "There's more to it than that," she said.

"More to it than what?"

"Well," she said, "she was *past* nine months pregnant when The Skipper took her on the ship. She was *due,* if you know what I mean."

Vincent and I had a quick dinner at home and then left the house to walk the beach down to the pier. We walked past the water where I remember my grandmother singing. Had there really been a child? Had it been thrown to the seas? How was it possible that so many in my family were in the clutches of the ocean? We watched the gulls floating on the water, riding the waves, staring back at us and mewing for food. The seals paddled along, barking and huffing together like a Greek chorus. They were all overweight and lazy since they spent their days following the fishing boats into Chatham to eat the overflow of culled fish before retiring to their rookeries for the night. The sky started growing moody, gray clouds were rolling across the bay, and the low growl of thunder echoed off the horizon. Black clouds started silhouetting over the dark gray with flashes of yellow outlining their edges like fringe. Lightning was starting to strike the middle of the bay. There was a fast chop to the water.

It was definitely time to reverse course. I turned back.

"We'd better skip the pier tonight," I said to Vincent. We both trotted back to the house, trotting together step for step, me and this faithful dog who would trot to the end of the earth with me. There was a loud crack and we picked up the pace. I love watching lightning strike its crazy-quilt patterns across the sky, but I'm not foolish enough to stay on the beach; I usually head the other way, to the safety of my kitchen, and watch through the back door, and that's where I was heading now. We ran as fast as we could, the rain now pelting our faces and the lightning glowering behind us.

My cell phone rang almost as soon as I got home. It was an automated announcement from my security company. The alarm had gone off at the Galley.

"I'll check it out in the morning," I said to Vincent after I hung up. "Maybe the storm set it off. There's nothing I can do about it now."

A bolt of lightning struck nearby with a simultaneous crash of thunder. The storm was overhead now, unleashing its full fury, rain slanting against my windows, with long tendrils of gold lightning stretching across the water, lighting it up in dramatic flashes. My house phone rang. It was Officer Joe Miranda from the Fleetbourne Police Department.

"Miss Aila," he said. "Your alarm at the Galley was ringing as I was riding by and I got out to investigate. You'd better get here. Someone threw a brick through your store window."

Chapter 29

By the time I got to the Galley, arriving like a Valkyrie, with thunder and lightning crashing all around me, there was a crowd of people there. A small crowd, to be sure, but when you live in a town where the most exciting thing to happen this year was that the bakery was putting seeds on its rye bread, an alarm ringing late in the night is big news. Several people had gathered around Officer Joe, under a huddle of colorful umbrellas and gossipy conjecture, while Officer Joe himself sat in his car out of the rain. He was waiting for me with his flashlight trained on the broken store window just in case a burglar decided to make an exit. The big front window of the Galley had been completely shattered, glass was all over the street, and the alarm was still ringing.

I couldn't fathom it for a moment. The Galley looked violated, like a hole had been punched into its heart. I took out my keys with shaking hands.

"Is it okay for me to go in?" I called over to Officer Joe.

He rolled his window down and cupped his hand to his ear over the alarm. "Eh?"

"Can I go in?"

"Sure. Go ahead!" he yelled back. "I don't think anyone is in there."

I rolled open the little wooden scissor gate, thinking how perfectly inadequate it was, then opened the door to the Galley and waited there, reluctant to enter by myself. I pointed my finger to the interior and looked back at Officer Joe. I wasn't sure what the protocols were now, since generally the first thing to do, notify the police, had apparently been done, but I was reasonably sure that letting me enter the store alone was not part of the procedure. Officer Joe got the hint; he climbed out of his car and we stepped into the store together, with him right behind me.

We were in pitch dark.

"You need to put some lights on," he said helpfully.

"I can't see the switch box," I said. "I need a light to see the switch box."

He shined his light back and forth, illuminating the walls. "Hey, that apple crumb pie looks good," he said, resting the beam on the dessert case.

"Today's special," I said. "Can you please move the beam up about two feet?"

There was the switch box and I crunched across the glass to turn off the alarm and turn the store lights on.

"Oh no. Oh no." It was all I could think of to say. "Why would anyone do this?" I asked. "You think it was teenagers?"

"Could be," Officer Joe answered slowly. "But usually if they're up to mischief, they wouldn't stop at one store."

"Who else would do this?" I asked, trying not to cry.

"Troublemakers," Officer Joe declared. "People do strange things if they don't like something. I know there is a rumor going around that you might be selling the store, and it could be that somebody doesn't like the idea."

"I am not selling anything to anyone," I replied huffily. "Just hired a new person to help me."

"Sometimes people around here don't go for change," he said. "I personally like having you here, Miss Aila, but if you wanted to sell, it's your business; it's your choice. I would still come in, s'long as the coffee's good, but—you know folks."

I was beginning to know folks more than I wanted to. He followed me through the rest of the Galley and, even though the lights were on, shone his flashlight into every crevice, onto every shelf, behind every display case. There were no other signs of damage. We went into the kitchen together. Nothing was stolen; nothing was out of place. Apparently, the damage had been confined to where the glass had fallen and to the old marble front counter that now hosted a moon-size crater with a white brick sitting in the middle. It would all have to be replaced. Officer Joe pulled the brick out and handed it to me.

"What an odd brick," I said. And it was. Regular brick size and painted white, it looked unusual. "I've never seen a brick like this."

"Must have come from some kind of demolition site," Officer Joe reflected. "Like a building or something that's being knocked down."

"Do you need it for fingerprints?" I asked.

"Nah," Officer Joe replied. "Not worth dusting it. But you might want to hang on to it for a while, in case you need evidence for your insurance company."

I put it by the front door as a doorstop.

Officer Joe began writing copiously on an official-looking pad. "So I'm calling it an act of vandalism." He looked up to give me instructions. "Call your insurance company first thing in the morning. Give them this report number and tell them to call us." I signed something and something else again.

We were standing in the middle of a thousand shards of glass. Rain was sweeping in through the broken window, leaving puddles; lightning hovered nearby. I needed to tarp the front of the store and there was no one I could call to help me. The Galley had been my total responsibility for two years, and I now had the dilemma of either leaving it unattended, in order to buy tarps, or staying overnight. Dan would have helped me,

I thought miserably. My father would have had ten solutions in half an hour while my mother would have made coffee for the whole town and wrapped everything in plastic.

Officer Joe was still standing there with his flashlight beam on the pie. Then I thought, *Well, what are taxes for anyway?* I asked him if he would mind keeping an eye on the store while I ran out to buy a tarp, promising him a piece of pie as a thank-you bribe. He agreed and an hour later I returned with a huge plastic trash pail filled with supplies. He helped me staple the tarp to the window frame; we were finished in twenty minutes and he left, happily drinking a large cup of hot coffee and clutching a brown paper bag that contained a Sandwich and a generous piece of apple crumb pie.

I pulled on my new heavy-duty gloves, grabbed my new heavy-duty broom, and began sweeping up the glass. It had the odd sheen and wavy lines of old glass and had been the front window of the Galley for over sixty years. Someone once told me that glass melts, that it's really a liquid, and slowly, over time, its molecules slide to the bottom, leaving the top thin and fragile. I remember how Dan had adamantly corrected me. Oh no, that was a myth, he insisted. The truth was somewhere halfway in between. Glass was a solid with liquid properties and its distinctive flow pattern was definitely a product of early, primitive manufacturing. He was precise like that, meticulous in his thoughts, careful in all his calculations. The houses he designed were perfectly, environmentally, beautiful. He had been sketching a new house for us with windows everywhere to capture the light. Windows were the soul of a home, he always said.

I needed to clean up the Galley window.

The heavy gloves made it safe for me to pick up the large pieces. They glimmered like broken rainbows, reflecting the lights from the ceiling as I heaped them into the trash pail along with the big piece that came from the center of the store window. It had the store name, *The Galley*, in large, old-style gold lettering, outlined in black, and the logo, a rolling pin and cup of coffee underneath it, painted a long time ago. I swept up the small delicate pieces that were shaped like little fairy swords. Then I swept up the tiniest glistening crumbs and mopped the rain off the floor until it was almost dry. I stood back to look. Everything was in place. In a few days, it would all be repaired. New glass, a new marble counter. No one would be able to tell how my heart had been fractured along with the front window.

I gated the front door, its spindly little scissor gate seeming ironically useless now, turned on the switch for the cameras and lights, and left for home.

The streets smelled fresh and clean, with that damp, intimate scent that bathrooms get after you take a shower. The storm was well past, the lightning was receding into the distance like a memory, but I could still hear the fading murmuring of thunder. I counted aloud after a flash, ending when I heard its rumble. "One, one thousand"—that's how you count off the length of a second—"two, one thousand . . . three, one thousand. . . ." Every five seconds equals a mile in distance: twenty-five one thousands, the storm was five miles away. My grandmother had taught me that.

I drove, weary and anxious to get home. I had always worried what I would do if there was an emergency at the Galley. I had set up protocols of what to do in an emergency after my father died and the Galley became mine. Call the police, call Shay, call the insurance company. I hadn't done any of it this time, but things still got done. I had handled it. The only problem was that I couldn't figure out was why it had happened. Was somebody taking offense that I hired Mrs. Ahmadi or was it just a random act? No matter what, I would handle it, but I was getting tired of counting my losses.

I pulled up to my house and let myself in through the back door. It was an old habit, learned in my childhood, to always use the back door to keep the sand out of the house. There, by the door, I glanced down the beach to the dock. It was dark. Sam wasn't there, a good sign, I thought. I was afraid he was going to take the boat out despite the storm.

Men and boats.

* * *

Vincent was waiting for me in the kitchen, sitting in a small debris field of garbage and very slowly and very guiltily wagging his tail. His head was dropped down and he was looking at me from the tops of his eyes, as if to say, *Sorry for the mess; I have no idea how it happened.*

I just flopped down into a kitchen chair and sat there staring at the clock. It was after midnight.

"I need to teach you how to use a broom," I said to him. He came over to me and put his chunky block head on my lap. I ran my hand over his body. His fur was growing in and actually had a shine to it. He was a sandy red color, the scabs were long healed, and even his once raw and battered ear had a coating of soft fur, as if it were natural for them, to have the lumpy, brutalized shape underneath. His eyes were filled with trust and shining up into mine. What did a few piles of garbage mean? Nothing. Nothing. His soul was pure; there wasn't a drop of garbage in his beautiful soul.

The real garbage was in the mind of the person who had thrown a brick into the Galley.

I pulled myself wearily from the chair and grabbed the broom. I swept everything into a pile and dropped it all in the trash pail, then mopped the floor. Vincent watched me with a remorseful expression the whole time.

I would take a shower, I decided, and call the insurance company in the morning and then close the Galley for the day or maybe until it got repaired. I had spent a lifetime there, anchored to one spot like a buoy sitting in the bay, marking the end of the shallow water. I didn't have to stay in Fleetbourne, I realized. I didn't have to stay anchored.

Maybe it was time to leave the shallows and get out into the ocean.

Chapter 30

Morning came and acted as though nothing had happened. The sun rose over the bay and turned it crystal and gold; the gulls were impatiently walking up and down the beach, crying for food; the waves were imperturbable, lapping rhythmically against the shore, rearranging the seaweed and the broken shells into free-form designs. The beach of broken shells. And a Galley of broken glass. There were a few boats out on the bay doing nothing in particular. I fed Vincent, had a cup of light, light coffee, found all my insurance papers, got dressed, and left for the store, leaving a ringing house phone behind. I didn't want to contaminate my home with Galley business anymore. My father always conducted all store business in the store. When he came home, he was *home*.

Mrs. A and Sam were waiting in front of the store and I realized, regretfully, that I should have conducted at least one little bit of business before I left. I should have called Mrs. A and told her not to come.

"Oh my goodness," she said as soon as she and Sam got out

of the truck. "What happened? I heard an alarm ringing last night, but I didn't know it was us!"

Sam patted me awkwardly on the shoulder. "What can we do to help you? I was just about to drop my mother off and head to the dock, but I can stay and help."

"Thank you." I was grateful for his offer. "But I don't know what I'm doing yet." I unlocked the gate and the door and we went inside.

The light coming in through the tarp cast a dark, eerie blue over the store; even with the lights on, we looked like Smurfs.

"Did the storm break the window?" Mrs. A asked as she looked around.

"No. It was a brick," I replied, pointing to the culprit, sitting by the front door.

"I hope I'm not the problem," she said quietly.

"You are not the problem," I said firmly.

There were little crumbles of glass around the counter. The paper bags and pastry papers, pretzel rods, food wrappers, boxes of gum, and other odds and ends, all had been sprinkled with glass. I would need a day, maybe more, to clean it up.

"I don't think we'll open today," I said to both of them. "Sam, you may as well go to the dock and work on your boat. I have no idea what I'm doing. I don't want to waste your time."

"No," he said. "I'm worried about you. I'll stay for a while."

Mrs. A just started cleaning. She pulled the trash pail over and threw everything away that had been on the front counter. When the pail was full, Sam carried it to the Dumpster behind the store to empty it. I spent the rest of the morning on the phone with the insurance agent, who insisted that perhaps the wind had carried the brick through the window, which made it my negligence because the window didn't have a grill to protect it. Mrs. A washed the area down, made coffee, and we began serving the customers who were timidly creeping in, looking around in bewilderment and peppering us with questions until I finally put the brick on the counter with a note taped to it: "I came in through the window. We don't know why."

Business was lagging badly according to the Baconometer, but Mrs. A convinced me to keep the Galley open.

"Be strong," she said. "People throw bricks all the time in Jordan. Pish! Bombs, too. It's nothing. We don't give in."

I knew what she meant, but I was worried. I worried even more when I saw a customer stretch up in order to see over the counter to look at Vincent.

"Isn't that the dog that attacked a salesman right in his store?" she asked.

"No," I said.

"The whole story appeared on the Wellfall Town Media Page," she countered.

"It wasn't my dog," I said. "In fact, the way I heard it, a cocker spaniel stole his lunch off his desk, I heard it was bologna, but it might have been tuna fish. You know how stories change."

"I guess," she said, giving me the squint-eye before ordering a sandwich.

I called Larry's cell phone.

He sounded shocked. "A brick?" he kept repeating, while Shay was in the background asking, "What? What? What? What's wrong?"

They arrived at the Galley within minutes. Shay rushed in and I shouted, "What are you doing? Sit down!" I pulled out a chair from behind the counter and she sat, but not before she gave me a big hug. "Are you all right?" she asked, over and over. I reassured her that I hadn't been anywhere near the brick when it was in flight, while Larry and Terrell went through the store to assess the damages.

After several minutes, Larry stood outside the front door, his hands on his hips, and was staring up at the eaves of the Galley. "That looks like a camera," he said, pointing.

"Oh God, I forgot. Yes!" I yelped. "My new security camera. I can play the video on my cell phone."

"I'm surprised the cop didn't ask to see it," Larry said.

I guessed that Officer Joe, his hands full of apple pie, wasn't all that anxious to spend another rainy minute at the Galley. I was so nervous, shaking so hard, that I could hardly play the app on my cell phone. Larry finally took it from me. Sam and Mrs. A and Terrell and Shay and I huddled around as he played with the buttons, peering at the screen.

"Here we go," he said. "Date and time." He fiddled some more and the camera app buzzed on and started replaying the previous night. He handed the cell phone to Sam.

"Whoa! I know who that is!" Sam yelled as soon as the video began. He gave the phone back to me and I watched it intently. A white car pulling up in front of the Galley, a man getting out carrying something dark that I guessed was the brick, his arm swinging back, and the object flying into the store window. The glass collapsed like a fainting movie star while the man jumped into the car and sped away. But not before the motion detector lights were switched on, illuminating his face.

"Bingo," Sam said.

I stared at the screen and replayed it. The figure, the car, the brick. I recognized the man right away. "You're right," I said, handing the phone back to Sam. "Bingo."

It was the car salesman.

It took a full week for the new glass to be delivered and installed and when it was finished it looked almost like the old window; *The Galley* was painted in the middle with old-fashioned gold lettering outlined in black. And the same logo, a cup of steaming coffee sitting on a saucer under one part of the lettering and an old-fashioned rolling pin sitting at an angle on the other side. My eyes welled up when I saw it. The window was shiny and new, the old glass gone. Glass that my great-grandfather had wiped clean daily, that my grandmother had complained about washing, before the ritual was passed on to me by my father. Forever gone.

"You can start again," said Mrs. A. "Modernize."

"You should have put your store hours on one side," Larry suggested.

"And your name in the corner as the proprietor," said Terrell.

"Leave her alone," said Shay. "This is hard enough for her."

* * *

The salesman, Frank Biljac, was arrested within a few days and charged. The complaint was going to be presented as a hate crime, Larry said, an important case for this little town, which hadn't had a lawsuit since the 1960s. We had the police report; we had depositions; we had the white brick; we had statements; we had the law on our side.

We had everything but a lot of customers.

While we waited for justice, Mrs. A was eager to learn all the workings of the Galley and had been quick to pick up the routine. She made coffee exactly as ordered. She made sandwiches, now wearing food gloves and comfortably using the slicer for the cold cuts. She decorated the tops of salads with parsley and kale and rings of red, green, and yellow peppers and carrot curls that made the food look more inviting. She even made suggestions, like putting two small bistro tables under umbrellas outside the store, and then she personally ran to the town clerk's office and got the permits as well as upgrades on the local gossip, though she didn't gossip. She wiped the new window into sparkling submission, and the front door, too. She even took over the task I least liked, ordering from my suppliers and keeping them all honest when the orders were delivered. She turned cartons of potato chip bags upside down to make sure the bottom hadn't been slit open and a dozen bags taken out without my knowledge. She counted the boxes of eggs and made sure there were none broken; she checked the sell-by dates, sniffed the meats, and checked the cheeses for mold. She was almost replacing Shay, but not in my heart.

In time, Mrs. A was making tabbouleh, the tomato salad she had made for me, and *om ali*, a sort of bread pudding, as well as special Middle Eastern pastries. She and I held bake-offs with customers voting for their favorite desserts. We started adding international cuisine to the old reliable Cape Cod cuisine, and a few other exotic dishes here and there that Mrs. A thought up.

But we still didn't have a lot of customers, not nearly the

amount we used to have. The town, it seemed, had divided up. There were those who supported a *patriotic* American, that being the car salesman, poor guy, who had been nearly mauled to death by some kind of wolf-dog hybrid, maybe a werewolf, which had been sneaked into the dealership by a terrorist intent on stealing a fleet of trucks to send overseas. The rest of the town was supporting a frail widow who was working day and night to make ends meet to pay for her dying mother's hospital care and who simply tried to buy a car with her fiancé, a decorated war hero. Though the war hero part was true, the rest of it was all ludicrous. There were stories about events that never happened, interviews with neighbors who had never really trusted me because everyone knew that my grandmother was a World War I spy who sang secret messages across the bay to aid the enemy, though no one could get straight who the enemy actually was then. A collection was taken up for me even though I was financially stable and tried to return the money, eventually donating it to the Humane Society. A collection was taken up for the car salesman, too, but no one ever heard what happened to it.

A court date was set and everyone was ready for an epic battle.

Chapter 31

The moon was in its third quarter, split nearly in half, like my life, like the Galley, like my heart when I was with Sam. We were sitting together on the big porch swing on my back deck, one of his arms around me, the other around Vincent. The dog and I had come home from a day at the Galley to find him patiently waiting there for me, stretched out on the big swing, his leg propped up on the seat of a nearby chair, as he sipped a lemon soda. He had rolled his jeans up, and his prosthetic leg gleamed in the sun. There was a pizza on the table and a cooler ready with cold sodas next to the swing. "I made you a gourmet dinner," he had said, grinning. "So you'll go boating with me."

"You are not going to butter me up with pizza," I said, opening the box and taking out a slice from the mushroom half. Vincent stood at full alert. Sam leaned over to pull off a plain slice and handed it to him. "Or my dog," I added.

"You need to relax," he said, patting the space next to him on the swing. "You need to sit it out for a day and let someone take care of you for a change."

I sat down. He put his arm around me and handed me a soda from the cooler.

"I never didn't want someone to take care of me," I said, then realized I had gotten myself into a grammatical complexity. "I mean, I like being taken care of. Sometimes I even *crave* it. It just hasn't worked out for me."

"Sometimes I feel like you push people away."

"Sometimes I think I do," I said remorsefully, then added, "Sometimes you do, too."

"Luckily we don't do it at the same time," he said. "So let me take care of you." He started nuzzling into my neck. The stubble on his face felt comfortingly scratchy.

"How?" I asked, giggling. "How will you do that?"

"Well, I made you dinner. I fed your dog. I brought dessert." He reached into his pocket and pulled out a crumpled bag of M&M'S. "And I am offering you a tour around the bay. We can go right after we eat."

My heart was beginning to pound just from the suggestion. "I can't," I said. "I just can't."

"Plus," he added, "I want to give you the honor of naming the boat. Maybe you can come by after work tomorrow. I don't think you've even seen it since I finished it."

We had a date.

Of course Mrs. A knew where I was going after work. It seemed there was very little she didn't know about what Sam and I were up to. Sometimes it left me discomfited; it seemed he was always reporting back to her. I knew he had been making the boat his big project and that his mother was very relieved he found something to occupy his time.

"It could lead to some kind of career," she enthused to me that afternoon after I mentioned that I would probably need to leave early to see Sam's boat. "A lot of people need their boats overhauled. Give it a good name when you see him later."

Sometimes I felt like I was dating his mother.

* * *

"Hey!" he called out when Vincent and I reached the pier after work. "Come on up."

We climbed the steps and I couldn't help but feel a little resentment that he had taken over my space. The pier had always been my personal spot, a sort of annex to my living room where I could sit for hours and listen to the water and think. Now it was lit like a Hollywood sound stage from the two floodlights that were plugged into the electric outlets on his slip. The same lights I could see from my bedroom window at night when he was working. He had them focused on the boat, spotlighting it.

He grabbed me up into his arms when I got near and gave me a long, hard kiss, then made a wide sweep of his arm that took in the boat. "What do you think?"

The boat had been completely transformed. Its old weather-beaten pink was gone and it now was a sharp navy and white. Its brass fittings had sprung to life, glittering from polish; there was neat black lettering on its side, the Hull Identification Number, allowing it to move legally through the waters.

"She's beautiful," I said. "I can't believe it's the same boat."

"I just spent the last three days tuning up the engine," he replied. "Bought a few parts and now it's purring. Next step is to name her and then we go on our maiden voyage. Would you give me the honor of naming her?"

I knew it was an honor but really had nothing to offer. "Well, 'Vincent' is taken," I said teasingly. "How about *Bob*?"

"Why would I name a boat *Bob*?"

I loved that he fell into my trap. "Because it's what they *do*," I said triumphantly.

It took him a minute. "Oh, funny."

"How about *Miss Phyllis*?" I said. "After your aunt."

"My aunt?" He made a face. "Actually, I wanted something nautical. After all, I was a Navy SEAL."

And then it occurred to me. I did have a name. I was keeping it for a special moment and a special time, but this seemed right. "I am going to give you the name of something that has a lot of significance to me," I said. "I give it to you as a gift."

He stood almost at attention and looked at me expectantly. "Go ahead," he said. "I'm listening."

I took a deep breath. "*The Wentletrap.*"

"Where did you get that?"

"Because it's shaped like a spiral staircase," I said, "that you can climb to the stars."

I could see he was turning it over in his head, sounding it out. "I know it's a kind of shell," he started slowly. "Climb to the stars. Even with my leg." He squinted his eyes as though to picture the name on the side of the boat. "Yes," he finally said. "I like it. *The Wentletrap.*" He took another moment. "I really like it! Maybe I could get someone to paint a picture of one on the hull." He took my hand. "Come inside the cabin and take a look around. In fact, I can offer you a cold slice of leftover pizza."

What is it with men and pizza?

"No thanks," I said. "I don't do boats. I'm going home to go over some papers Larry gave me about the broken window."

He took my hands. "I want to ask you something," he said, his face growing serious. "That guy you are always talking about— Larry—are you and he . . ." He drew in a deep breath. "Does . . . he mean something to you?"

"No," I said, incredulous that Sam would even think like that. "I just met him. He's my lawyer."

He nodded. "I hope you're leveling with me. I mean, I was crazy sick thinking about him and you for the past few days." He gave me a quick kiss on my cheek. "I'm going down into the cabin," he finally said. "Come with me. I'll just turn the engine on, so you can hear how it sounds."

"I don't do boats," I said, moving away from him toward the dock steps. "I've got to go. I'm going to have dinner that isn't pizza."

"Please," he said, still hanging on to my hand.

"No. I can't."

"Is it because of that guy?"

"No!" I felt a quick flash of anger and pulled my hand away. "Don't you get it?" I shouted back at him. "I won't go on your boat because it's a *boat!*" I was immediately sorry I yelled. He looked crushed.

"But you have to come with me on its maiden voyage," he said. "That goes with naming it."

"Then find another name from someone else. I don't even swim anymore."

"Listen, I can't go alone," he said, suddenly serious. "If I get into trouble, I may not be able to get out of it."

"Your aunt Phyllis should really go on its maiden voyage," I replied. "After all, it was her boat."

"No," he said. "It has to be you." He lifted my chin up to kiss my lips. "You, me, and the bay," he whispered. "It'll be okay. I will help you forget everything you remember. And you can help me remember everything I've forgotten."

I wanted to say yes more than anything, but I was bound by anchors to a memory that wouldn't let go. I turned my face away. He took it in his hands and turned it back, so that I was looking at him again. Then he kissed me tenderly.

"One trip," he said softly. A light breeze ruffled his hair; it fell across his eyes. He looked so earnest, so sweet.

"Let me open your heart," he said. "It'll be okay. I'm a Navy SEAL. What can go wrong?"

Chapter 32

Of course we went home together. My home to be exact, since its main appeal was that it offered privacy from his family. As we walked along the beach back to my house, Sam leaned on me a little since the deep, wet sand has always been a challenge for him. He had a strong grip around my waist, pulling me close to his side while he nuzzled my neck and ear and face. He was eager to spend the night with me. How good that felt. I thought of nothing but bringing him into my bed, eager to be with him, too.

We locked Vincent out of the bedroom and I could hear him settle happily in the kitchen, banging the lid off the trash pail. Hardly the kind of sound that made for a romantic evening.

"Garbage," I moaned.

"Stop worrying," Sam said to me. "I'll clean it up."

We were in bed together. He had removed his leg and laid it next to the bed like a metallic blue sentry and it made no difference in how we moved toward each other. He pulled me close and then held me tight in his arms while pressing his lips hard against mine. I was lost in the warmth and urgency of his body.

I wanted to remember every touch, every breath, every word. I wanted to trace my fingers along the fierce outlines of his tattoo with intimacy. These things can be taken from you in a flash and I was acutely aware of that. I closed my eyes and we kissed for a very long time, until our eagerness overruled us both and we made love.

He stayed the entire night—I heard him slip from bed to pray—and we alternately slept and woke each other up, returning to a dream state of nearness after intimacy upon intimacy.

"I'd better get home," he said as first light radiated over the water, reflecting pink and gray shadows shimmering across my bedroom walls.

"I have work," I said dreamily, my head in the crook of his arm. I didn't want to wake just yet. I wanted to stay afloat in this feeling of timelessness. It was like breathing underwater, something impossible but something that came as easily as if I always had done it.

"We are taking a boat ride tonight," he whispered against my ear. "Yes?"

"No," I said, drowsing off, unable to fight against the tide of sleep.

"Yes," he whispered into my ear. When I awoke again, he was gone. The kitchen was immaculate—he apparently had done a bit of garbage control—and there was a note on the table telling me that Vincent had been out. There was also a fresh pot of coffee on the stove and a paper napkin twisted into a heart.

Mrs. A had the Galley already open and was casting what I thought was a judgmental eye upon me. She knew, of course, that Sam had been with me all night. It may not have mattered so much to her before, but every moment Sam and I spent together, our relationship grew stronger and I don't think she wanted that. She said nothing except, "Good morning," and continued getting the Galley ready for the day. Though she was usually friendly and chatty, describing her life in Jordan, talking about her husband's family and how she faithfully cared for them in their later years, I knew, by the set of her lips, that she had something on her mind. She finally turned to me while she was making the coffee.

"Sam woke me up this morning when he came in," she said matter-of-factly.

I had a rebuttal in my head. That Sam was an adult, a former veteran, and quite capable of having an independent life without his mother's interference. But all I did was make an *umm* sound and take over the next customer.

About an hour later she said, "You know, in my day, a proper woman would not let a man spend the night." I just nodded, biting my tongue so that I would not feel compelled to point out that things were different now and frankly, I didn't care if I were a proper woman.

We were working together stocking shelves when she turned to me and said, "I am trying to accept that Sam needs to have his own life, but I am worried that you are not right for each other."

"That's something Sam and I need to figure out," I said.

An hour after that she stopped mopping to tell me, "You know, Sam prefers the food he grew up with in Jordan."

I wanted to mention the astounding amount of pizza that he put away during the week but still kept my lips sealed. That seemed to be the end of it.

The rest of the morning was slow and, caught up in routine work, we spoke very little. We had customers—not as much as I would have liked; I could see by the Baconometer, that business was slow, but Larry had predicted there would be a dip after the broken-window episode. "People don't like to step into where there's been trouble," he had said. What he hadn't predicted was how long it was going to last, and though I had been thrifty over the years and had managed to accumulate a nice little nest egg, I was still worried.

Business ground to a halt after lunch and I made myself a Sandwich, even putting on the marinated artichokes that Larry had suggested, which took it in an interesting direction. Mrs. A made herself a cheese sandwich and a cup of coffee with three sugars and we sat down behind the counter to eat together.

She put her hand on my arm. "I didn't mean to speak harshly to you earlier. It's just that I don't want ideas to develop between you and Sam unless the right things are in place."

"What things?" I asked.

She took a sip of her coffee and seemed to be collecting her thoughts. "You know, you have to share the same values. Family is very important to Sam. He misses his father and his brother very much. Nothing can take the place of family."

"True."

"And the woman he marries has to know this."

I hadn't thought about marriage. Okay, that was a lie. But it wasn't something I had planned to do for a very long time.

"And," Mrs. A continued, "she has to meet my approval."

Sam came in later in the day to invite me to a launch party—he being the one getting launched—given by his mother and his aunt. He was going to test out the new leg in the bay. He had just come back from his CP—the Certified Prosthetist—for his final fitting. His face was flushed with excitement as he rolled up his pants to show it off. I could see right away that it looked different from his walking leg. It was black and made of special material with a more triangular foot that had small holes in it. For drainage of water, Sam explained. He lifted his leg up and extended it to show it off.

"That's an awesome leg," I said.

"Yup. Come to the pier later." He paused. "Wear your bathing suit and swim with me."

"I am sorry I forgot to invite you," Mrs. A, who was right behind me, said. "I was planning to leave the Galley early. We're all so excited."

"Please come," Sam said.

"I'll be there," I said. He reached over to give me a hug, glanced at his mother, and stopped short, ending with a friendly pat on my shoulder.

* * *

Three o' clock and Mrs. A was out the door. "You are welcome to come!" she called to me as Miss Phyllis's pink Cadillac pulled up to the Galley door. "You can celebrate with us."

I wanted to go, but I felt guilty for shutting the Galley so early. Then I thought, *Who appreciates that anyway?* I shut the door behind me and locked up.

Vincent and I walked along the shore to the pier. The day was quiet. Ahead of us were the cars belonging to Miss Phyllis and Sam, along with a car or two belonging to some Fleeties, who were beachcombing despite the protests of nearby seals.

Sam was already on the pier. He was in swim shorts and doing stretching exercises. Miss Phyllis and Mrs. A were sitting on the last bench at the end of the pier with a pile of beach towels on their laps. I hadn't put on a bathing suit since I was not a major fan of the bay and wasn't planning, in the least, to join Sam.

Sam saw me and waved. "You're just in time!" he called to me, grinning.

Vincent and I made our way to the end of the pier. I sat down and watched as Sam stretched his arms over his head, then shook them out, then stretched each leg carefully.

"Be careful," his mother warned. "The pier gets slick."

"The new leg is slip proof," he reassured her and continued warming up.

His body was beautiful. Lean and muscular and strong. His arms and his good leg were sculpted with large, strapping muscles, while the other leg looked like just a natural part of him. When he turned away from me, the tattoo seemed to stand guard over his body. He turned back and caught me staring at him.

"It's been over two years since I've been in the water by myself," he said. "I hope I haven't forgotten how to swim."

"You won't forget," I reassured him. "The sea never lets you forget."

This is true. How many times have I been tempted to dive in, then had to remind myself that this was a grudge match that I could never win?

He stretched some more, then walked to the end of the pier

and stared down into the water. I rose from the bench to watch. I knew what an important moment this was for him. The last time he swam, he was whole and both his legs had propelled him naturally through the water. How hard it is to find mechanics to imitate what comes so natural to our bodies! He stood there, mesmerized. The bay was calling to him, I knew, summoning him, coaxing him to follow it and be enveloped, promising it would carry him to another world. It wanted to hold him like a lover and lead him someplace secret and mysterious. I also knew it was something his body craved, maybe as much as sex.

He raised his hands and sprung off his feet, curving high and graceful into the air, then forming a downward arc into the water like a rift had opened just for him, closing behind him and taking him into its core.

I gasped before I could catch myself. His mother and Miss Phyllis jumped up and down and cheered, then danced with each other, crying with joy. His head emerged within seconds and his face was ecstatic. He had a natural affinity and strength. He bobbed up and down a few times, testing his power against the pull of the bay, then lay on his side and began swimming with long, elegant strides that carried him away, almost to the buoys that marked the deeper water. A few seals turned lazily to watch him, wondering perhaps if he were one of them. His head turned from side to side with each stroke. It looked effortless, though I could hear his breath, raspy and struggling, as his lungs fought for air. He was safe, I told myself. He was safe.

Vincent stood on the pier and barked, his tail wagging madly. He started running the length of the pier, back and forth, watching Sam intently. Sam was meant to be in the water; his every move proved it. And Vincent wanted to join him. I was jealous. I wanted to swim, too. I wanted to feel the water surround me, its cool silkiness, its undulating caress. I suddenly wanted to feel it more than anything. I watched hungrily as Sam floated, then disappeared beneath and emerged, wet and joyful, water cascading from his head and shoulders.

He swam back to the pier and called to Vincent, "Come on, boy!" He slapped the water. "Come on!"

Vincent jumped in and dog-paddled out to where Sam was. They played in the water, Vincent barking happily and Sam laughing, coughing, laughing.

His mother and aunt watched him for a while. Mrs. A still had tears in her eyes.

"The new leg is a blessing," she declared. "Praise be to Allah."

"I haven't seen him this happy in years," Miss Phyllis agreed. They gathered up their things.

"We're going home. Make him dry off when he gets out so that he isn't chilled," Mrs. A instructed.

I promised I would.

"Remind him not to overdo it," she continued. "He isn't as strong as he thinks."

I promised I would remind him.

They left in the pink Cadillac and I sat in the sun, my hands around my knees, feeling its warmth on my back, half dozing, half watching Sam swim, letting the bay swirl around him, encircle him, letting its small, tender waves envelop him, tease him to swim with them more and more, greedy, it seemed to me, to claim him.

He climbed the boat's boarding ladder onto its deck several times to catch his breath before he dove again. Vincent followed him faithfully.

I dozed off, my head warm and muzzy. I was swimming. The water was my best friend now, teasing me to let down my guard, to follow it to the beginning of all the oceans.

I was awakened abruptly by a few drops of cold water on my face and looked up. Sam was standing over me with Vincent, who was shaking himself off.

"You've got to jump in with me," Sam said. "I'm good. I can watch over you."

"I'm not afraid," I said. "I can swim. I just don't want to."

"You'll feel different about it after you go in," he said, then bent down to take my hand into his sea-cold hands. I pulled away.

"Don't overdo it," I said. "Why don't you towel off and come back another day. Give yourself a chance to recuperate. I hear you whistling while you breathe."

He recognized the truth of this. "Okay," he said, "but the next time you are coming in with me." He grabbed one of the towels and began to dry himself off. Then he took another and toweled Vincent.

"It'll change your life," he said.

I looked away from him, out to the sea, past the buoys, past the glimmer bay, past the horizon and the boats and the delicate, clinging white foam and the undulating waves, and said, "It's already done that."

Chapter 33

When the Royale Pavilion calls, my world stops. It's my mother's nursing home and the call is usually to report some new catastrophe involving my mother. The last important call I got from them was when she broke her hip.

"Your mother isn't feeling very well," her nurse informed me early one morning. "You might want to visit today instead of your usual time."

"I'll come this afternoon," I replied.

"She just seems weak," said the nurse. "The doctor checked her this morning and said she might be in congestive heart failure. He'll call you later, but he put her on oxygen and that seems to be helping her with her mental status; she's clearer than she's been in a while."

I was impatient to go. My mother's mind had been obscured by clouds on previous visits and I looked forward to seeing her improved. I instructed Mrs. A to close the Galley at a reasonable time, knowing reasonable might just be ten minutes after I left. I packed a small cup of chocolate ice cream in a bag of ice and left for the ocean side of Fleetbourne.

It takes only fifteen minutes or so to drive from the bay side of Fleetbourne to the ocean side and I drove it filled with anxiety. I wasn't ready to lose my mother. Though I knew I had pretty much lost her, I wasn't ready to have no one left. Just the act of visiting her gave me a connection to her, and I didn't want to relinquish it.

The facility sits on a bluff overlooking the Atlantic Ocean and its white Victorian structure starkly contrasts against the deep blue of the bay and the brighter blue of the sky that rises over it. The sun sat warm lemon yellow at its post in the sky, the waves rolled toward the rocky beach, sending blankets of effervescent white foam across the sand that quickly bubbled away like champagne, and the sound, the sound mesmerizes and comforts with its hypnotic rhythms. Someone was standing on the beach in a bright yellow jacket, feeding the gulls as they flew low over the undulating water and crisscrossed one another's flight path. They swooped in great curling loops with their sharp-angled wings carrying them on the sea breezes. The braver gulls hovered in place, letting their webbed feet dangle while they snatched up pieces of bread from the person's outstretched hand. Several elderly residents were sitting out on the porch wrapped in plaid blankets and cheered the gulls who flew down for food. A few other gulls, maybe not so brave, marched in unison along the beach, the breezes ruffling their pale gray feathers.

I love watching the gulls. They are tough and practical and everywhere there is water. I turned toward the building and opened the gate to the front yard. There was a chorus of friendly greetings from the residents sitting on the porch and I waved to them. Though they were all calling hello, no one remembered that I had been coming here for years; I knew that. They just sat, tucked in their blankets, insulated against the breeze and their memories.

"Hello, Miss Aila!" one of the nurses called out. "So glad you could come today." She was the nurse sent to supervise the porch dwellers. "Your mother is in the Memory Garden." She pointed left. "She wanted to sit in the sun. She has an aide with her." The rule here was that no resident was ever left alone, and I was thankful for it.

I crossed the front walk to the Memory Garden located on the opposite side of the building and went through the special swinging gate. My mother was sitting in a wheelchair, her eyes closed to the day. An oxygen tank sat next to her with a small, delicate filament bringing oxygen into her nose. An aide sat on a nearby bench reading a book.

"Hi, Mom!" I called out, as if it were any ordinary day and I was fourteen and just coming home from school. Her eyes fluttered open and she looked at me.

"Aila," I announced.

"I know," she said.

My heart burst with gratitude. She recognized me! I pulled the ice cream from the bag, and the small white plastic spoon, and sat down on the bench next to her chair. "Brought you your favorite ice cream." She looked at the cup I was holding up. "Chocolate."

"I like butter pecan," she said. I sighed.

"You'll be here for a while, won't you?" Her aide stood up and stretched. I allowed that I would be.

"Just push this button when you want to go," she said, pointing to a silver button clipped to the back of my mother's chair. "And I'll come back so you can leave. Or if you want to bring her in, you have to unlock the wheels from this side and make sure her feet are on the foot stand." I thanked her. She bent over to make sure the chair was locked before she left. She didn't have to instruct me, I thought ruefully. Almost everyone I knew used a wheelchair.

"Would you like some chocolate ice cream?" I asked my mother.

"I like butter pecan," she repeated.

"Okay," I said. "Do you want ice cream?"

She didn't answer me, just looked confused. "I don't have any ice cream," she said, her voice taking on the singsong rhythm of a child.

"I have some for you," I replied.

"They took my menu away," she said.

Oh, how could I ever have thought she would understand me? *Keep it simple. Keep it simple.*

I showed her the spoon and the ice cream. "Would you like some?" I asked. She nodded. I took a little bit on the spoon and she opened her mouth like a hungry baby bird, with the plaid blanket wrapped around her and the sea breeze blowing her white hair off her face. She opened her mouth for ice cream. I forced myself not to cry. It broke my heart, watching her take spoonful after spoonful when I brought it to her mouth as she opened it, leaning toward the spoon, trusting, vulnerable, in-nocent, waiting for me to place the ice cream on her tongue, her mind going so far back in time that she was eating like a baby.

"Do you like it?" I asked. She nodded and opened her mouth for more. There were maybe one or two teaspoons left—I wished I had brought a gallon, to prolong this moment. I fed her again and once more, then showed her the empty cup. "All gone," I said, hearing those words echo forward from my child-hood. Someone had said that to me so long ago. All gone.

My father and Dan. My grandfather. My grandmother. All gone. All gone. The words suddenly seemed so significant.

Then I had an idea.

"Mom, do you remember Grandma?" She nodded.

"Ida," I said. "Her name was Ida."

She nodded again. "I know," she said clearly. "Ida."

"Yes," I said.

"Do you know the story that she loved The Skipper?" I said, leaning in toward my mother to keep her with me. I don't know why I asked that. I didn't know what I expected, but this was my last opportunity. Who knew when the clouds would part again, if ever?

"She loved Grandpa."

My heart jumped. She did know. She was able to pull that much from the past. I tried again.

"She went on the boat," I said. "*The Man in the Moon.* She had a baby."

"*Man in the Moon,*" she said.

"Grandma had a baby?"

"A boy," she murmured. She closed her eyes and lifted her head to the sun, finished. What else could I say? "How do you know?" I managed, praying, praying that the door hadn't closed, the clouds hadn't come back, hovering over her mind, layering thickly, shrouding all of its content. "How do you know?" I asked. "Did she tell you?"

"You have to move the rocks." She pointed at the decorative rocks tucked between the flowers. They had inspirational words painted on them. "Joy," "Hope," "Good Journey," "Smile." "They're in the way of the flowers."

I knew she was gone. She starting dozing now, her face turned up to the sky like a sunflower, and I sat next to her, thinking about what she said, pieces of my family's history falling into place and out of place. How could I know if what she said was true? How would I ever know?

The aide came over. "It's getting chilly," she said. "All the others are being brought inside. I'm going to take her inside, too. Do you want to come in?" I shook my head. "Did you have a nice visit?"

"Yes," I said, and stood up. I gave my mother a kiss on her cheek and put the empty ice-cream cup and the spoon into the little paper bag. The aide held out her hand. "I'll take that, honey," she said. "I'll take anything that's been emptied."

And I watched her, tears streaming down my face, as she wheeled my mother away. *If only you knew.*

Mrs. A was in great spirits the next day. Sam had been swimming and came home happy. She hadn't seen him like that in years. It would open his life up to new things, restore him to the way he was before he joined the navy, assure his future. She could even see him marrying sometime in the near future, Inshallah.

I hadn't thought of that for us yet. It seemed the two of us, Sam and I, were stepping along a suspension bridge, balancing each and every footfall. Still, I said nothing to Mrs. A: there was nothing to tell her.

But it seemed she was looking at me in a new and different way. From the corner of her eyes, so to speak, as if she were stealing glances at me and trying to figure things out.

"I am trying not to care that Sam stays at your house sometimes," she finally said to me, as the afternoon wore on. I was making English tea breads to sell for the next day and she had come into the kitchen initially to watch how I made them. "Phyllis tells me that it's what everyone does nowadays and that I should just accept it."

"True."

"I know that family is very important to you," she started.

"Yes," I answered.

"And family is everything to Sam."

I didn't know where this was going. She was going to either welcome me into the family or warn me away. I sighed and put four loaf pans in the oven before starting a second batch.

"Does he pray?"

"Yes," I answered truthfully.

She looked satisfied. "May I ask you something else?"

"Of course," I said.

She handed me the canister of flour. "Are you planning to become a Muslim for my son?"

The question took me aback. I had no problems with Sam's religion, or anyone's, for that matter, but I was quite content to remain in my own.

"We aren't even in that stage of our relationship," I protested. "We are just friends right now. He hasn't even thought of proposing or anything." I thought Sam and I felt a deepening affection for each other—the paper napkin, twisted into a heart—but if I had to twist a napkin to express how I felt, I would have twisted a knot.

"But if he were," she pursued.

I considered this. "No," I said truthfully. "I will remain whatever I am and believe in what I've always believed in. But I wouldn't marry him unless I loved him deeply."

She knit her brows and set her lips in a tight line. "I have to tell you," she said quietly, "I want my son to marry a nice Muslim girl to please his father. It's very important that he pleases his father. Don't ever forget that."

Chapter 34

How could I forget that?

There it was. My sort-of boyfriend's mother speaking for him in matters of the heart. It was disconcerting. I bit my tongue because I wanted to be respectful, but I felt like the floor was shaking under my feet. Religion had never come up between me and Sam. I knew he was observant, but I just assumed that if it had been important he would have mentioned it earlier. What a fool I had been! To think that things were going to be that easy. Boy meets girl; they fall in love; everything works out. Fool! Fool! Hadn't my life with Dan showed me that nothing works out? Death intervenes. Things are waiting in the wings for the sole purpose of breaking your heart!

I needed to talk to someone.

I needed to call someone.

Someone who knew how to navigate the crap that falls into your world. Someone who cared about me and knew all about me and how I think and could tell me what to do or not do. Someone who had common sense and experience. Someone whom I hadn't spoken to for a few days and whom I missed like crazy and whose voice I craved and whose face I missed.

Shay.

I left Mrs. A tidying up the kitchen and slipped behind the counter in the front of the store to pull out my phone with shaking hands. Shay was delighted to hear from me and fell into a torrent of loneliness as soon as she answered the phone.

"I'm going crazy," she said. "Terrell spends all day giving music lessons or working in his garden and I sit here all day planning to eat everything he grows. I'm hungry all the time. I haven't eaten since breakfast an hour ago. I need lunch. I am even starting to eye Dude's cat food. It's got rice and these little slices of shrimp."

I interrupted her. "I need to talk to you. Let's go somewhere."

"Let's have lunch. I love lunch." Then her voice rose in surprise. "Wait! It must be something bad. You never leave the Galley."

"It's not terrible. At least, I'm not sure."

"Let's go to P-town," she suggested. "I'm jonesing for clams."

"Give me two seconds and I'll pick you up."

"Hurry," she replied. "The cat is giving me funny looks."

I told Mrs. A that I needed to run errands and asked her to close the Galley sometime in the afternoon.

"I was going to leave early," she said. "Sam is taking the boat out for the first time and my sister and I are going to be his first passengers."

I felt a pang of jealousy but reminded myself that I had refused to go.

"Have a great time," I said. "Wish Sam good luck for me and tell him to call me later."

"I'll try to remember," she said evenly.

With Shay's wheelchair and Vincent squeezed into the backseat and Shay in the front seat, trying to adjust the seat belt around her burgeoning figure while urging me to drive faster so she wouldn't pass out from hunger, we got to P-town in record time and parked at the first clam shack we saw.

At Shay's insistence, we ordered four dozen clams, two baked potatoes, a big salad, and a pitcher of iced tea. I added a hamburger for Vincent and we settled down at an empty table facing the wharf.

"So what's going on?" she asked, propping her legs up on a nearby chair.

"Stuff," I said, now wondering if I was making a big issue out of nothing. "How are you feeling? You look great."

"I feel terrific. I just know that everything is going to be fine," she answered, rubbing her basketball stomach with great satisfaction. She looked so contented and settled in. Her face glowed with an inner joy. *Creating life,* I thought. *Is there anything more sacred?*

The waitress struggled with the huge tray she was bringing us and went back for more. The clams were artistically arranged on platters of shaved ice, decorated with lemon slices and horseradish sauce. I just managed to squeeze the lemon juice on everything before Shay slid a dozen onto her plate.

"Whose hamburger is that?" she asked.

"Vincent's," I said, handing it to him. She looked disappointed.

"So, what's going on? Did you break up with Sam?"

"Were we ever really together?"

She shook her head. "I could never figure that out. So, who broke up with who?"

"Whom."

She gave me a snarky look. "You can't be grammatically correct when you're pregnant because you're speaking for two. In my case, three. I'm guessing Sam was the initiator."

I let out a long, heavy sigh. "Actually, it was his mother."

She looked shocked. "His *mother?*"

I shrugged. "I didn't know she was part of a package deal. She told me she decided that Sam is going to marry a Muslim. To be handpicked, I'm guessing, at some future date."

I waited while she slurped up three or four clams, then slipped one to Vincent. "What did Sam have to say?"

"I haven't spoken to him yet."

"Ohhh," Shay said, opening her baked potato and covering it with sour cream. "You got to give the guy a chance to explain. Do you love him?"

"I think so," I said. "I mean, he's a great guy, but he's so careful. He just has a lot of baggage."

She hooted. "And you don't? You have more baggage than an airport."

She was so right. I hung my head. "I don't want to look like I'm pressuring him into something both of us may not even want."

"Call him," she said, "and tell him you want to talk to him." She was piling salad on her plate now. "Invite him to the house for dinner or something."

"I can't," I said miserably. "I don't want to invite him to the house because—"

"Because you don't want it to lead to sex, now that you know his mother is looking over his shoulder. Big ick factor there, true."

"And I really like being with him." I said. "But if his future is all sewn up . . ."

"Listen." Shay took my hand in her clammy one. "Here's a good reason to call him. There's an eclipse tonight. Invite him to watch it with you. Act like his mother never said anything to you and give him a chance to speak for himself."

Then she scooped up all the remaining clams and both baked potatoes before I could get to them. "Problem solved. Let's get dessert."

I left Sam two messages as soon as I got home. He didn't call me back and wasn't on the pier later when I left my house to sit by the water and watch the eclipse. The seals quietly went about their business, dipping in the early evening water like sea nymphs, barking softly to one another while the gulls bobbed up and down on the gentle waves, dozing. A cool, light wind busied itself around my shoulders as I sat on the edge of the pier, dangling my feet over the water. Vincent sat next to me, smelling like clams—dogs always seem to magnify the aroma of whatever they've eaten.

There were a few Fleeties sitting along the beach, far from the shoreline, in chairs and staring expectantly at the sky. We were all waiting for the moon. It had taken its place in the sky early in the evening, large and pale gold in a dusky pink sailor's sky, slowly rising, rising above the water and the boats and the birds below, commanding the day to retreat. Now it sat, shining brightly, waiting for the moment it would be obscured by the penumbral shadow of the Earth. For the first time this year, the light of the full moon was being diminished, its dominion challenged, and I watched, feeling a little bit triumphant. Though it wouldn't be totally darkened, I would know by its bronzed glow that it was sitting in the outer shadow of the Earth, chastened, its luster and beckoning luminescence fading. Its power to move the seas and create madness in people's souls momentarily weakened.

We waited on the pier, Vincent and I. The moon waited in the heavens. I couldn't take my eyes from it. My husband and father had been lured by its promise to light the night sky for them, its promise to light the seas for them, but were only lured to their deaths.

I was waiting for the apology.

"Aila!" A voice rang out. "Aila!" It was Sam, making his way across the beach in his familiar swinging walk, using his cane for support. "Aila!"

He climbed the stairs to the dock and made his way to stand over me. "Sorry I didn't call you back. I took the boat out!" His voice was jubilant. "There was no cell service and my radio keeps crapping out. I gotta order a new radio. I didn't know you had called until I got back. Come sit next to me." He headed for a bench and I followed with Vincent at my side.

"Sit down. Sit down." Sam patted a place next to him. I sat warily. He immediately put his arm around me and leaned over to give me a kiss. I allowed it.

"How did it go?" I asked.

"Perfect," he enthused. "The boat is in perfect shape. I took my mother and my aunt. It was great."

I turned away from him to watch the sky.

"Oh yeah," he said. "The eclipse. Is anything happening yet?"

"It's just starting."

"I wished you had come with me today," he said. "I wanted it to be you who came with me."

The Earth had started moving into place, into perfect alignment with the sun behind it and moon in front.

"Look." I pointed at the shadow stealthily creeping across the face of the moon, starting to dim its bright silver light into a pale yellowed pewter.

"I think I see it," he said, then pulled me closer to him. I didn't curve into him, didn't fill the hollow of his arm and body. I just sat there, watching the moon.

It was barely perceptible, but the eclipse was inching itself across the surface. There was a shadow, creeping slowly, just the whisper of a shadow, bronzing the surface below.

Sam kissed the side of my face. I didn't respond.

"What's wrong?" he asked, puzzled.

"Your mother had a long talk with me today," I said. "She wants you to marry a Muslim woman. Obviously not me."

I could hear him pull his breath in.

He dropped his face into his hands and groaned. "Oh, I'm so sorry! We had an argument. I don't want to disobey her, but I care about you so much. I don't know what to do." He took my hands in his. "She gave me life. She was with me, sat with me—lay next to my bed at night for almost two years. Can you understand?"

"I'm trying," I said.

The shadow was deepening, the moon grew darker.

"And my father. My father is so proud of me. How can I hurt him?" Sam was pleading with me now. "He's lost everything."

"So that's your decision, too?"

He didn't answer me, which was an answer.

"When were you going to tell me this?" I asked angrily. "You, with the paper napkin heart!"

"I care so much for you," he said, pressing my fingers. "I don't want it to be like this. She came to me a few days ago and begged me not to tear the family apart. I don't know what to do. I never thought she would be like this."

"Being with me would tear your family apart?"

He nodded. His face was a study in misery. "You don't know how it is. Our religion is very strong in our lives."

The eclipse had done its job, dimming the moon, holding it in the shadows.

"I guess I *don't* know how it is," I said. "I thought you were being on the level with me." My stomach was churning. I had actually started allowing myself to . . . love him. What a fool I had been to think that the universe would allow this for me. "We can be friends," he added. "We can always be the closest of friends."

"Closest of friends while you're off dating someone else and planning to marry? How does that work? I don't want to be your fuck buddy," I said, my anger growing. "I don't do that."

"It wasn't my intention to make it into that." He dropped his face into his hands again. "Oh God. I don't know what to do. Don't leave me."

I sat next to him realizing there was nothing more to say. I couldn't promise him anything, and now I could see that he couldn't promise me anything, either.

"I didn't want it to be this way," he said. "I don't want it to be like this. But it was how she raised me. I have to honor and respect my parents."

"I suppose you're lucky to have her," I said, rising from the bench. "I wish I had my mother. But I need someone to honor and respect *me*. I wish you all good things, Sam."

The people below us were standing now, folding their chairs, ready to leave. "It's all over," someone was saying. "It's all over. The moon is dark. What else is there to see?"

"Let's go home," someone else said.

And I stood up. Vincent went to my side and we walked the pier together, starting for the beach and home, leaving Sam sitting there, him and the darkened moon, to come out of the shadows by themselves.

Chapter 35

Vincent was starting to smell. Just around the edges.

It wasn't surprising since he spent a great deal of his personal time rolling around on the beach or rooting in house garbage. Since he was going to attend the impending court date of *Cordeiro v. Biljac,* the car salesman, he definitely needed to be spiffed up. It's not good to have your star witness emitting the pungent odor of food scraps and dead fish. I made an appointment to bring him to the dog groomer at Dr. Susan's office, where he was booked for the full treatment: a scented bubble bath, skin conditioner, a tasty snack, a mani-pedi, or in his case a pedi-pedi, all the luxurious things that any human would like to be pampered with, except for maybe the flea and tick medication at the end.

And in anticipation of my own deposition, I made an appointment for myself. With Miss Phyllis, at Follicles.

Her salon was in a renovated beach cottage at the edge of town on Beach Twenty-One. It was painted rose pink and white with *Follicles* spelled in gold lettering over the front door. And on the mailbox. And the pink sign next to her driveway, and the pink Cadillac sitting in the driveway. And over the pocket of her pink uniform.

The interior sported pink and gold marble floors, pale pink walls, and pink furnishings. Décor by Pepto-Bismol, as Shay used to say. She had her own hair done at Slash in P-town, where they were a bit more edgy and fashion forward.

Miss Phyllis was pleased to see me. "Are we going to be relatives?" she asked me as soon as I walked in.

"I don't think so," I said. "Things got complicated."

"I'm sorry," she said, patting me on the arm. "My sister shouldn't be trying so hard to influence Sam's life." She led me to the pink porcelain sink in the back of the store and wrapped a plastic cape tightly around my neck. I loosened it with a finger in order to breathe. "Sam's a good son," Miss Phyllis continued, then let out a long sigh. "She wants what's best for him, but it's for him to decide."

"Why wouldn't my friendship be what's best for Sam?"

Miss Phyllis shrugged. "She has devoted a lot of time helping him heal," she said. "All those years while he was on suicide watch at the hospital. You know, they never have enough staff and she came right away to stay with him. It was a great sacrifice for her to leave her husband and Sam's brother behind. And now they're stuck with immigration problems. Who knows when she'll ever see them again. Come sit and I'll wash your hair."

Suicide watch. *Suicide?* So that had been his problem! He had lost the drive to live. He had lost his appreciation for life. This beautiful man.

Miss Phyllis was waiting for me. I sat down and leaned back. The water went through its usual rotation of scalding and Arctic—these old beach cottages are notorious for their temperamental plumbing. She washed my hair with her long pointed pink nails digging into my scalp until my head felt like it had been surgically opened. After towel drying it, she led me over to a creaky salon chair.

"So how do you want it?" she asked as she pulled out her scissors and combs, and stood back for a moment to gauge how much to cut off in order to whip me back into the seventies.

"Not short." I gave her my usual instructions. "Just kind of casual and loose and modern." Her specialty was the Partridge Family look.

Of course she didn't listen to me and snipped away until there was nothing of interest left. I rose from my chair, disappointed, made my usual vow to myself never to return, and headed for the door where I thanked her, as always.

She had followed me to the door, where she took both my hands in hers when I tried to pay her. "Don't worry," she said. "I can tell that Sam is getting stronger. Do you love him?"

I couldn't answer her. She looked into my eyes. "I think you do," she said. "And I think he loves you. Give it time."

"I can't do that," I said miserably. "I don't want to get hurt."

"No, no, of course," she said, and gave me a hug before taking the money from my hand. "Remember, life is like a bad haircut. It all grows out in the end."

My next stop was at the vet to pick up Vincent. He looked like a new dog. His coat gleamed like copper; his toenails were trimmed; his teeth had been brushed. He smelled like a new dog, too. And just in time—our court date was the next day.

Larry called me early the next morning. "I'll meet you on the steps outside the courthouse at eight. Shay and Terrell are coming. Bring the dog."

The courthouse steps sound impressive until you realize that it is also the same building that houses the Department of Motor Vehicles, the town clerk's office, and everything else from Assessments to Zoning. As I had expected, it had been recently painted the usual super-white with touches of authoritative black trim. Red flowers overflowed from two large troughs that followed the steps up to the bricked landing by the front doors. The bronze plaques commemorating the year it had been built, sometime in the 1800s, gleamed; the glass doors on the directory sparkled; it was postcard perfect. My town takes pride in such things.

What I didn't expect were the protest signs. And the small group of marchers, carrying clubs and torches. There was even a police escort in the form of Officer Joe, who was sitting in his squad car with the red, white, and blue flashers on, talking somberly into his radio.

"What's going on here?" I asked Larry, who trotted down the steps to talk to me, leaning into my car window.

"I don't know," he said. "Apparently, the salesman is a member of some kind of alt-right group and they came out to support him. I don't like it."

"I don't recognize any of them," I said, searching the crowd for a familiar face. "They're not from town."

"You're right. Their cars are from out of state," Larry said.

"But where are *my* people?" I asked. "The people from town to protest back?"

Larry shrugged. "I don't know."

The marchers picked up a chant. It was ugly. The words were ugly. They were ranting against blacks and Muslims and Jews and Mexicans and just about everyone who wasn't marching with them. My stomach lurched and I had a sour taste in my mouth. I could feel my heart slamming into my chest.

"I'm scared, Larry," I said breathlessly. Shay and Terrell pulled into the parking lot. "Tell Shay to go home," I said. "It doesn't look safe for her." A brick suddenly flew from one of the marchers and landed near Terrell's feet just as he was getting out of his car. A white-painted brick, like the one that had come through the Galley window.

Two more squad cars pulled up. Now there were eight officers standing at the bottom of the steps facing off about four times as many marchers. One of the policemen picked up the brick and looked at it carefully.

"Follow me," Larry said. I parked the car and got out, holding Vincent tightly on his leash as he walked quietly next to me. Larry stood on the other side of the dog. "I don't want him injured. They may try to provoke him."

And then my fear turned to anger. No one was going to threaten Vincent. I straightened up and brought my shoulders back. "Shay!" I called out. "Walk next to me."

She was more than happy to comply, but I could see that her hands were shaking. "Remember how we stood up to Tommy?" I whispered to her. "These are just like him. Cowards and creeps."

We walked toward the courthouse steps. I could feel the heat of the torches. Vincent started growling. I turned to look one of the marchers in the eye. He looked like a normal person, brown hair, blue eyes, wearing a white button-down shirt, black pants. He could have been anyone. Hatred is so ordinary looking. His face flushed and he stopped chanting as he passed me. Someone pushed a club at Vincent's face. He yelped and pulled at his leash to run away.

I turned around to face the man. He was wearing a black shirt, this one with some kind of ugly symbol on it.

"You touch my dog and you die!" I shouted at him. "I promise it will be the last thing you do."

He lowered his arm and turned his face away from me. Larry said, "Shut up," into my ear and pulled me straight ahead, up the steps. "Don't talk to them. Don't look at them. I hope they're going to win our case for us."

The police formed a semicircle around us.

"Thank you, Officer Joe!" I called out. He nodded back at me.

We made it into the courthouse. Me and Shay and Larry and Terrell and Vincent.

Shay and I hugged each other with trembling arms in the lobby of the building. Her face was grave.

"You have to keep your mouth shut," she said into my ear.

"I didn't want him to hurt the dog," I whispered back, and suddenly we were both in tears.

"They're cowards," Larry said. "That's why they carry all that shit with them. But you have to be smart about things. You don't engage them. Now let's get upstairs."

The actual courtroom was somewhere in the warren of old-fashioned rooms on the third floor and we couldn't wait to get there. We all squeezed into the elevator at the same time, and didn't say another word until the doors opened to the hall in front of the courtroom.

Our instructions were to sit and wait in the large anteroom. It was all old-fashioned mahogany floors, walls, and very hard benches. Shay took her place on a bench next to Terrell and Vincent while I sat on Vincent's other side. Mr. Biljac, of brick-hurling fame, tiptoed in with his lawyer and took his place on the far side of the room. The court officer asked us to turn off our cell phones and then summoned the lawyers to the judge's chambers and the three men disappeared behind a carved wooden door. We quietly waited for them to emerge after their deliberation.

Mr. Biljac shot angry glances over at me every once in a while, to let me know that he felt innocent. Apparently, brick throwing in his social circles was a perfectly acceptable way to protest disputes. He had been charged with vandalism and now the judge was going to determine how much his court fine was going to be in addition to his restitution to me for all my damages. In addition, Larry told me that the marchers gave him an idea. He was going to try to link the brick throwing to a hate crime, since it apparently was being supported by a mob of white supremacists. That would make it a federal crime.

We were all somber, even Vincent, who finally decided to nap on the bench.

"Vincent smells different," Shay whispered. "I can't quite put my finger on it."

"He had a bath," I whispered back.

"I guess it's the *lack* of smell I'm smelling," she replied softly. "Nice touch."

And we waited. After about half an hour, I could hear faint chanting from outside, below the window. Apparently lacking other forms of entertainment, the marchers were planning to make a big show of it. Suddenly there was shouting. Curious, I got up from the bench and walked over to the window. Vincent followed me, still leashed.

The window overlooked the steps to the courthouse. Down below was the photographer sent by the *Daily Fleetbourne Herald*. To preserve their anonymity, the marchers were quickly pulling on white masks. They shook their signs, mostly misspelled, showcasing their illiteracy, and shouted several unoriginal but markedly ugly slogans. The photographer took some shots and left. With no audience left to impress, the men suddenly started melting away.

If they were hoping for some kind of altercation, it failed to deliver. They weren't in a mood to continue marching in an empty parking lot and go unnoticed. It had been a bust.

The door creaked open and the judge poked his head out and looked around. "Is that the dog?" he asked Larry, who said, "Yes." I wondered why there would be a question about it since Vincent was the only dog in the room. The other lawyer peeked out, too; they all nodded at one another and withdrew back into the chambers.

We waited some more. The car salesman continued to glare at me and I glared back. Vincent looked at him, too. The man started to squirm.

Finally, Larry appeared. He came over to me and started whispering. "The case against Victor was dismissed. No corroborating evidence of any dog bite and the judge could see that Victor is a calm dog, even with the crap going on outside."

"Vincent," I said.

"Who's Vincent?" he asked.

"You know," I said. "Van Gogh."

"Go?" Larry looked confused.

"The dog is *Vincent*," I hissed. "Vincent. After Vincent van Gogh. It's the ear thing." I pointed to where Vincent was missing an ear.

"Victor, Vincent, it's not important," Larry replied.

"It is to him," I said. "It's his name."

"Vincent," Larry conceded. "Now, the second case, concerning the brick through the window, was also awarded to you. You are getting damages from Mr. Biljac and he has to perform a month of public service. I tried to get him prosecuted for a hate crime. After the marchers today came out to support him by throwing a brick at Shay's car, they apparently have a stockpile of white-painted bricks; it linked him to them, but it's not enough. Same kind of brick, same paint, but not enough for evidence. Sorry. Hate crimes are taken very seriously."

Well, it wasn't the epic battle I was prepared for, but at least I had my dog's name sort of cleared and my expenses covered.

Shay got to her feet and applauded; Terrell joined in; Vincent barked; Mr. Biljac said something to his lawyer, who took him by the shoulder and marched him out the door.

Larry invited all of us back to Shay and Terrell's house for a celebration. "My treat!" he exclaimed in a flush of triumph to me. "I planned a party—I'll run to P-town and pick up a few dozen clams and some other stuff and we'll cheer you up. You need to celebrate."

Not sure how he would react to Dude, Shay and Terrell's cat, I dropped Vincent off at my house and called to tell Sam the outcome of my case. His phone answered with the message that he was out on his boat where there was no service and he would return all calls as soon as he got back. I told him he didn't need to call me back.

I deliberately drove past Town Hall on my way to Shay. It looked normal and quiet and a sweetly old-fashioned relic of Cape Cod. Official, secure, a refuge, a sanctuary, my Town Hall, in my town, in my country. The malicious ghosts of old years had come back to inhabit the souls of the weak and the hateful. How had that happened? Who had summoned them forward and promised them protection? Where did it get sanctioned, this raging malevolence?

I stopped my car for a moment. There was no one around. The building gleamed white in the sun. The windows looked officially friendly. The red flowers had been recently watered and stood up fresh and strong. The flag was still in place, flying and casting its shadow into the very parking lot that had been filled with the cars of the malicious.

I had won my small case and could now put it behind me, but I wasn't ever going to forget how easily my town had played host to such evil.

Chapter 36

Larry really knew how to throw a party. He had decorated Shay and Terrell's backyard with CONGRATULATIONS, GRADUATE signs, which apparently was all that was left in the P-town party store on short notice, and had trimmed the rest of the area in orange and black streamers. He had purchased an overload of food and beverages from the local supermarkets, a huge American flag from somewhere, which was immediately planted in a corner of the garden, a large poster board stork carrying a baby boy by its diaper with *X 2* written on it, a red and green wreath that read: "Merry Christmas," and a big bunch of flowers, which he presented to me.

"What are we actually celebrating?" I asked Shay later.

"Oh, Larry's been planning this for about a month," she explained. "It originally was to celebrate my pregnancy and his promotion at his firm, and then he added your case and Memorial Day and whatever else was available at the Party Hearty store. He likes to be thorough."

"Awesome," I said.

"Plus he invited a few people from his office."

They arrived later in the afternoon, a party brigade from Larry's law office in Boston, looking to let their hair down for the weekend. They had even booked rooms in P-town. I volunteered to help cook and serve, but everyone seemed to know what to do to keep things running and Shay didn't have to leave her comfortable patio chair even once. Apparently, Larry's parties were a fixture and he had them down to a science.

"He has parties all the time in Boston," Shay explained to me. "Everyone just sort of falls into a job and it all gets done."

Larry himself was a bottomless source of energy, dancing, pouring, serving, passing out the paper plates and napkins that said "Happy New Year" on them, directing where the food should go, and making sure to come over to me periodically to ask if I was enjoying myself. I was. There was always someone interesting and pleasant to talk to, and I was never left to sit alone. I danced until my legs ached and laughed until I was breathless. We were all moths drawn to the light, and the light was Larry. His jokes about them made the courthouse marchers look dim-witted and ludicrous, though we all knew they were an omen.

"Are you cheered up?" he shouted into my ear during a particularly loud song we were dancing to.

I nodded, but that didn't satisfy him.

"Are you cheeeered up yet?" he sang into my ear.

I shouted, "Yesssss!" and he shouted, "Excellent!" and looked satisfied. He brought his light to every corner.

By the end of the day and after several mango mojitas, I had almost forgotten that I had come alone.

The party was winding down pretty much by the time the sun was; a cool dusk moved in. Larry brought out a sheet cake that read: "A Piece for All of Us," complaining it was supposed to have read: "Peace to All of Us." Shay and I were sitting at a table outside with our coffee when Larry came over with two plates of cake, one each for me and Shay, then left to get a plate for himself.

"What do you think of him?" Shay asked with a smile.

"I like him a lot," I said. "He's so much fun. So upbeat all the time."

"He likes you. He thinks you're smart and brave."

I groaned. "I am so not brave."

Larry appeared with a plate of cake for himself and a cup of tea. "How are you doing?" he asked as he seated himself next to me. "I thought you would bring that guy with you—the vet."

I shook my head. "It didn't work out," I said.

He seemed genuinely sorry. "He *was* a bit somber," he said.

"Time for me to get another piece of cake." Shay left us sitting alone.

Larry pulled his chair closer to me and leaned over. "I wanted to talk to you about the Galley," he said. "I have some ideas. You should do some upgrading. Modernize it. You know what it needs?"

"A nice café," we said in unison.

"Right," he said. "You can start now and have it ready before summer ends."

"I've been having some ideas, too," I replied, thinking they probably weren't the same ideas. I was tired of the Galley. Tired of getting up in the morning to open it, then wondering where my customers had gone. Tired of talking about it. "I'm thinking of closing or selling it and walking away."

"No, no, no." Larry shook his head. "You can't. It's a great place. You just have to get your mojo back. I'll write my ideas down before I leave for Boston. When I come up to the Cape again, we can talk about it."

I resented that a little. The few times he had been in the store, he had been pretty vociferous about the things he thought needed updating and I had graciously tried to entertain his suggestions. Running the store had been my responsibility for the past two years. I had been part of the Galley even before I was born. Larry had been acquainted with the Galley for less than a month.

"Thanks," I said, rising from my chair. "I appreciate your concerns." I gave him a smile and got up for more coffee.

Later, Terrell turned on the backyard lights and emerged from the house holding his fiddle. He played a few notes of the Bob Marley song "Everything's Gonna Be Alright." Shay started singing with her clear soprano and gestured for me to join. I picked up the harmony, Larry tapped the beat on the table and sang with us. Some of the others picked up the words, their voices sailing over the backyards and up into the darkening sky. Dan would have been playing his guitar, I thought. And singing louder than anyone else.

It was time for me to leave.

I kissed everyone good-bye, was given a piece of cake to bring home. They were still singing as I walked to my car. Terrell's voice was strong; Shay sang in her usual lilting tones, but she was totally right.

Larry, with the deep and thrilling baritone voice, sang flat.

I sat in the car in front of my house for a while. My head was still full of songs and music and cake and dancing and I wasn't ready for my quiet, quiet house. I rolled down the window and leaned back, letting the car run. If I sold the Galley, I should sell the house, leave Fleetbourne. After all, what would be the point of staying?

Vincent started barking at the sound of my car. Okay, maybe my house wasn't all that quiet. I went around to the back steps and let myself in. Vincent ran right over with potato peels hanging from his chin.

"Garbage boy!" I chided him. He jumped up to kiss me.

The house phone was blinking and I pressed the button. There was a message for me to call the Royale Pavilion.

I sighed. They were so conscientious. If my mother needed as much as an extra Tylenol, they immediately phoned to let me know. I pressed the number and identified myself. The call was directly transferred to the Nursing Director.

"We tried to reach you all afternoon," she said. "Your cell phone just kept going to message."

"Oh! I'm so sorry," I apologized, remembering that I had to turn the phone off in court.

"I apologize to have to tell you like this, but we need you to come as soon as you can," she went on, her voice full of sympathy. "Your mother passed away this afternoon."

Chapter 37

The nurses were lined up in an arcade, four on each side, flanking the entrance to my mother's room. I imagined myself marching to her door under crossed syringes, but each nurse only shook my hand, expressed her sympathy, and returned to her duties. The nurse who usually cared for my mother opened the door and led me in.

The room was immaculate as always, a light glowing softly from the lamp next to the bed where my mother lay. She was groomed; her hair was combed, a smudge of lipstick on her lips in an attempt to restore her to the look of health and dressed in a fresh yellow nightgown that I did not recognize. Her face had eased into peaceful repose, unlined, blessed with grace, her soul in a place beyond us.

Her nurse had packed up my mother's personal items and put them in a plastic bag to give to me. I peeked in. A picture of my father and one of me. *How ironic,* I thought. My mother had owned houses and a business, cars and trucks, furniture, an old upright piano, good china and everyday dishes, so much over the years, and now all her worldly possessions were two old pictures in a small plastic bag.

I stood next to her bed for a few minutes, not really knowing what to do. Her nurse stood next to me.

"We have in your original application that she wanted to be cremated," she said softly. "You need to make the arrangements."

I had no idea how to go about that. Did they roll my mother down the hall, setting her bed ablaze like a funeral pyre, and then hand over the remains in an asbestos bag? I was getting giddy, I warned myself. It had been a hard day—the courthouse marchers had frightened me, I'd had too much to drink at Larry's party, and now my mother's death. The nurse took notice of my befuddlement. "Just call the funeral director; he'll take care of everything," she said.

"Okay," I said thankfully.

She gave me a little hug and left. I stood by my mother and leaned over to kiss her forehead. "Mom," I whispered. "Mom. I'm sorry I didn't get to say good-bye."

I would never see her again. How could I bear to never see her again? How do you get used to someone you love just disappearing from your life like a magic trick?

I stroked her hair. There was nothing more to say. The room felt eerie. Occupied but strangely empty. "I will miss you," I said, and studied her face. I wanted to remember her face. I stood there for a while, trying to memorize her features, her hair, her hands.

I was suddenly very tired. I touched her head again as though bestowing a benediction and said, "Bye, Mom," like I would be back later. It sounded foolish in the empty room. "I love you."

I thanked all the nurses, donated her barely played television and the rocking chair I had purchased in order to sit in her room at night, and walked down the hallway, acutely alone.

Of course I had expected her to leave me at any moment, and yet, somehow, I still expected her to remain in her condition forever. I had expected that I would visit her every week and bring her chocolate ice cream and talk about the world beyond her bed, even knowing that she couldn't comprehend it. It had given me a sense of security that I wasn't yet the last of my family, that she was still my buffer against our total extinction.

Once outside, I stood on the front walk and looked up at the lovely old building. Some of the rooms were lit pale yellow against the darkness as they played host to other visitors, other families, other stories. Mine was over. The porch chairs were vacant and waiting for tomorrow. The gate to the Memory Garden was closed. I followed the ground lights along the walkway, stepping through their soft puddles on the way to my car, and, weeping, left the Royale Pavilion forever.

Fleetbourne loves a good death.

They'd had a heartwarming and very long and public memorial service for my father and Dan. My father was a respected businessman and had served at the Galley for many years, food, groceries, postal services, carrying the economically deprived on his books until either the person or the books crumbled from age; he lent his tools, his car, his brawn to wherever it was necessary, his services to the volunteer fire department. His memorial service had been arranged by the minister, flowers were delivered, the Ladies Auxiliaries from both the church and the fire department prepared tables of food while I sat in my kitchen, in shock. I had to face it all alone, as my mother was already at the Pavilion and never knew she had been widowed.

Actually, that we had been widowed together.

The whole town had attended. Filled with love and respect and sympathy and more than a little morbid curiosity. Shay ran interference for all of it and I was able to breathe.

Dan's memorial was held in Beaufort, South Carolina, where he had been born and raised and which was the geography behind his always-delightful soft southern accent. I flew there for the service—his parents had handled it all—and flew home again, my life upended.

There had been no caskets, no funeral cortège to the cemetery, no burial, all of which usually eases the transition from living to dead for the family. They were just gone.

Magic.

It was my mother's turn now.

Not one to be fussed over, she hated anything ostentatious. Her birthdays were celebrated with a simple card and a gift that she always declared we really shouldn't have gotten her. Valentine's Day was considered well done with a single red rose that my father brought home after work. Mother's Day was a hand-made item and the biggest hug and kiss I could muster.

Her memorial, a few days after her death, was modest, in keeping with her manner; I didn't want to embarrass her with excess. The church was filled with her beloved red roses, and the minister spoke of her with an intimacy that stemmed from knowing her almost her whole life—and I appreciated that.

I had prepared a eulogy.

I stood up and looked out at Shay and Terrell and her parents and Larry, who were sitting in the first pew, representing family. Shay was smiling affectionately. Sam was sitting right behind her, his head bowed, with Miss Phyllis and Mrs. A, whom I had asked to close the Galley for the day. The other rows were filled with almost everyone from town, their faces benign and filled with affection. Even The Skipper and his wife. He sat upright, shoulders back, his face very solemn. Mrs. Skipper wore a blue feathered hat that perched in her white hair like a seabird. There was Mrs. Hummings, the town clerk, and Dr. Susan and Officer Joe. How could I ever have doubted these people? They were my neighbors and friends. There were even acquaintances and fellow merchants from P-town.

I thanked my mother for my life. I thanked her for her goodness, and kindness, her great cooking and baking and how she taught me these skills so patiently until I loved them, too. I thanked her for the love she had raised me with. There was little else I could say except that I would never stop missing her.

I chose "Amazing Grace" for the choir to sing. The Ladies Auxiliary prepared a luncheon in the church basement, which brought tears to my eyes as I remembered my mother volunteering her own time to ease the burden of other families so many years ago. Shay's parents hugged me tightly; Sam paid his respects and quickly left, Mrs. A blessed me in three languages; there were kind words everywhere.

I knew that my family had almost completed its cycle of life and death; the final chapter was waiting for me. I told this to Shay as she sat at a table next to Terrell, two plates in front of her, one of macaroni and cheese, the other holding a large salad, since everyone knows that salad erases macaroni calories.

"No," Shay said, in the middle of a huge mouthful. "Let your grief turn to good memories and tell yourself that you are the beginning of your own chapter and you can take it wherever you want. It can be the best chapter ever."

I watched her fill her plate again and smiled. I wanted to tell her to take a lot of pictures of her baby and pictures of herself and Terrell and pictures of her parents and pictures of her friends and to take even more pictures of them and to save them forever.

I had so few pictures. Why hadn't I taken more? I looked around at the room full of people. I didn't want it to end and have everyone disappear out the door and leave me with no one.

I leaned across the table to talk to Terrell. "Can you take a few pictures?" I asked him. "Just a few pictures?"

"Sure thing," he said and stood up with his cell phone and snapped some photos. "I'll send them to you."

I put my hand on his arm to say thank you and he hugged me. "You're an okay chick," he whispered into my ear and I liked that very much.

I gave a brief speech, thanking everybody for coming and caring and for honoring my family. There were hugs and kisses and sweet remembrances of my mother and then it was suddenly over. I put a large bouquet of roses in my car, shook the last hand, kissed the last cheek, and drove home as alone as I had ever been.

* * *

Vincent met me at the door with a ball in his mouth. Dogs know about these things, life and death, and handle it in their own doggie ways. They mourn and they play and then it's time to eat. Later, they mourn again and play again, maybe followed by a snack. Life and death are simple cycles to them. He rolled the ball across the floor and then chased it. He picked it up in his mouth and looked at me hopefully. *Why not?* I thought. What is a pit bull for, if not to take you away from sadness by delighting you with their unending goodwill and effervescence? I changed into jeans and we headed for the pier. It was vacant and I was grateful for that. As I started up the steps, I suddenly realized that *The Wentletrap* was missing from her slip. Sam had gotten to the pier before me and had taken his boat out. Just as well. We had been avoiding each other for days and this was not a time I wanted to talk to him. You cut your losses.

I threw the ball onto the beach for a while, while Vincent made it his responsibility to dash after it and return it to me as fast as possible. "My mother would have liked you," I told him as he dropped another drooly ball into my lap, then sat and waited for the next throw. Life was simple for him: I envied him that.

Suddenly the buzzing of a boat engine from the distance caught my attention. I recognized *The Wentletrap,* her new running lights ablaze, coming across the bay, I recognized Sam standing at the wheel inside the cabin. He waved to me and I waved back.

"I'm sorry to disturb you!" he called to me as he slowly and skillfully eased the boat into the slip. I reassured him that he wasn't. He tied it up and stepped out onto the pier, then climbed up to where I was sitting. "May I sit here?" He sat down on the bench next to me.

I shrugged. "It was kind of your family to attend the services," I said. "Thank you."

"It was a very nice service," he said politely.

We had nothing more to say and just sat there. Vincent dropped the ball into Sam's lap and looked up at him, wiggling his stump tail in anticipation. Sam threw the ball down onto the beach and Vincent was ecstatic to go after it.

"I miss you," Sam suddenly said in a quiet voice.

"I miss you, too," I replied.

"We have to talk," he said, taking my hand and kissing it. I allowed him. But it was going to come to nothing; we both knew that.

"There's nothing to talk about," I said. "We're at an impasse."

"We don't have to be."

"I'm not converting," I said.

He just sighed.

"How's the boat?" I asked.

"It's working great. Put in one of those fancy positional things," he said. "You don't have to drop anchor; it just keeps the motor running and holds you in place. All I have to do is remember to order a new radio."

"Well, it looks great."

"Thank you," he said. "It clears my head."

"Great."

We sat for a while, letting the sound of the bay fill in the blanks.

"Listen, Aila," he started. Vincent interrupted him by dropping the ball into his lap. Sam took it and threw it into the bay. Vincent galloped off.

"I don't want to live without you," Sam finished. "I just don't know how to work this all out. Just give me some time."

"I'm sorry it's so hard for you," I said, realizing with a rush that my words were true. "I don't care what your religion is. I can live with it. But I have to stay who I am. And I have to be so important to you that I matter above everything else. That's the kind of love I need." *And once had,* I wanted to say.

He dropped his face into his hands. Vincent was barking madly from the beach, trying to command his ball, floating on the water, to return to him.

"Sorry," Sam said.

"That's okay," I said. "It's just a damn ball." I guessed our conversation was over.

We watched Vincent plunge into the water and swim to the ball and grab it, then swim back to shore.

"If there's anything I can do for you," Sam said, pulling himself to his feet, "just ask. I always offer my boat and the sea." He started to leave. Maybe I wasn't going to see him again. I stared at him, realizing how many times I had pictured his face, wanting to remember it, to carry with me all the time. Faces fade. In time, faces fade like old flowers. He leaned over and gave me a kiss on the top of my head. Vincent bounded between us and dropped a wet ball on my lap, waiting for his next assignment. I patted him on the head. Then Sam walked back to his truck.

I sat on the pier for a long time, staring out over the water. The bay had been part of my life since the day I was born. I knew every molecule that spun and churned against the coastlines, knew every thrash of the waves, every color that was influenced by the sun and the moon and sky. I knew what it wanted from us and how it managed to get it. The water had been part of my family since the beginning of oceans. And, I suddenly realized with a start, my family was part of it as much as the fish and the seaweed and the shells and the sea glass. As much as the tossing waves and lathering foam, we were part of it. We just couldn't help ourselves. A forbidden thought had been in the back of my mind since my mother's death. Triggered by Sam's words, it pushed forward to my consciousness. I thought of my father and Dan and my grandmother's mystery child and my mother, who would be forever separated from my father. I remember when I was a child and they spoke of family plots that had been set aside in a corner of an old cemetery in Orleans, a town not far from us. My great-grandparents had been buried there, then my grandfather and grandmother. But my father, who had been lost at sea, had broken the continuity. He would forever be separated from his family and my mother.

I suddenly realized how wrong that was and stood up. My breath came in gasps. I was being tasked with a responsibility.

I had to set things in place. The continuity would be up to me and suddenly, suddenly, I just knew what I had to do. There was no other way to fix my family.

I called Sam, my heart pounding. He answered right away.

"You were right and I need you to help me," I said, terrified of what I was about to ask him.

"Of course," he said. "Anything." He paused. "What?"

My voice shook as I got out the words. "I need you to help me. Please. I want to spread my mother's ashes over the sea."

Chapter 38

My mother's ashes belonged to the sea as much as they belonged to my family.

It was where she was destined to be, next to my father, next to her possible brother, to comfort and be a mother to Dan. The stars and the moon and the heavens and the sun all had known that this was her place, too. They had known this since my father's and Dan's deaths in the time before time, and now, since my mother's death, they had always known that they would call to me and ask me to set things right for my family. They had drawn me to the pier for years, night after night, after my father and Dan died, to fill my head with moonlight, in all its iterations. The bay would whisper only parts of its secrets to me, knowing that I would be compelled to pursue them. The water would hypnotize my soul and draw me close, always asking me to pay attention, pay attention, murmuring that when the time was right I would know what I needed to do.

It was all so perfect, as only could be arranged by an infinitely wise universe.

The tiny, pearlescent wentletrap had been sent to me, found

by an animal that was pure of heart, my Vincent, who has carried it to me without injury to it. It was necessary for me to give the right name to Sam's boat, to make it the proper transport for a holy chore. I knew I would have to cast away my fears and rage and board *The Wentletrap* as she was carried on the sea. I would have to summon the courage to do this, from every part of my soul, so that I could complete my sacred and preordained task.

I saw it all so clearly. I trembled from the weight of what I was being asked.

Sam, for his part, was more than thrilled. He would be the one to take me on my first trip. He said he felt honored; he promised that he was strong enough for the two of us, that he would take care of me.

He checked and double-checked the equipment; he would plot the course this very night, he was so anxious and proud and ready. We would go right away, tomorrow.

The boat seemed to buck a little as soon as I stepped down into it. Like an unbroken horse, it was testing my strength and resolve; it was warning me, letting me know that it wanted my respect, that we had a connection in all of this, that it would be a vehicle of dignity and dispatch.

Still, my legs shook. I needed to trust it. I needed to let it carry me out to the ocean and trust that it would safely return us. I needed to trust that I was doing the right thing. I felt my heart pounding. I resolved to proceed with what was being asked of me, to ask Dan and my father to watch over me. I straightened my shoulders, standing on the deck and feeling the water beneath us. How familiar. How gently it rocked us. Sam had checked the weather repeatedly for me. No rain or storm would interrupt us; I just needed to have courage.

I carried aboard the roses that I had brought home from the church and the silver urn that held my mother's ashes. Vincent followed me, wearing a doggie life jacket with a red rose tucked into a buckle, to mark the occasion. He found a place on the deck under a seat and lay down to nap as though he had done this forever.

Sam had been watching me from the deck, leaning on his cane for balance. He was wearing jeans, a long-sleeved tee, and his swim leg. I ached to be held by him, then chided myself. But he caught me staring and held his arm out to me. I reached for his hand and he pulled me close.

"It'll be okay," he said into my ear. "I will take care of you." He kissed me hard on the lips and I kissed him back. I had missed the wrap of his arms so much, the press of his body against mine, I almost couldn't bear it.

"I'll take care of you," he said again, and we held each other. "Let me."

He started the engine and let it warm up as he untied the boat from the pilings, then backed it out of the slip with great skill, gently and carefully and very straight before he turned it starboard. The open bay was ahead of us.

It was a perfect day for this. The bay was calm and quiet, dotted with private sport boats, water-skiers, kayakers, and fishing boats that buzzed across its surface like mosquitoes. We passed P-town and the crowds of people waiting on the wharf for the ferries to take them out fishing or whale watching.

It was a smooth ride. We eased past the Race Point lighthouse that was nestled in the dunes and was the marker for where the bay met the sea. It stood resolutely at the very tip of the Cape, usually whipped by brute winds and blowing sands and unpredictable currents. The mercurial combination used to cause shipwrecks, catching boats unaware before the lighthouse itself was built to aid sailors coming in from the ocean. Today the juncture looked calm.

And inviting.

The Wentletrap purred onward. There were boats in the distance, cruising quietly. We turned eastward into the waiting Atlantic Ocean.

The water changed from calm and respectful, a mirror reflecting the glowing sun, to a more challenging chop. The boat handled it well, rising and falling with the waves, rolling side to side like a pacing horse. I closed my eyes, letting my knees open and close slightly, riding the deck like an old hand. I had almost forgotten this, the feel of the ocean pulling you forward, ready to hypnotize you with its undulations. I held tightly on to the railing and stared out over the water, my tears falling, joining with the spray that kicked up against my face, joining with the salt of the spray and the salt of the water. We were all the same elements, born of original seas. Somewhere in the deep. Somewhere ahead, somewhere, my father and my husband were waiting for me to complete my task. This was a homecoming and I almost couldn't bear it.

Sam made a slow turn with the boat. In the far distance was a whale-watch boat, cruising the waters with its load of passengers. The whales had migrated down from the Arctic Ocean around January to start feeding and wouldn't be leaving yet for the Caribbean—that came in late August and early September—but there were a few here and there, signaling their imminent appearances with a spout of white spray that shot straight up into the air, followed by gray behemoths rising gracefully from the depths of the ocean, giant mouths agape as they strained fish through their baleens and took another long breath before diving again to catch more. They were magnificent, their backs curving in slow, graceful arches as they sliced through the water leaving only their perfect tails to hover above the surface for a moment before disappearing. I loved watching them.

There was an odd sound from off in the distance, distorted by the air and the buzz of the boat's motor. A splashing. A cry. Some kind of gurgling call I didn't recognize. I tilted my head to listen, but the sound got caught up in the resonance of the wind and the water whipping against the boat.

"Did you hear that?" I called back to Sam.

He shook his head no. A few minutes later, the boat eased to a slow pace; he had cut the motor. Now it quietly rocked back and forth, hypnotically, like a child's cradle.

"I think this is a good spot!" Sam called from the cabin. He pointed to the port side of the boat. "It's calm here. What do you think?"

I looked around. Here and there the blow from the humpbacks betrayed their positions in the distance with a fine, white mist that spouted up from the water, accompanied by a huge sigh of release. The water was respectful. On the horizon, in the distance behind us, was the lighthouse, barely in view, a reminder of the cape, so my mother wouldn't lose sight of where she had come from. Ahead was the freedom of unending seas.

"Yes," I called back. "This is where she should be."

Sam came down from the cabin and stood quietly next to me. "It's a good spot," he said.

Together we watched the shearwaters, the small seabirds that follow the humpbacks, fly close to the water's surface, swooping in small flocks, waiting for the tell-tale white bubbles to rise from the depths, indicating a whale was coming up to feed. The birds would feed, too, with bravado, as they dove into the whales' mouths to snatch a fish or two before the huge jaws closed. My mother would be surrounded by life. A whale suddenly spy-hopped, balancing its body upright in the water, and stared at me with its dark, unfathomable eyes as though it were reading my soul.

The sound I had heard before echoed from a distance. A splash, a haunting cry. A call from the deep. Perhaps another species, whose voice I didn't know.

But it was the right place for my mother; I knew it. I reached under the deck seat and brought out the urn and the bouquet of roses.

What to say? I hadn't prepared a prayer, though I should have. A dedication. I opened the urn and held it upside down, shaking it gently. The contents quickly flew away, at first carried on the wind, then settling on the surface of the water, then dissolving into the waves and foam before they disappeared. I dedicated her to the seas, to its protective depths during battering storms, to its rolling majesty under the warming sun, to my waiting family.

She needed to be rejoined with my father. She needed to let Dan take care of her like the good son-in-law that he had always been. She needed to bring family to a possible brother who had been abandoned to the sea.

It would be the last thing I would ever do for her. "Goodbye," I said into the wind. "I hope you find one another and find peace. I love you all." I threw the roses, one by one, onto the waves. They bobbed and floated, red petals against the inscrutable blue water until the current carried them all away. A whale blew a stream of white mist as though it were playing taps.

I had completed my task. I felt my heart draining off its last supply of sorrow. I went up to the cabin with Sam, ready to return home.

The strange sound was back, a mournful note, deep and low, along with the hard splash of water.

"Sam," I said. "Listen. Do you hear that?"

He leaned out of the cabin and tried to concentrate. "Not sure," he said.

I picked up the binoculars from him and adjusted them. There was a roil of water, in the distance, white and heaving with a dark center. It splashed a soft rise of spray, then stopped. Another call, like an oboe playing a dirge.

"What is that?" I said, pointing in the direction of the object. I handed the binoculars to Sam, who strained to make sense of it. There were no boats in the area; they had gone about their business farther out. There was nothing but the roll and thrash of something dark, covered with white foam, and the deep timbre of something that needed to be given a voice. For a moment I thought it was some kind of apparition. Some omen from the sea that, in this final moment, it had accepted my family into its depth. No. I was wrong. It was something living. The water was rolling in a rhythm that only something alive could fuel.

"Let's just go over there, take a look," Sam said. "It doesn't appear to be that far."

He turned the motor on once again and pointed the bow of

the boat to the odd shape. It appeared to be stabilized in one spot. The motor hummed to life and the boat eased forward.

Another sound that faded back into the depths. I took the binoculars from Sam for a hard look as we drew closer.

I could see clearly now what it was. A chill ran down my spine as I realized with horror what I was seeing. I ran from the cabin to stand at the bow, pressing myself against the rail for support. "Oh, Sam!" I cried. "Hurry! Hurry!"

It was a humpback whale.

And it was drowning.

Chapter 39

With the engine pushed to full speed we reached it within minutes.

Sam stopped the boat and came down from the cabin to stand next to me and peer over the side. What we saw made me sick.

"She's twisted up in a gill net," Sam said. "It's pretty bad."

Only the front part of her body was visible. Something had caught on to her flukes and she was being pulled down almost vertically, deep below the water. About a hundred feet away was her calf, distressed and swimming in circles, blowing spouts and diving, to re-emerge moments later.

The whale's pectoral fins were pinned to her sides and her dorsal fin was bound with the same fine, almost invisible white nylon netting that tightly wound around her body. Unable to move, she barely seemed to have enough strength to breathe. How long she had been struggling was anyone's guess.

I knew it happened frequently, whales getting caught in fishing nets, fighting for hours, twisting and thrashing to break free, but only entangling themselves further, struggling until they die of exhaustion.

"I'm going to use your radio," I told Sam as I started for the cabin. He had sat himself down on the padded deck bench and was pulling his jeans off.

"There's a place to call!" I yelled back to him. "In P-town. Center for Coastal Studies. They do rescues."

"Turn on the automatic positioner," he called back. "It'll give our location."

"Don't jump in," I said. "Please don't jump in. Wait for me to call the rescue first."

I left him sitting on a bench while I went topside to the cabin. I turned on the automatic positioner, which kept the boat in the same position without needing an anchor, and then called the number to the rescue. The radio cut out before the call could go through. I stuck my head out of the cabin to relay the information to Sam.

"She won't last!" he yelled up to me. "We've got to cut her free."

"They have rescue teams!" I yelled back at him. "I'll keep trying. They have equipment."

He glanced over the side again. "Are you crazy?" he yelled back. "Equipment is going to do her shit, if she dies."

In fact, the thrashing had stopped. She was barely moving now and looked exhausted from her efforts. We had no idea how long she had been struggling.

Sam had stripped to his bathing trunks leaving his tee on. "I'm coming up to the cabin!" he called. "I want to check the radio. Damn cell phones are useless."

He came into the cabin. "I want to find my knives."

"I'll try the rescue center again," I said.

Vincent started barking on the deck. I called him to me. "He knows there's something wrong," I said to Sam.

"Tie him up," he replied, busy looking through a cabinet. "We don't want him leaping into the water."

I fastened a rope I found to his collar.

"Sam, you can't do this by yourself," I said. "It's too dangerous for you."

"There's no time," he said.

"You could get killed," I argued. "That's a forty-ton animal thrashing around."

He held his hand up. "We're not arguing about this," he said. "I've made up my mind. I just have to find my stuff."

"She could kill you with a flip of her body," I argued.

But he wasn't listening. "We need knives," he muttered as he searched the lower cabinets. "Where's my dive knife?"

He pulled out a black plastic tackle box, set it on a bench, and opened it. Every tool inside was neatly wrapped and had its own place. Bait knives, utility knives, even a round knife sharpener. On the top of the equipment lay a pair of goggles and a black knife sheath that was attached to a belt. He took the goggles and put them over his forehead, then reached for the sheath.

"My dive knife," he said, pulling the sheath off, revealing a thick knife with a serrated edge. "I used to take it everywhere." He ran his finger lightly across the blade, then buckled the belt around his hips before putting the knife back into its sheath. "Okay," he said. "I'm ready. I'll start by trying to free her flukes. Once I get them free, it'll release her tail. Then I can work on her midsection."

I followed him to the lower deck. The whale let out a loud, shivering mist of breath through her blowhole, the same sound I had heard before, stressed and terrified.

Sam pulled the goggles down over his eyes and peered at her from the side of the boat. He had positioned the boat about twenty feet from her to allow himself some room to work without being knocked into the boat if she started thrashing.

But she lay in the water, just floating, still as a log. For a moment I thought the worst.

"Let me try one last time," I begged. I ran up to the cabin and banged the top of the radio with my fist. Still no service. When I came down, Sam was already mounted on the side of the boat, sitting with both his legs poised over the water.

"Please be careful," I pleaded.

"Get the other knives ready," he said. "I might need them all. And be ready to pull the netting into the boat when I toss it up to you." He took a deep, noisy breath. "Here goes," he said, lifting up on his hands. "I'm not waiting anymore. This is how I lost a man. Waiting to be evacuated. It's not going to happen to me again."

There was nothing more I could say to warn him. Swim leg and all, he slid down into the water, barely making a ripple in the surface.

Now I realized the reason behind his decision to try the rescue by himself, his impatience to get it done now. It was his compassion for the whale, of course.

It was also Corporal Mike Edison, KIA.

Even with a handicap, he was an amazingly strong swimmer. He had once described the training for a Navy SEAL, and it was brutal, beyond brutal, even, to build nearly superhuman fearlessness, strength, and endurance. Now I watched his arms pull against the water, like it didn't exist, as he glided effortlessly and silently to the whale.

As I watched him, I knew this was a man I could love deeply. He was kind and caring and had a goodness that matched the depth of the ocean and beyond. He was a good man, he had compassion and a good soul. "Please take care of him," I prayed to the sea. Her eye followed Sam, but she continued to lie quietly as he swam to her flukes. They were wrapped in the netting as though it had been knit into place. He reached toward her and touched her gently. She still didn't move. Then he reached down and pulled the dive knife from its sheath, bringing it close to her body. He started sawing at the nylon strands very slowly, holding them away from her body. A few threads flew apart. He worked at it some more. Another blow of mist and air, loud and long, startled him, and he paddled backward, away from her. She moved sideways toward the boat, and managed to hit it. It wobbled. Sam swam behind her, waiting another minute until she settled before he started cutting again. She could kill him with one move.

It was going to take hours, it seemed. He cut relentlessly into the nylon, strand by strand, pulling it with his fingers, forcing it to unravel faster. He pulled a handful upward and cut again and again at it until it suddenly released into a knotted bundle of mesh, which he tossed up to me to get it out of the way. I dropped it onto the deck. Freed from its tangles, her tail suddenly slammed the water.

"Whoa!" Sam yelped, startled. It sent him flying several feet. I could hear his labored breathing. His lungs were struggling to support his efforts.

She was trying to free herself, but she was still too trapped. She tried again to push away and her tail slipped under the boat. It rose and dropped suddenly, knocking me off balance. I pulled myself back up and braced.

She blew again. I hoped she wasn't getting impatient. Or angry? Vincent was getting frantic in the cabin and I went up to calm him and try calling the rescue again. No luck. I grabbed Vincent's rope and he pulled me down to the deck to the freed gill net. I tied him to a cleat and commanded him to lie down, out of the way. He knew what I wanted and lay quietly, his head between his paws.

An hour and a half passed, and Sam had worked his way to her dorsal fin cutting at the net with meticulous slashes. The work was tedious, thread after thread, the remaining mesh pieces growing taut as the weight got transferred to them. Slice after slice, when suddenly it gave way. Her top fin was freed. She shuddered, but remained calm.

He slipped between the whale and the boat to cut the netting from her ventral fin. She blew weakly several times in succession, but lay in the water without moving. Her baby was swimming in frantic circles, blowing loudly, diving, coming closer. Sam moved quickly, and I could hear him reassuring them both, patting the female's massive side. She was more than twice the length of the boat, I estimated a good forty feet. She moved sideways and almost caught Sam. He quickly pushed himself toward her flukes to avoid getting crushed. She tried to move again, maybe she was in pain, or thought she was free, but she swung her body back and forth for a few minutes and he stopped working on her. It wasn't long before she exhausted herself again.

"Good girl!" I called softly over the side of the boat. "Be calm. Be a good girl."

Sam worked tirelessly. Cutting methodically, pulling the net away from her, cutting at it some more. It was slow, painstaking work and it endangered him every second. I lost track of time, the hours of the day seemed to crawl past us, time hung still as Sam worked, and this behemoth creature, understanding somehow that we were trying to save her, stayed calm.

"I think I'm nearly finished!" Sam finally called. His voice was raspy and his lips were dusky from the cold. He swam back into position next to the boat and handed his dive knife up to me. "Give me the other knife!" he called up. "The big one." I reached down and we swapped knives. Only a little more netting wrapped around her second pectoral fin, but it took another hour. His face was drained with fatigue now and I worried for him.

"She's free!" he suddenly called out. He looked jubilant. He threw a large swirl of gill netting up to me; I just barely caught it. The nylon threads were jagged where they had been cut apart, a wild mess of clear, wiry strands that were invisible to oncoming fish. Its whole purpose was to entangle, and it had done its job exceedingly well. The whale shook herself for a moment, then, realizing she was free, dove, disappearing under the water. She emerged about twenty feet ahead, the calf next to her, and blew hard and long.

We cheered. There is nothing more redeeming than to save an animal brought nearly to its death by the carelessness and indifference of humans. She was a mammal, and she needed to breathe air. A few minutes later she was turned in the water in order to nurse her calf.

"I need to get into the boat." Sam suddenly sounded exhausted. He reached for the boarding ladder, struggled up the vertical steps, and finally hoisted himself over the railing and fell into the boat. He had given almost more than he was capable of giving and was totally spent. He sat down on the padded deck bench, leaned back, closed his eyes, and fell into a wordless stupor.

"Sam, look," I said as the two whales leapt together in the water. Our whales. He turned around and watched with me.

She knew she was free. They dove down together and an instant later both emerged about several hundred feet away from us, breaching the water, rising jubilantly through the air, then diving again, their tails silhouetted against the sky like pieces of art, before vanishing into the ocean. The mother was exhilarated, fired up with the knowledge that she had been freed and she was still alive. She breached again and again, joyful and full of life. She knew she had almost been lost and seemed grateful, wanting to show us that she appreciated what Sam had done for her.

Life, life, she seemed to say. She was so full of energy now. She would live. She would flourish. Everything was forgotten in the joy of being alive. She vanished beneath the water again and leapt up, filled with elation. The water splashed like a monument around her. A large, noisy spout blasted from her blowhole, and she leapt again. A moment later, she breached with her whole body and allowed it to fall against the water's surface with a huge slapping sound, as though she wanted to feel the water hit her with the fullness of its element, a jubilatory acknowledgment of her existence and her triumph and her continuing existence. The baby swam in happy circles around her.

"Wow, look at that," Sam said, awed. "She *appreciates* it. She knows—she *knows.*"

I knew what he was saying, I felt it, too. It was an epiphany. Life was precious, and precarious, and she was celebrating her return to safety. Her joy touched me. It was something Sam and I would remember forever.

He watched her intently until she and the calf were gone from the horizon. Her mood had stayed celebratory;; she dove and leapt and played with an abandon that made me jealous. It was pure love for life, pure joy for being free to live it. Sam watched her with a greediness. "Wow. That was so good," he murmured. "That was so good!" He had tears in his eyes, watching her, and reached over to take my hand.

"You gave her that," I said. "She is thanking you for her life."

He looked up at me. "I did, didn't I?" he said softly.

We sat together on the bench, not budging for a long time. Sam's eyes were closed and his head was tilted back. The boat rocked gently on the waves, keeping its position, and I stared out over the water, watching the blow of other whales in the distance, watching as fishing boats began moving past us, heading for the harbor, gazing at the whale-watch ferries sailing past, passengers waving. I realized how much I loved the water as I sat there quietly, next to Sam, watching, the whales rising from the ocean with their mouths agape, the shearwaters risking all for a quick steal of fish, the gulls cutting sharp angles of air above. I loved the water. I loved the feeling of the sea lifting the boat across its back, the cutting salt in the air, the air, the air was just a lighter part of the sea. How had I lost that part of myself? How had I forgotten how deeply this all ran within me? The sky was growing overcast. We needed to get back. I touched Sam's arm and he sprung awake.

"I wasn't asleep," he said. "I was thinking about things. It all disappears so fast, I was trying to put things together and make it all fit."

"And did they fit?"

He looked beleaguered. "I'm trying so hard."

And then he took my hands in both of his and looked into my eyes. "Give me time, Aila," he said. "I have to get myself together. Please give me time. You won't be sorry."

Chapter 40

We were ready to go home, but neither of us made a move to do it. We sat on the deck, weary, hypnotized by the movement of the water, lulled into a reverie by the cry of the gulls and the feel of the sea winds on our faces. We didn't speak, and Sam looked like he had dozed off a little. The sun was moving behind us, finished with the day.

Vincent was getting restless. He'd had enough of the sea and his dinnertime was approaching. He walked over to Sam and started to lick his face, paying special attention to Sam's eyes and mouth, then tried to revive him by barking straight into his ear. After all, what is a pit bull for, if not to keep you on your toes? Sam opened his eyes and smiled at the dog.

"You want some coffee?" I asked.

He nodded and stood up and stretched. "I better get us home," he said, and gave me a quick hug with his ice-cold body before heading for the cabin.

I went belowdecks to make us coffee in the small galley. I hadn't seen it before and it was a typical boat galley, set up neat as a pin. I looked around, poking into the cabinets and the dorm-size fridge, turning on the small four-burner stove, open-ing and folding the table, testing out one of the two chairs like Goldilocks. It was a perfect little kitchen, a *real* galley, and I thought about my own, more commercial one. This was every-thing to me. I realized how much I loved being able to tinker about in it, proud that it was my family establishment that had been named for the heart of a boat. I loved cooking food and serving it up, knowing that the customers who came in were happy and satisfied with my efforts and returned to me, again and again. Where would I go if I gave it up? I loved the water. I couldn't live without seeing it every day. I had made it an en-emy, but truly it wasn't. My father and Dan had made a foolish mistake and the water takes what it takes, indifferent to the consequences, like any predator in nature.

The coffee was ready, and I poured out two mugs and caught myself smiling. Maybe Sam would be at my side someday, maybe not, but for the first time in two years I was happy again with my place under the stars.

I brought the mugs of coffee topside and handed Sam his. He sipped it gratefully. I also found a blanket and wrapped it around his ice-cold shoulders.

"Are you okay?" I asked. He nodded. He was at the wheel and I sat in the cabin and watched him. Sometimes there was a spout on the water and we both turned to it, wondering if it was our whale.

The trip home was quiet. By the time Sam steered us past the Race Point lighthouse, it was dusk, but we could see its white structure standing a stark forty-five feet against the graying sky.

"That's the marker that we're going to be all right," he said, pointing to the lighthouse. "The light tells us that we have re-turned from the end of the world and we're going to get home safely, and see our families and live out the rest of our lives well."

I left him steering the boat and went down to stand on the bow because I've always loved the view coming into the bay, sail-ing past P-town, sailing toward the slips and familiar lights of the houses that lined the beach of Fleetbourne, there was such peace in it. The pain and the ghosts and the fears had been left behind; ahead of me was my life and whatever I would make of it.

We sailed across the bay and I watched as Sam docked the boat with skill. I helped him tie it up and we gathered our stuff and stepped onto the slip and climbed the stairs to the pier.

Sam took me into his arms and kissed me. "I'll call you tomorrow," he said. "I promise. There are some things I need to get a handle on."

I opened the Galley the next morning with a certain anticipation and happiness. It was all mine, from the unfashionable T-shirts, to the cheesy postcards, to the Portuguese rolls that sat in the front cases.

I didn't know if Mrs. A would show up, I didn't know if I would hear from Sam again, but no matter. I turned on the flattop and started the coffee and checked the bacon and listened to the Maritime station so I could write the forecast on the whiteboard and Vincent ate his breakfast behind the counter and I set up the day's mail in the back room and it was all good.

Mrs. A came in, wearing a pretty red and gray print blouse over jeans with a red hijab. I always looked forward to her color combinations and rather enjoyed them. She was reserved and polite and went about her normal chores as she did any other morning. She had just finished carrying in the bread and doughnuts for the day when she turned to me.

"Okay," she started. "Sam talked to me last night, and tells me that he is going to make changes in his life."

I didn't know how to answer that. "I don't know what to say to you," she went on. "I am not angry with you. I don't own him and I have to respect what he wishes to do, though it breaks my heart into a million pieces."

"I understand," I said. When Sam and I rescued the whale, for a little while, we felt as though we almost owned her. She was *our* whale, her life was under our management. I wanted to call out to her to be careful. To watch out for danger. I wanted her to stay around so that I could protect her every day. Of course I knew it was silly. That she was the curator of her own life, that she had survived by her skills all these years and would do so again. Sam and I had been given a small opportunity to ensure her survival and it was part of our stewardship to leave her alone after that.

I touched Mrs. A's arm. "He loves you so," I said, but she looked sad.

"I love him, too," she said. "But he is a man, and I have to let him make his decisions."

"He's a wonderful man," I said. "Because of you."

"So are you planning to marry him?" she asked.

"I don't know. I care for him a great deal," I said honestly, "but we're not up to that yet. I promise that when we decide, you will be the first to know."

She acknowledged my words with a shrug. "He could do worse," she said, and finished setting up the doughnuts.

I didn't hear from him for two weeks. I guessed that he was busy, I know I was. I was reluctant to call him, whatever he was deciding would have to be of his own desires, without interference.

Larry called me to set up a date, a calendar date, not a social date, to talk about the Galley, and I was curious. He picked me up in his weather-beaten blue car, looking cheerful in a yellow shirt, jeans, and his red sneakers.

He drove us to Orleans, a lovely little town about half an hour south of Fleetbourne, to a breakfast place that served hubcap-sized waffles that Larry had read about and now needed to carry out his "research."

He was not disappointed. His plate came stacked like a tire store, and he rubbed his hands together in anticipation before digging in. I had an omelet. We ate in silence for a few minutes before he pointed to my plate with his fork.

"So, how's that omelet?" he asked, flashing his eyebrows up and down a few times.

"Great," I said, then understood what he meant. "Want to try it?" He forked up some of my eggs in a nanosecond. To be fair, they were replaced by a generous portion of waffle. We swapped my English muffin for two pieces of his bacon, he tasted my coffee, and I sipped his chai tea and we both shared a piece of cherry pie. I loved his enthusiasm over food.

"So," he finally said, "I wanted to talk to you about the Galley."

"Talk to me."

"I think you've got a great place there," he started, "but I think it could be better. It's an anachronism."

"That's part of its charm," I countered.

"But it could use some modernizing," he continued. "Some upgrades that would make it easier for you."

I listened as he outlined a few ideas he had, ending with "I know it'll increase your business, and I think that's what you'd want, a single gal like yourself. A thriving business."

I promised him I would think about it and keep my options open. We enjoyed a second cup of coffee and tea together and climbed back into his car.

He drove me to the Galley and we parked outside for a few minutes, trying to stump each other with old show tunes, two-bar maximum, and laughing at each other's singing. His laugh was infectious, and I was enjoying his company.

"Don't let your guard down," he said, suddenly serious. "I have a feeling that fool who broke your window is not finished."

"I guess we'll see what happens," I said. "I can't do anything until he does something."

"True," he said, then got out of the car to open my door.

We stood there for a moment, grinning at each other. "Thank you for a great morning," I said.

"All options are on the table," he said, and leaned over to give me a little kiss me on the cheek.

* * *

I heard from Sam a few days later. "I would love to see you," he said. He had called my cell phone while I was at the Galley. I didn't give Mrs. A any indication that I was talking to him. "There's something I want to ask you," he added.

That night Sam came to my house with a dozen roses, a box of chocolates, and a dog biscuit in his pocket, right out of the Manual of First Dates. Vincent and I invited him in. He was so polished up. His hair was neatly trimmed; he had a brand-new shirt, new slacks; even his leg was polished. He came into the kitchen, filling it with his height and big frame, like a gentle bear. I offered him iced tea and he sat down, looking earnest and nervous. Vincent immediately felt the need to comfort him by shedding some fresh hair over his slacks. Sam reached down absentmindedly to pet him.

"So what's on your mind?" I said, handing Sam his iced tea and sitting down opposite him. He gulped his drink. Vincent hit him on the arm just in case I had served Sam something and forgotten to serve him.

"Should I send him out of the room?" I asked. "Is he bothering you?"

"No, no," Sam said. "He's part of everything."

Right answer.

Sam sipped at the iced tea and sipped again. I got up to pour some for myself. It looked like it was going to be a long conversation.

"I just wanted to let you know that I am looking for an apartment for myself somewhere around here so that I can move out and be more on my own."

"That's a good idea," I replied. "It's a big step for you." Then I thought "big step" might not have been the most sensitive thing I could have said.

"And I was thinking, I really loved restoring *The Wentletrap*. I want to set up a shop to repair and restore boats. Maybe here or maybe in P-town."

"I'm glad you're planning to do something you love," I said.

"And"—he took my hand and held it across the table—"you

know how I feel about you. You're one of the best things that came into my life."

He stood up and held out his arms. I stood up and went to him and got enveloped. He kissed me very gently. "And then," he said, "and then I would like to court you and Vincent properly. Real dates, and dinners, and everything you deserve."

So I didn't get a proposal; I got a plan.

And that was fine with me.

Chapter 41

Maybe it was the bright sparkling window and the new white marble counter, or maybe it was Larry calling it an anachronism, but suddenly the whole Galley looked tired and old and shabby in contrast. Suddenly the old wooden floors that had been trod upon since the time my great-grandfather became postmaster and decided to set up a milk and egg stand next to the mailroom looked beyond worn. They had bevels and dips and more than one customer carrying a cup of coffee had taken a funny step that resulted in a messy spill. I remember a favorite game that Shay and I played as children consisted of each of us holding a little ball and letting it go to see whose rolled downhill to the opposite wall the fastest. The food display cases had been installed around World War II so that the locals— women whose husbands and sons had been sent to war and who didn't have transportation to the big stores—were able to shop. Though the cases still kept everything cold and fresh, their aging lights were starting to flicker and dim and sometimes turn colors that gave the food an unearthly glow. Even the flattop had problems in the form of cold spots that Shay had dubbed the "no-cook zones."

I had two solutions. Modernize or modernize.

I discussed it with Shay and she had a dozen suggestions, like adding a café, a bakery, and a dog rescue that she claimed Vincent told her he wanted, since there wasn't one in all of Fleetbourne. I discussed it with Larry, who was ecstatic and had a dozen more ideas: table service, Wi-Fi, a small stage up front for musicians, and possibly a large rack for newspapers and magazines from all over the world. Mrs. A was taken with the idea of a little café like the ones in Jordan, filled with pastries and jams and sweet teas and coffees that came, finally, with enough sugar. She even volunteered to run it and I knew she would be perfect, since she was naturally bossy and always more than happy to run anything. She had the drive to organize the entire Middle East, put everyone in their place, tidy up the borders, and have them all fed by five p.m.

I put a suggestion box for customers on the front counter and it was filled in two days, most of the suggestions dealing with food service: they loved the food, hated eating it in their cars.

It seemed I had no choice. We were destined to redo the Galley and build a café.

Dan's architect firm generously donated the plans. In keeping with its name, the Galley café would be bright and nautical but not enough to make you seasick. I sent out for bids, which came back ranging from practical amounts to prices high enough to build the café on the moon and provide bus service, too. Larry helped me sift through all the offers; Sam helped me interview the contractors, his six-foot-three height and bulky muscles intimidating them into sincere contracts.

We pulled it all together and were ready to build in one month. Larry helped me secure a government loan for single businesswomen with one dog, apparently overlooked by the current administration. I chose tiles and colors and windows and light fixtures and a new flattop and several new cold food cases, and eventually I decided to keep the old-fashioned look for the original store, only with new fixtures. "Otherwise," I told Sam, "my family ghosts might think they're in the wrong place and get themselves lost."

It was almost as much fun as shopping for shoes.

The construction finally started. We kept the Galley open for business while the word got around that the Galley was being turned into a spa, a car wash, and an amusement park. I said yes to every inquiry.

But the days dragged on. We went through two more full moons and one scary night when Shay had early labor pains. She was fine and spent her days sitting in her wheelchair at the construction site as honorary general contractor.

Sam found a house to buy with a veterans loan, right in Fleetbourne, with a huge garage that he immediately turned into a boat shop. His neighbors immediately complained about the noise and he turned it back into a garage, then found a garage in P-town that had been a house that had been turned into a head shop, which he turned into a boat shop.

We kept building.

The building inspector, Mr. Harry Dickman, weighed in on the project. He found that the roses that served as foundation shrubs were planted half an inch too close to the foundation and had to be moved so if there was a fire the firemen could squeeze behind them with their hoses. He decided there should be a sink behind the front counter because we needed to wash our hands before we made sandwiches and the sink by the food cases was too far away to be hygiene effective. And that we needed a second sink at the front counter for pots and pans even though I didn't cook anything at the front counter and had a sink in the back kitchen for that. He decided that we couldn't use the Marine Conditions Board because we weren't an official organ of the National Weather Service and we might be endangering people with our handwritten information. He determined that the potato chip rack had to be moved away from the breads because they could cross-contaminate. "And do what?" I asked him, but he wasn't sure.

"He sure lives up to his name," Shay sighed one day when I was complaining/whining over Sandwiches with her.

"*Harry?*" I asked, baffled.

"His other name," she said.

It was August when we got our Certificate of Occupancy. The parking lot had been moved twice because the original site hosted a nest for the piping plover and it couldn't be disturbed. The bathroom was finally working after a three-day discussion as to where to build the septic tank if it couldn't be built near the inlet from the bay that ran behind the store, making us the only establishment with a sewage pipe running under the roadway to a vacant lot across the street.

We even built a secure chain-link-fenced backyard for Vincent with an all-weather doghouse and security camera that transmitted to a TV monitor behind the front counter.

The end of the tourist season was upon us. We made hundreds of lunches to go, answered hundreds of questions, and gave hundreds of directions on the best way to leave Cape Cod before Labor Day. There was really only one way, we told our customers, one long road, the Grand Army of the Republic Road, but they kept hoping for a side road, a secret road, to beat the traffic. Shay and I always get a private giggle out of it when they ask how to beat the traffic. I always think, *Beat the traffic? You* are *the traffic!*

The café was finished and ready to officially open. I hung an OPEN FOR BUSINESS sign across the new front window and people came in to ask where the new business was. Mrs. A got everyone confused by greeting them by the front door with a bow on her head and the Jordanian custom of a tiny welcoming cup of strong, bitter Arabic coffee, which immediately killed coffee sales until I could convince her to use American coffee with milk and sugar.

Miss Phyllis donated 10 percent off coupons to everyone who came into Follicles for a haircut.

We christened the café like a ship, with me smashing a bottle of champagne across the white-painted post and chain fencing that had to properly observe town rules and match all the other establishments with white-painted posts and chain fencing, giving Fleetbourne the air of a pristine brig.

Mrs. A ran the front counter. We ultimately decided that people could order their food and carry it themselves to the café to eat and chat. I ran the kitchen, with Mrs. A's unsolicited and chronic input and guidance, and we ran through a variety of stock clerks, cleanup crew, errand runners, kitchen helpers, and dog walkers, sometimes all on the same day.

But we had all our customers return. Mrs. Skipper and The Skipper, her homicidal husband, and Mrs. Hummings, the town clerk who dropped by on a regular basis for coffee, a buttered Portuguese roll, and a lively exchange of town news about all the other residents who made Fleetbourne the town it was. I was pretty content with the way things were going and went to bed at night, sometimes alone and sometimes not, with a sense of satisfaction.

Like the steady light of the sun and the varied light of the moon and stars, I thought things would always be so, the constant stream of business, daily and seasonal and lasting forever.

But there were stirrings of trouble.

Larry heard the news first and then there were murmurings here and there from customers. There was going to be a demonstration. Another march. Something evil was coming my way.

The success of the Galley was irking someone. Perhaps a certain car salesman with nefarious ties who skulked around in the darkness with white bricks in his hand. He had finished paying for his crime by reimbursing me for damages and had spent two months working at community service, which had really stuck in his craw. Plus I had hired a Muslim, I had a black lawyer, and it apparently gave him no rest. He felt he had been punished for accidentally breaking a window; I needed to learn a lesson and he just happened to have a group of supporters who were able and ready to teach it.

I was to be targeted for another round of hate marchers. And there was no telling what they would do.

The thought of it frightened me. I was proud of what I had built and dreaded seeing my Galley ruined in any way. The prospect of my customers being terrorized to the point of deciding it was too daunting to patronize the store anymore broke my heart. Sam steamed clean his old uniform and promised to locate and round up the men from his old unit, or at least some of the men he had met at a Veterans' Hospital outpost in P-town where he went for therapy.

"To do what?" I asked him. He didn't answer me.

"What if it gets ugly?" I asked Larry, remembering the torches and the clubs.

"I'm training people to respond a certain way," was all Larry would tell me. "I'll take care of everything. I have a few ideas." He put his arm around my shoulder reassuringly.

I was given a list of things to bake, loaves of white bread, angel food cake, sugar cookies. Mysterious phone calls were made from the Galley kitchen and things were arranged behind my back, which left me plenty of time to agonize over what was coming.

"You've been through enough," Larry kept repeating. "Let me handle this."

"Exactly what are you handling?" I would ask him, but he never answered me.

The hate march, Larry learned, was set for Friday morning, when the Galley, as usual, was filled with customers shopping for the weekend. I made Shay promise to stay away and decided to keep Vincent home that day, for his own safety. But Larry took me aside and gave me a big hug to calm me down.

"You know how I love parties?" he asked.

I nodded.

"Well, this will be the best party I will ever throw," he reassured me. "I promise."

Chapter 42

I awoke early on Friday morning, only to find that a mist had slipped in from the bay and had blanketed Fleetbourne in a soft fog, giving the streets a benign, velvety appearance. It was deceptive. Fleetbourne is an old fishing village and fishing villages are tough. The folks are used to brutal storms and dangerous water, and boating mishaps, and tough fishing seasons, and still they thrive, optimistic and strong. There is little that can cow them, and I should have remembered that.

The hate marchers were due in front of the Galley by noon. Apprehensive, I called Larry. He had found himself a little apartment in P-town by now, as Shay and Terrell had turned their guest room into a double baby room.

"What should I do?" I asked Larry.

"Open as usual," he said, "and get ready."

Ready for what, he didn't say.

Sam had spent the night with me and left even before I awakened. Vincent was sitting by my feet waiting for breakfast. It almost seemed like a normal day.

* * *

The Galley was already opened by Mrs. A when I got there. She was wearing a red blouse with her blue jeans, and a red, white, and blue hijab with a fresh apron. She had the new flat-top already warming up, the two coffee dispensers that were sitting at their own new coffee bar filled with water, and a basket of coffee pods next to them. The newspapers were displayed on their new rack, the Portuguese breads were in their new cases, and a peek into the café revealed that each table had a centerpiece of red, white, and blue plastic flowers with a small American flag waving from the middle. It was a statement to be sure, but one I hoped would not be hosting the hate marchers.

Larry arrived with a clipboard filled with papers. And a whistle around his neck.

"You think the hate marchers are going to listen to your whistle while they're burning down my store?" I said to him.

"No," he said. "It isn't for them." He paused. "And the only thing that'll be burning today is the barbecue."

"We don't do barbecue," I reminded him.

"You will be."

Hosting the hate marchers with barbecue seemed a little too hospitable for me, but before I could ask him anything further Terrell pulled up outside and parked. Terrell hopped out and took Shay's wheelchair from the backseat, then helped Shay out of the car and into the chair.

"Oh no," I moaned. "If there's a problem, Shay can get hurt. Those thugs won't respect a pregnant woman in a chair."

Larry just opened the front door to let them in. Terrell wheeled Shay up the new ramp and through the door. Shay was wearing red and white and her chair was festooned with red, white, and blue streamers woven through its wheels. Apparently, Larry had established a dress code for the hate march.

"I had to come and support you," Shay said to me as I leaned down to give her a hug, but my heart was fluttering with fear.

I offered to make breakfast for anyone, but everyone had already eaten.

My stomach had joined my heart flutters and I passed on

breakfast as well. "Why don't you just relax with a cup of coffee?" Larry suggested, but I was too nervous.

Of course my first customers of the day were The Skipper and Mrs. Skipper, determinedly earlier than anyone else, so that Mrs. Skipper could get first pick of the freshest cherry Danishes we had. First she needed to buy a box of Cheerios. "The Skipper likes Cheerios if he can't have his kippers," she told me when she placed the box on the counter. "And I'll have two teas with my Danish this morning."

"I like Cheerios also," I murmured as she pored over the Danishes, selecting the two plumpest. "I also like cherry Danish."

"Well, if you had been my child, I would have given you Cheerios for breakfast instead of that awful garbage you were fed," she said. "I felt very sorry for you."

"I thrived on whatever I was given," I countered. "My grandmother did the best she could."

"I felt sorry for her, too," Mrs. Skipper said gently. "Very sorry."

It was a strange comment. I wasn't quite sure what she meant; but it was something I was going to find out. She paid for her purchases and turned to her husband. "Donald, I'm ready to leave."

The Skipper joined her by the front door. "We're going to stay right outside," Mrs. Skipper announced before leaving. "Brought two lawn chairs and we're going to watch the festivities. I hear it's going to be a hoot."

At ten-thirty the streets outside were beginning to fill. I recognized the demonstrators. They were Fleeties, almost all of them, dressed patriotically and setting things up along the street. Someone parked an ice-cream truck and someone else parked a huge barbecue van. There were hot dog trucks and taco trucks and balloon and hat vendors. American enterprise was catering a hate march.

"No," said Larry. "They all came here to support you. You'll be glad later that they are here."

* * *

Someone was setting up a table next to the Galley and some-how had all the loaves and cakes I had baked for the day. Over their display was a sign of an upheld fist holding a loaf of bread. Underneath, in big letters, it read: WHITE FLOUR, NOT WHITE POWER! GET IT HERE. An obvious mockery of the white power hate marchers.

There were other signs, too. HATE ONLY BELONGS IN THE DICTIONARY being held, of course, by one of the English teachers at Fleetbourne High. And GO BACK TO YOUR MOTHER'S BASEMENT AND GET LAID, YOU'LL FEEL BETTER. And rainbow flags all over the place. The crowd had not only come to support me; they had come to support everybody, and I felt my eyes fill with tears. The Galley started to overflow with customers who wished me luck and stayed to order Sandwiches and some of Mrs. A's more exotic foods. Mrs. A and I worked the front counter pretty much like Shay and I used to.

At eleven, Larry held the door open and summoned me out-side. "Listen," he said, pointing down the road. I stood there in front of the Galley to listen. The crowd cheered when they saw me and yelled their support. I waved, but I really wanted to throw up.

"So you hear them coming?" Larry asked.

I didn't hear anything.

And then I did. A soft roar from somewhere that seemed to float from the road that led to P-town. A roar? It had a rhythm to it. I didn't get it at first.

Then the marchers appeared as they came toward the Galley and I heard the chanting. "Oh God," I murmured, and felt my muscles tighten, thinking it might be the last day my beautiful new Galley would be standing.

Suddenly the chanting became clearer. "Bigotry! Spot it and stop it!" over and over.

They were coming down the road in a ragtag fashion. Not really marching, more like strolling. And chatting. And laugh-ing. They couldn't possibly be the MARCHERS.

They weren't.

Apparently, P-town was emptying out and heading for Fleet-bourne in support. They filled the road, not in the least bit organized. There was a painted school bus somewhere behind them, driving about six miles an hour, filled with the drag queens from the theaters on Commercial Street waving from the windows and hooting and hanging on to their wigs. There was the P-town Ukelele Finger-Pluckers, a marching band of no real renown but overflowing with goodwill, playing a ragged version of "Here Comes the Sun": there was the tuba player who often gave spontaneous one-man concerts in Portuguese Square: playing something unidentifiable. There were demon-strators from every business, every local home, every building, every vacation home, swelling through the streets and totally blocking the road. Some were dressed in shark costumes, some dressed as mermaids, while some wore humpback whale hats, pinwheel hats, baseball caps, and live parrots on their shoulders. They carried fishing poles over their shoulders, poop scoopers, rainbow-colored flags and posters with pictures of pandas that read: "Black, white, and Asian, what difference does it make?"

"I told them to bring whatever they have," Larry whispered into my ear, sounding pleased.

Next came the contingent of dogs. P-town is famous for be-ing dog friendly, and strolling through its streets with your dog has become a rite of passage and a beloved tradition. The dogs were now here, marching, being carried, some of them sitting in baby strollers, some wearing signs proclaiming that Dogs Love Everyone and So Where Are the Cats?

When the bus reached the front of the Galley, its doors opened and twenty drag queens gingerly stepped out in their sparkling stilettos and joined the marchers. I recognized my friends Lynne Guini and Ella Vator and Cherie Danish among them. They brought signs that read: Free Willy and Free My Willy and carried bags of sparkles that they liberally distrib-uted at the crowds in an airborne manner.

One of the last to arrive was a bus from the Veterans Ad-ministration. It also pulled in front of the Galley and stopped.

The doors opened and Sam was lowered to the ground on a hydraulic step. He was in his old uniform and he looked striking. I ran to his side and we kissed. Behind him were thirty or forty veterans being helped from the bus, men and women who received their rehab from the VA outpost in P-town. Wheelchairs were snapped together; men with arms missing, legs missing, all veterans, all heroes, had come to protest hate and declare their support for all Americans.

It was a demonstration of love, a block party, a street festival that ran the length of Fleetbourne and overflowed back to P-town, that went on for hours. They sang and they cheered and they hugged one another and they gave spontaneous speeches about nothing and everything that mattered.

By ten at night, they started dispersing. The hate marchers couldn't make their way to Fleetbourne since all the streets had been totally blocked off. They had been stuffed back into the holes they had crawled out from and no one missed them and no one cared.

"I heard that they're going to try Boston tomorrow," Larry said. "We'll see how that goes."

He informed me the next day that Boston had totally blocked off the hate marchers with hundreds of peaceful demonstrators. Apparently our little town of Fleetbourne, with some help, found itself ahead of the curve.

But I had no illusions, not anymore. There are good people and there are morally undeveloped people who skid off on the wrong path. The Galley remained standing, proud and unmolested. It had been tested and it had prevailed.

Chapter 43

The summer ended with a full moon. A perigean super moon, in fact, extra big and extra bright, with high tides and a spectacular cosmic show. And it was well deserved by us below.

It took two days to clean the streets of Fleetbourne. The Fleetbourne Highway Department, which was a misnomer since we didn't really have any highways, swept through the town and then pumped water from the bay, an illegal act, to wash it all away. The Galley received the bill for it, and I filed a protest with Lorna Hummings, the town clerk.

"You wanna play, you gotta pay," she told me when I visited her at Town Hall. I sighed. It seemed back to business as usual for my town, so I paid it. It totaled only 102 dollars and 49 cents, the 49 cents being used to cover the cost of the letter sent to the Galley to inform us of the charges. I did receive a discount, though, of 15 dollars, since I had never gotten money back from Vincent's license when he got his dangles cut off.

The Galley became a popular hangout spot. The little bell that tinkled over the door never stopped ringing and Mrs. A finally pulled it down. "It is not music to *my* ears," she declared. "I will find something else." She brought in an electronic chime that went off every time the door opened and closed. It sounded like the chime on the new microwave and sent her galloping to check on phantom food. After a week she complained that her feet hurt and we reinstalled the bell.

The super moon was affecting everyone. People seemed politer, calmer, kinder. Of course, it could have been fatigue from partying for twelve straight hours that Friday, but it seemed we all learned something about one another. We weren't perfect, some of us were just wonderful and some of us were far from perfect, but we had learned we could live together and respect one another and help one another out as most of us had always done. The rest were learning a thing or two about compassion and inclusion and acceptance, and as long as they were willing to change, we would be willing to associate with them and guide them further.

Shay informed me that she had raised several thousand dollars while sitting in her wheelchair with a collection box on her lap and a large sign asking for donations for a dog rescue. "Everyone just looked at me and was just so kind!" she marveled more than once. She had been moved to the parking lot during the street festival and I suppose that the sight of a beautiful pregnant woman sitting in a wheelchair with a donation box just might have stimulated public sympathy and generosity.

Mrs. Huggins agreed to put the issue before the town board and hinted that she had enough information on every board member to get the proposal for a dog shelter ratified. It was to be built next to the Galley and called Vincent's House, which gave me a sneaking feeling that the Galley was going to foot a large part of the bill for it.

I also had been thinking about The Skipper and Mrs. Skipper and her remarks about my grandmother. A few days later, when I just accidentally happened to be taking Vincent for a stroll down their street, I felt emboldened to pay them a visit. Their house was a small cape with pale green shutters, the name Healey on the mailbox with a gold anchor painted underneath, and a large crab apple tree that draped over most of the front lawn. Their old green Ford was in the driveway and The Skipper himself was asleep, stretched out in a lawn chair, sunning himself on the porch. I tied Vincent to the mailbox and walked right past the snoring Skipper and rang the bell. Mrs. Skipper answered the door in good time, frail and bent. She didn't seem surprised to see me.

"Aila!" she said, opening the door wider. "Come in. I thought you might be paying me a visit."

"I hope you don't mind," I said. "I wanted to talk to both of you. Should we waken The Skipper?"

"No, let the old fart sleep," she said, and gestured for me to follow her inside.

She walked bent over, weighted down by her years. We passed through a sea blue living room with old photos of fishing boats on every wall; I followed her into the kitchen. "Would you like some tea?"

"Thank you," I said, then realized my mistake. She was in her nineties, as far as I knew, and moved very slowly. Ten minutes later, she had the teacups on the table. Ten minutes after that, the tea bags were in the cups.

"So you came to talk about your grandmother," she said, shakily holding a pot of boiling water over my lap. I nodded. "Well, she once was my best friend, you know."

I didn't know.

She filled our cups, more or less, then returned the pot and tugged at a cabinet drawer.

"Trying to get us spoons," she said. I opened the drawer for her. She took out two spoons and set them by the cups. "Do you take sugar? Cream?"

Realizing that each ingredient was going to add half an hour of extra time, I lied. "Thank you, no. I take it plain."

"Well, I take both," she said, and proceeded to the refrigerator, where she stood, tugging on the handle.

I got to my feet again, opened the refrigerator for her, and took out a small container of cream.

"Not that one," she said. "That's Donald's. I like the skim."

Another several minutes more we were finally settled. She carefully put sugar and skim milk into her coffee, offered me half a cherry Danish left over from her breakfast, and then leaned back in her chair.

"So, Lorna told me that you were around asking her questions," she said.

"Is what she told me true?"

"What did she tell you?" Mrs. Skipper asked in a patient voice. "Tell me everything." I realized, suddenly, that Mrs. Skipper was lonely. Donald was sleeping like a dead man on the front porch and very likely would continue on to dinner like that. The phone hadn't rung once; no one was rapping on the door to visit. She wanted my visit to last. I quickly shared the information I had gotten from the town clerk. Mrs. Skipper showed no surprise.

"Your grandmother and I were the dearest of friends," she said again. "And I was keeping company with Donald. She hurt me very badly because she flirted with him behind my back."

"She was wrong to do that," I agreed.

"Yes, she was." She took a sip of tea. "And he was a fool," she added. Her eyes were fading into the distance. I know that look. "She was always very pretty, much prettier than me, and he had a fling with her and she got—you know—in the family way."

"I'm sorry," I said.

"And they didn't know what to do when she was ready to have her baby," she continued. "So *my* mother found a place in Boston who would take the baby. They left on the boat when your grandmother was very close to delivering."

I could picture my grandmother bundled up, sitting in the boat, worried and scared.

"I know everyone thinks that I told Donald to throw the baby overboard! What kind of person do people think I am. I *helped* Ida. She had her baby in Boston, a boy, and then they came back." Her voice shook with emotion, I couldn't tell if she was angry or close to tears.

I felt a thrill of relief, though. The child had lived! "I'm so sorry," I said again, reaching over to put my hand on hers.

"The crew was sworn to secrecy, but you know men. After a few drinks, their lips just started flapping," she said. "We were trying to protect your grandmother. She could have had her baby in the street, for all I cared. Her mother didn't want her in the house with a baby! Donald begged me to help."

I felt awful for Mrs. Skipper, betrayed by two important people in her life and gossiped about forever. "Do you know whatever happened to the baby?" I asked.

She shrugged. "Adopted. A nice family. Owned apartment houses. The Winstons or something. That's all I ever found out. It wasn't *my* baby."

We both stood up. I thanked her for the tea and moved to hug her. She grabbed me around the waist and held me tight for a moment, then let me go. "Donald married me after that," she said. "He married me for my money. I knew that. But I didn't care—I just loved him so. Still, I couldn't get over it, I was so hurt—I never gave him the opportunity to sleep in my bed, if you know what I mean. He got his boats, but he never got me."

I hugged her again and she sniffled onto my shoulder.

"Thank you for sharing that with me," I said. She slowly led me to the front of the house.

"She didn't deserve a pretty little girl like you," she said, opening the front door.

I sighed. What could I say about my own grandmother? "She was crazy," I said. "She was just crazy." And heartbroken.

"I always said that," she agreed.

The Skipper was up from his nap and had untied Vincent from the mailbox and was back in his chair, petting him.

"I was right, Florence," he said to Mrs. Skipper as we stepped out to the porch. "I told you we had a dog named Katy. Look! She's finally come back!"

The super moon hung over the nights like a revelation, its light so strong that I couldn't sleep. It was my pleasure now and my nightly custom to sit on the pier with Vincent and sometimes Sam by my side and look straight up, at such an exceptional moon, an optimistic moon, as it bathed us in its radiance.

Sam had moved from his aunt's house and broken his mother's heart, all on the same day. Mrs. A was mostly forgiving, and just to show how much, vowed to bring him his favorite foods every single night.

He was very proud of the little house he had bought in Fleetbourne, and was painting it with his buddies and doing a few repairs before he wanted me to see it. That meant he was making friends at the Veterans Service outpost where he had started therapy, and I was happy for him. He also had a few people who wanted their boats customized and he was excited about that.

Occasionally he would make an appearance at my house with dinner, grinning at the back door with a bag of food and a bouquet of flowers.

But something was bothering me. Of course I had to talk to Shay about it, which meant a trip to her house, since she swore she couldn't even pull on a pair of Terrell's fishing waders over her swollen feet.

The first thing she did, when she met me at the door of her house, was grab my left hand and scrutinize my ring finger. "EH?" she asked.

"That's what we need to talk about," I said, watching her waddle into the kitchen in front of me.

"So what's going on?" she asked over coffee and cakes.

I couldn't put my finger on it, I told her. I always thought that when you fell in love, you were excited and thrilled and wanted to be with your love all the time. It had been that way with me and Dan, and Shay agreed, she and Terrell had spent every moment together. Sam was a wonderful man, I told her, and I loved being with him. Sometimes he brought dinner, sometimes he suggested a movie, or a night out driving somewhere and it was always fun.

"But it's like he's holding something in reserve," I said. "I want to be the most important thing in his life. I want him to break down my door if he can't reach me. Call me all day long until he becomes a pest and I have to tell him to give me space. I want us to talk all night making wonderful plans for the future.

I want him to feel ecstatic to be with me. I want him to shower me with silly little gifts—and occasionally a really nice one."

"Hmmm," was all she said as she rested her hand on her chin, her eyes scrunched together as she listened.

I raised my left hand. "Do you see a ring?" I asked. "Do you see something sparkly that I could show off at the Galley while I'm slicing bologna?"

"First thing I looked for when you came in and I did not see a ring," she agreed.

"I want him to tell me why he bought himself a little house in Fleetbourne without talking to me, since he told me he was making plans for us," I said.

"Hmmm," she said. "Maybe he meant plans for a new boat."

"I want him to be crazy in love with me," I added. "I want *passion*."

We sat together for a long time, sipping coffee and eating our way through a chocolate cake and a strawberry shortcake.

"Okay," I finally said. "I'm going home."

She gave me a hug and waddled next to me as we made our way to the front door.

"By the way, does Larry ever call you?" she asked, just as I was ready to step outside.

"Almost every night," I replied. "He's always got something to tell me, something he read somewhere or heard in his office or recipes he found for the Galley."

"Hmmmm," she said. "Hmmmm."

Chapter 44

The super moon, full of ostentation, was gone and the skies were dark again. Most nights, I sat on the pier, always with Vincent, but less and less with Sam. He was busy, he was working late into the nights on his customers' boats. He was tired, he was fixing his house—I had seen it by now and it was actually a very nice little cape. He had adapted the stairs and put up railings and changed the bathrooms so that he was able to get around comfortably and safely and I knew all of that took a lot of time.

I went boating with him sometimes, enjoying it more and more, and he was finding the freedom to relax and heal. Though we hadn't gotten any closer to following the plan, it didn't bother me as much as I thought it would. We had been good for each other. There are all kinds of moons and all kinds of love and maybe we were just going to remain like a moon in its first quarter.

The summer was recently gone, too, along with the last tourist, the last humpback, the last of the farm-stand tomatoes.

The beach plums were finished and the pumpkins and bushels of corn had arrived. The super moon had yielded its hold on the sky and, a month later, was followed by the affably orange harvest moon. It is the time of the autumnal equinox and the harvest moon rises early in the evening sky, even before the sun sets, bathing the Cape in extraordinary light. It is the time to harvest apples, the last chance to reap what was ripening throughout the summer.

It was the time for Shay to deliver her sons.

An early October morning, and Terrell called me as I was just opening the Galley, to tell me that he was rushing Shay to the hospital.

"We're on our way," his jubilant voice boomed over my cell phone as I was just unlocking the front door. It was a dark morning, a fall morning and the sun was still behind me, not ready to rise yet, but I snapped fully awake with Terrell's words.

"I'll be there," I said, catching his excitement. It was going to be a morning of babies!

I shut off the alarms and turned on the lights and started the flattop and hurriedly ran through all the morning work while waiting impatiently for Mrs. A to arrive. Larry called just as I started setting out the Portuguese rolls.

"Let's go, sister," he fairly shouted into the phone. "We're going to be an auntie and uncle. Do you want me to come get you?"

I answered him with a breathless yes, and cut two generous slices of cranberry pecan bread and made two large cups of coffee to go since we were going to need nourishment for the long ride. Mrs. A finally arrived and I gave her the news.

"Oh!" She clapped her hands together. "We are going to have the babies! I'm so happy. A glorious morning! Praise be to Allah! I can't wait until Sam has children." She would first have to approve of a wife for him, I thought ruefully.

Larry pulled up half an hour later, his brakes squealing to a stop. I jumped into his car and we raced off to Cape Cod Hospital in Hyannis, about forty minutes away.

"I'm so excited," I crowed. "It was a tough pregnancy."

"I know," he replied. "I could barely get through it."

We sipped our coffee and I fed him pieces of bread because he didn't want to be distracted while driving. "Hey," he said. "I don't know if I told you, but I'm opening up a new office in P-town. I love the area and I don't want to commute to Boston anymore. Tons of work here—discrimination cases, mostly, some other stuff, too."

"You're almost a Cape Codder," I said. "You know you have to ride into town on a humpback to make it official."

He shot me a look and we both laughed. The rest of the ride was spent playing our favorite game, guessing show tunes, the new rule being we couldn't hum more than a single bar, although his off-key renditions put me at a disadvantage. We picked up flowers along the way, Larry chose a huge arrangement; I bought two blue teddy bears to sit underneath.

"Planning to spoil them from their first breath," he said.

Shay was in her room asleep. The babies were in the nursery, and Larry and I elbowed each other out of the way for the first glimpse. They were small and tender and so full of innocence that I was brought to tears. They lay next to each other, pale mocha skin, heads full of dark fuzz, so beautiful, in a drifting, gentle sleep.

Larry stood quietly, then bowed his head. "And from His fullness, we have received, grace upon grace," he said, and I looked at him.

"That's biblical." Our eyes met, and suddenly we were hugging each other.

"Always wanted kids," he said.

"Me too," I replied.

We tiptoed into Shay's room. Terrell was sitting next to her bed and took the flowers. Shay's eyes flew open.

"I did it," she said, between kisses and hugs. "It's over."

I laughed. "It's just beginning," I said, and she smiled and fell asleep.

"We named them Lawrence Shaquille and Alonzo Rasheed," said Terrell. "For their meanings."

"They're perfect," Larry and I said together.

Terrell took Shay's hand and stood over her, smiling down at her sleeping form.

Larry took my hand, put a finger to his lips, and led me out the door. We left the new family to be alone, but not ever to be alone again.

The harvest moon had prevailed for almost four nights, its glow not even starting to diminish. The nights were getting chilly, and the skies were brittle with stars. Sam visited me the next night. We ate dinner in almost silence and I knew that things had changed between us. I didn't see him on the pier anymore; I guessed he didn't need to be there.

"Let's take a walk," he suggested after we finished eating our tomato soup and cheese sandwiches, and I agreed. He helped me clear the plates and scraped a few leftovers into Vincent's bowl while I found myself a jacket.

We walked the shoreline and listened to the waves. Vincent followed faithfully, the air was misty from the spray coming in off the bay, and held a real chill. We stood together on the beach and looked out over the water. It reflected the full moon, a harvest of light that covered the bay in a reddish glow.

"I have a few things to tell you," Sam started, and I had a sudden funny taste in my mouth.

"I'm listening."

"You know I go to therapy," he started. "And it's really helping."

I had to agree. It had been a while since he entered a room, and slipped around corners, or sat with his back to the wall, afraid of becoming a target.

"I feel stronger than I've felt in a long time, and I want to say thank you for being there for me."

"It was good for me, too," I said.

"I don't know where things are going," he started, "and I'm grateful you're being patient."

"Mmm."

We walked a little more, then turned to the sea again. It was lapping at the shore like a faithful dog.

"I wanted you to know—we just got a new guy," he said.

"Okay," I said encouragingly.

"Frank Biljac. I guess you know the name."

I did. It was the brick thrower.

"He came in for therapy. He's a vet," he said. "Iraqi War. He helped get rid of Saddam Hussein. But he's really fucked up. He vibrates with hate. His probation officer sent him."

"Ugh."

"Yeah, well, he would like, at some point, to apologize to you."

"No thanks."

I said no more, and we let the matter drop. I could hear him breathing next to me.

He took my hand and faced me. "You know I care so much for you," he said. It was the wrong thing to say. You are not in *love* with somebody if you *care so much* for them. You are not *crazy* in love. I took my hand away.

"Don't," I said. "We were good for each other and we needed each other. I'm so glad for that. Let's keep things the way they are. We are great at being friends." He dropped his head for a moment and then nodded. We started a long, slow walk, side by side, from the water's edge to his car before we kissed good-bye.

I went home and wept. The moon glowed softly through my window, across my walls and my pictures, and I got up to close my shades. There are things that you need to sit in the dark to think about properly. Vincent licked the tears from my face and I wrapped myself around his soft and well-nourished body and we fell asleep together.

Larry called me two nights later.

"Are you busy?" he asked, as he usually did. "I made a duck terrine with haricot verts."

"Did you put slivered almonds on the haricots?" I asked.

"It's implicit in the recipe," he replied. "Are you up for it?"

I had nothing planned for the evening and it sounded wonderful.

"I'll bring it over in about an hour," he said. "And a bottle of wine. Dessert's on you."

"I'm a working girl," I said. "Would you settle for a box of cookies?"

"Depends on the cookies."

I laughed. "Okay," I relented. "I'll see what I can whip up in one hour." I raced through my kitchen; plenty of sugar and flour and butter. I had sugar cookies waiting on his arrival.

True to his word, there was a knock at the back door an hour later. Larry was standing there, holding the terrine, one hand up in the air like a waiter and a bottle of wine under his arm. He gave me a peck on the cheek and I invited him in.

Vincent sniffed him approvingly and settled himself under my chair.

Larry helped me set the table, pour the wine he had brought, and set the terrine out like a centerpiece. "Just experimenting with cooking," he said. "You might want to make it for the Galley."

"It's too grand for the Galley," I demurred.

"But not too grand for us," he proclaimed.

We ate, we toasted the harvest moon that was peeking through my window, we ate cookies and drank wine and talked for hours. Before he left, he stood in front of me by the back door as though pondering something important. "Yes," I said, and he leaned over and kissed me on the lips.

"May I see you again?" he asked.

"I already said yes."

The harvest moon hung so large and fulsome in the night, I could barely sleep. It left rose-gold shadows across my room and was urging me to come outside. I dressed in warm clothes and took a walk with Vincent. There were things that lay, unsettled, within me that I had to think about and try to put them all neatly in the right drawers. I felt a keen loss over Sam, I had thought we would end up in love, though I know love is elusive and can't be summoned like a well-behaved dog.

Vincent and I stepped over the seaweed, and the slick little stones that returned sly gleams back to the moon, making our way across the broken shells. This is a beach of broken shells.

But I know now, every once in a while, you can find a shell that is whole and perfect.

I had family out there, somewhere. A great uncle, whom I was sure, had married and had children who had married and had children, so there were cousins yet undiscovered. Someday I would make it a project to find them, but at least I was not the last of my family, and that felt good. And even if I never found them, I had Shay and Terrell, who were true and good and had become family. I had nephews to spoil. I had a good and loyal dog who had brought love and companionship into my life, because that's what pit bulls are really for.

Vincent and I climbed the steps to the pier and I sat down on the edge. I let my legs swing over the water. I was happy. Sam and I would always be friends, I knew. Larry—I didn't know where that would lead, though I had grown to really care for him. I loved his compelling personality, his sense of fun—but I was keeping my options open and felt very optimistic.

The moon was above us, so full and joyous that its luminescence overflowed and encircled us in a golden halo, so filled with pure light, so full, so full, that it couldn't contain itself, and its enchantment escaped from its surface and spilled down across the bay and the sand, to be magnified and mirrored. My little house on stilts glowed as though possessed by magic. The seaweed looked like silken scarves. The little stones and sea glass were sparkling gems and all the broken shells had become porcelain lace. The night sky was filling with light pirated from faraway stars and distant planets, from all the moons and suns that ever existed, fusing it with this moon, this radiant, moon, this ever-present gift that, it seemed to me, was making the whole world glow with splendor and contentment and peace and such pure love that it would soon saturate the entire universe with eternal happiness.

Like my heart.

AND ALL THE PHASES OF THE MOON

Judy Reene Singer

ABOUT THIS GUIDE

The suggested questions are included
to enhance your group's reading of
Judy Reene Singer's
And All the Phases of the Moon.

Connect with U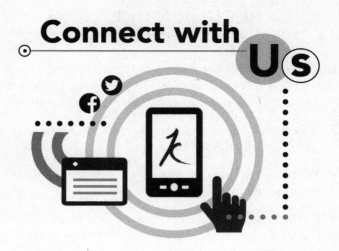s

Visit us online at
KensingtonBooks.com
to read more from your favorite authors, see books
by series, view reading group guides, and more.

for sneak peeks, chances to win books and prize packs,
and to share your thoughts with other readers.

facebook.com/kensingtonpublishing
twitter.com/kensingtonbooks

Tell us what you think!

To share your thoughts, submit a review,
or sign up for our eNewsletters, please visit:
KensingtonBooks.com/TellUs.

DISCUSSION QUESTIONS

1. Two years after her father's and her husband's deaths, Aila is still barely functioning. Do you think that's too long a period of time to mourn? Is there a right way to mourn?

2. Was it dangerous and foolish to bring home a beaten-up stray pit bull without checking him out more thoroughly?

3. What do you think of Aila's predilection for sitting alone at night on the pier?

4. In the beginning of the book, Aila paints a bucolic and peaceful picture of Fleetbourne. Were you at all suspicious of her rose-colored view?

5. Do you think the scene concerning Sam trying to buy a truck was realistic or way over the top? Did the car dealer's punishment go far enough? This scene is based on a real incident that happened at a New Jersey Mercedes dealership, when the salesman refused to sell a car to a man of Indian origin in 2016. How would you have reacted if you were Sam?

6. Do you think Mrs. A was too overprotective or did Sam need that much emotional support until he healed?

7. Was Shay right in keeping Aila out of the picture while she struggled with bigotry during her youth? What are friends for in situations like this? How does race play into that decision?

8. How can one fight vicious hatred and bigotry?

9. Did learning about Mrs. Skipper's background change your opinion about her? Do you think Aila's grandmother was really crazy, or heartbroken? How much of her tragedy did she bring upon herself?

10. Were you surprised at Aila's choices at the end?